THE AURIGA MADNESS

BRIAN CALLISON was born in Manchester in 1934. He was educated at the High School of Dundee before entering the merchant navy in 1950 as midshipman with the Blue Funnel Line, sailing mainly on cargo liners to the Far East and Australia. On leaving the sea he studied at Dundee College of Art. He has held several administrative posts, including managing directorship of a construction company and general manager of a large entertainment centre.

He also served several years in the territorial army with the 51st Highland Division Provost Company, Royal Military Police, and now maintains an active connection with the sea as Head of Unit, Royal Naval Auxiliary Service.

His first phenomenally successful novel *A Flock of Ships* was published in 1970 and has already been translated into nine foreign languages. This was followed by eight more novels, of which *The Auriga Madness* is the most recent. No less an authority than Alistair MacLean has said, 'there can be no better adventure writer in the country today'.

BRIAN CALLISON

The Auriga
Madness

FONTANA/Collins

First published in 1980 by
William Collins Sons & Co Ltd, Glasgow
First issued in Fontana Paperbacks in 1981

© Brian Callison 1980

Made and printed in Great Britain by
William Collins Sons & Co Ltd, Glasgow

Prologue

It was one minute to eight British Summer Time — on an extraordinarily pleasant Scottish morning at that — when William Dornoch of the Forth Pilotage Authority stepped easily from the deck of the fast motor launch *Leopard* to the bottom rung of yet another ready-prepared boarding ladder.

Even with both vessels making considerable way it was still a simple manoeuvre for Pilot Dornoch, a routine part of a working day. For the past nine years Willie Dornoch had been embarking in similar inward-bound ships, subsequently either guiding them from this present position under the shadow of Inchkeith Island to their allotted berths in Leith Docks some six miles to the south-west or even further up-river, to the port of Grangemouth.

Today did offer something a little different in that Dornoch had not come alone. This time he preceded a rather more unusual companion; a Port Medical Officer who, apart from being a specialist in the treatment of toxic illnesses, was also currently preoccupied with the initial symptoms of a much more personal malaise called sea-sickness — for even when calm the Firth of Forth can be spitefully cruel to those not hardened to the gyrations of craft such as the *Leopard*. In fact the pallid countenance of the accompanying P.M.O. already betrayed distress at such a nauseatingly unconventional start to *his* day. However, the doctor was a man of firm resolution, and not only had the new arrival relayed a specific request for his services, but the content of her somewhat mystifying appeal had generated hasty preparations in certain Edinburgh Infirmary wards ...

It took the experienced Pilot Dornoch less than one full minute to climb the carbon-copy ladder of a thousand vessels before. It should merely have demanded a further brief moment for him to swing lithely across the bulwark capping and down to the inward-bounder's deck, only this time, he didn't.

He didn't move at all, for that matter. Simply hung there high

5

above the corkscrewing pilot cutter as if frozen; white knuckles betraying the tension of his grip on the ladder and one foot still half raised in arrested motion; gaze ever-widening to take in the incredible things happening before him on the strange ship's forward deck.

. . . and then William Dornoch began to whimper.

Chillingly, and with ever-increasing hopelessness. Just before the blade of a shiny red fire axe, wielded by a creature with staring and terrible eyes, entered the crown of his uniform cap and split him like some slaughter-house carcass.

It was precisely eight o'clock British Summer Time on that suddenly quite frightful morning when the shocked and now totally confused toxicologist was also swept from the ladder by the plummetting parts of ex-Pilot Dornoch, to vanish below the foamsmashed gap separating the two moving vessels.

It was also the moment when an inexplicable squall disturbed the surface of the water. While that could only have been a meteorological phenomenon induced by the adjacent Scottish hills, a fanciful observer might have imagined that the Firth of Forth itself had trembled briefly at the monstrous prospect presaged by Pilot William Dornoch's end.

Because eight o'clock also marked the time when the ten thousand tons of steel and wood and plastic and men, known collectively as the Motor Vessel *Auriga*, finally went mad.

Chapter One

It had begun some twenty-four hours before Pilot Dornoch's bizarre and untimely death — the affliction that was to become The Madness; only a short time after the *Auriga* had rounded the Skaw marking the northernmost tip of Denmark and settled on her final 430-mile leg into the Firth of Forth on the other side of the North Sea. 257° true on the autopilot heading indicator left the spindle-legged flare-offs of the Ekofisk oilfield to port and the carnal delights of Helsinki just a niggling memory for certain members of her complement.

In a way The Madness was conceived out of conflict within that same band of jolly fun-seekers; because of a fight which took place between Assistant Steward Baird and Ordinary Seaman Grainger to be precise; with the provisions store providing the battleground, and a somewhat devious Finnish lady called Olga fuelling the fires of resentment.

Not that the aggro involving Baird and Grainger was in any sense a symptom of The Madness. No! It was more a case of their untidy bout of fisticuffs providing the catalyst, the vehicle by which an already existing but dormant foulness would be stirred into reaction. Anyone surviving the next thirty hours aboard the *Auriga* could have vouched for that because, at the time, Messrs Baird and Grainger merely betrayed a normal healthy desire to punch each other's bloody heads; the sort of reaction any close shipmates would display at abruptly finding themselves double-crossed in love. By each other.

The Madness, when it finally did contaminate *Auriga*, was to prove a hideous affliction which would contort men's bodies and derange their minds, and drive them to acts obscene in their conception. But that ultimate manifestation of the power of The Madness was to require time to spawn, to grow, and to subjugate all reason; to destroy the seaman's instinct which carried countless ships like *Auriga* safely across the oceans of the world. It

7

wouldn't reveal itself quite so blatantly for some hours after the fight in the galley store room; not until the flares of the Ekofisk were well astern, and the ship was closer to the ever-narrowing waters of the Firth of Forth with that waterway's unsuspecting traffic, and its Naval dockyard at Rosyth, and its supertanker terminal off Hound Point.

And its two great bridges.

And its vulnerability. To a ship the size of the *Auriga* at least. When The Madness had charge of the watch.

Olga of the Nordic skin and the statuesque beauty really did have a great deal to answer for.

She would never know it. In fact she probably never thought much about what happened after the *Auriga* sailed from Helsinki, despite the fact that the story dominated every headline from Toledo to Tokyo, because Olga wasn't the sort of girl who gave a damn what sailormen did — or had done to them — once the bedroom door had closed between her and their wallets. Even if she scanned the Finnish press, and glanced at the photographs detailing *Auriga*'s terminal insanity she could never have associated such a grue of once-humanity with the anonymous grinding torsos which had been the Baird and Grainger of a few days before.

So Olga never would grow haggard with guilt; though maybe she wouldn't have done so anyway. Olga the Finn was a very hard lady despite her tender twenty years and her ability to inject, into every commercial coupling, a conviction in each temporary partner's mind — namely that he, and only he, wielded the key not merely to Olga's eternal devotion but also her subsequent moral redemption.

It meant it was the easiest thing in the world for a sexually immature young sailor to fall desperately in love with Olga. Both Assistant Steward Baird and Ordinary Seaman Grainger did so, but on separate occasions; having wistfully generated identical fantasies involving potential sea-wives who would await their return with compliant fidelity, yet still copulate to order like a salacious wanton. They were only fleeting dreams — but pure magic nevertheless — and the shipmates regaled each other with their mutual yet curiously parallel hopes over and over again, as slightly bored seamen are wont to do; while with each successive telling the memories of their Helsinki conquests grew more and more enchanting and seemed much more a reality. Neither, unfortunately, appreciated that the bond between them embraced not only their dearest ambitions but also the same lady; the nubile and thoroughly professional Olga.

Or not until that breakfast time off the Skaw anyway, while Assistant Steward Baird was working in the provisions store forr'ad of the galley and Seaman Grainger just happened by as the spearhead of the deckwash party under the command of Bosun Peak. Naturally they dallied yet again, and talked of many things. All involving love.

Then it happened.

Grainger suddenly gripped the handle of his deck brush tightly, staring in dawning disillusionment at the still reminiscing Hughie Baird. '*What* did you say wus the name've that tart you been screwin' the ass off've, Steward?'

The remark did insert a somewhat misplaced crudity into the previously genteel conversation, but was induced by Grainger's conclusion that *his* Finnish affair bore an ever-increasing similarity to that of Assistant Steward Baird's.

Baird stopped tallying bottles of sauce and turned irresolutely. He didn't know why, but suddenly the euphoria embracing them both had soured to a perplexed resentment.

'Beg pardon?' he said. Ominously.

'You jus' said your tart's name,' Grainger pressed on recklessly. 'What wus it, that name?'

Ever so carefully the Assistant Steward placed his tally board on the sacks of flour behind him and clenched his fists. Then he thought a moment longer, and grinned uncertainly.

'O.K., what's the game, pal? You kiddin' me on or somethin'?'

The rest of the deckwash gang turned the corner of the deckhouse with Bosun Peak dragging the splashing umbilical cord of the hose. A fine salt spray of deflected water began to speckle the hooked-back store room door but Grainger ignored approaching authority in his mounting fury.

'Her name, Bairdy? That Scandinavian tart you gone fruit cake about?'

Baird's pacifist resolve began to crumble fast.

'Ah'm givin' you fair warning now. You call mah future fiancée

9

a tart again an' ah'll have ye, Grainger. She'll no' be like yon bucket o' worms you been tellin' *me* aboot f'r the past three days an' that's f'r sure. You remember ah've seen the kind you fancy, especially once youse is too smashed on aquavit tae care aboot the bloody quality.'

Grainger, quite uncharacteristically, ignored the unkind slur on his personal love goddess's image and jabbed Assistant Steward Baird with the end of his scrubber.

'I'm askin' her NAME, you Glasgow ponce,' he bawled. 'That bloody tart o' yours!'

The deckwash gang stopped washing and clustered round with interest. Even Bosun Peak hesitated, with the hose directed into the scuppers and a look of mystified anticipation on his normally morose countenance. Baird wasn't giving a damn who was watching by then, though.

'Right!' he screamed back, finally goaded beyond restraint. 'Right then, ye Birmingham fairy. Youse has been askin' f'r it, an' ah'm just the lad tae gie it tae ye. Hughie Baird's no' a man tae stand back an' let his Olga be insult . . .'

Grainger flung the brush away and smacked his rival hard in the mouth. 'So she *is* the same one — Olga! Excep' she wus *my* bird, you double-crossin' bastid. Blonde, greeny-eyed, tits like an Amazon an' a scar above her . . .'

Baird's fist counter-attacked in a wide raging arc and caught his apoplectic assailant squarely under the left ear. The seaman lashed back with his foot and took the Steward's legs from under him. Baird cannoned into the storage racks and went down under an avalanche of sauce bottles, tinned fruit and a sprinkling of powdered mustard.

'Gerrup!' Grainger demanded, weaving and feinting theatrically; aware, despite his amorous disgruntlement, that he was being assessed by an appreciative audience.

'Kick 'im in the slats, Grainger,' advised one relaxed pundit, enjoying this fortuitous break in the daily routine.

''E's gonna bloody kill you. When 'e gets up,' predicted another with relish.

'*If* 'e gets up,' speculated the first.

'Pack it in, Grainger, an' get back scrubbin',' growled Bosun Peak, but without any great enthusiasm. He was torn between the need to maintain discipline and his natural desire to see that cocky bastard Grainger done over proper. All the same, the deck hose had a fair old pressure on it and his arms were getting tired.

'GerrUP then,' Grainger challenged, conscious of the need to maintain his unpremeditated but not unwelcome new hard-man image. 'Gerrup, Baird, so's I c'n knock yer down again.'

Which Baird obligingly did; erupting through a clatter of pots and pans and mustard dust. More by accident than design he kneed his adversary in the crotch on the way up, and miraculously planted an untidy karate chop on the back of Grainger's neck as the seaman went down instead. Then, recovering from his surprise at accomplishing such an unexpected counter-stroke, he felt obliged — for the sake of the viewers — to start kicking the vociferously swearing Grainger for an encore.

'Told yer. Din't I tell yer 'e'd kill you, Grainger?' queried the second deckwasher sagely.

'I'll murder you, Baird . . .' Grainger shrieked between kicks as he tried desperately to scramble out of range. 'Oh I'll bloody *murder* yer, you sneaky Scotch . . . Awwww! Ah!'

'Well, you'll 'ave ter hurry up, Graingy boy,' offered the first deckwasher helpfully. 'Seems like the Steward's got the same idea.'

'Christ, but I wish I was retired,' the Bosun brooded wearily. 'Seagoin' hasn't never been the same since most of us proper sailormen was killed off in the war.'

Grainger was retreating fast now, heading towards the open door in an attempt to get out of range of the Assistant Steward's boot. First Olga, an' now a bloody mini-Scotsman . . . Burning with humiliation he flung himself over the coaming and out on to the deck, eyes searching for something, anything, to use as a weapon against Baird. The comedy was over; suddenly there really was murder in the air aboard the *Auriga*, and Bosun Peak sensed it too.

He would have liked to restrain Grainger but he couldn't; the hose hampered his freedom. All he could do was snap urgently, 'Grab 'im, you lot. The fun's over . . . an' you, Grainger — get off've yer ass an' start scrubbin'.'

'Ah'm gonna kill 'im,' Grainger was babbling. 'Oh I'm gonna crucify that back-stabbin' git of a steward . . .'

But the lid was blowing off in the store room too. Baird, frustrated by his rival's lunge for safety, was searching grimly for a longer range missile to consolidate his victory. He wanted to hurt Grainger now; savagely and uncaringly. His Olga ... HIS Olga, not only defiled by a randy yobbo like that, but bein' called a tart on top of everythin'! Yeah, well, maybe she *was* a tart ... but she wasnae *that* sort of a tart. Not wi' Hughie Baird, she wasnae ...

Someone walked out on the port bridge wing and stared irritably aft towards them. 'Christ!' muttered the Bosun a bit too late. 'It's the Mate.'

Panicking, he began to yell officiously above the din. 'Belay that, both've yer! Cut it out or I'll have yer both up before the Chief Officer.'

An impeccably directed mango chutney bottle completed its trajectory from the store room doorway with a dull *thunk* on the back of Grainger's skull. Bellowing with pain and rage the seaman clawed to his feet and lunged again.

Though not at Baird, this time — but towards Bosun Peak.

'Gerroff!' Peak squealed in sudden apprehension. 'Get away from me, Grainger ...'

'Stop that man, dammit!' blasted commandingly from the bridge. Chief Officer Temple abandoned all traces of senior dignity by sliding angrily down the ladder rails, en route for the fray. But David Temple's reactions invariably tended to be liverish by the time he'd spent four hours on watch dreaming of his precious breakfast.

Grainger didn't care any more about the sanctity of Officer Temple's bloody breakfast. Or any soddin' thing else, f'r that matter — apart from Baird's imminent decease. But killing his oppo wasn't exactly practical, hampered as he was by rapidly closing authority.

So he did the next best thing.

'Screw YOOOOOOU!' he shrieked hysterically — and snatched the deck hose from the Bosun's disbelieving grasp. He didn't even notice the grins of ecstasy on the faces of those other crewmen who ... 'Well, we *woulda* stopped 'im, Mister Temple, sir. Excep' 'e wus too quick f'r us.'

The hose jet caught Assistant Steward Baird unawares and off balance, hammering him back through the door and following him tenaciously into the store itself. There was a sort of aquatic explosion from within as the pressure cleared every remaining gastronomic delicacy from the already decimated racks, whereupon Baird was submerged under a waterfall of pickle bottles, tomato sauce, canned savouries, brown sugar, salt, pepper and flying things unidentifiable.

The *Auriga*'s current stock of baker's flour erupted from its sack, curdled into a marmalade and mustard-laced porridge and finally cocooned the Assistant Steward under a batter shroud before launching him into the convoy of idly swirling goodies passaging the flooded deck.

'Oohhhhh shit!' muttered Bosun Peak.

'Peak!' bellowed Chief Officer Temple, arriving just too late to do his chief petty officer's job of maintaining discipline for him.

'What'll the cook say . . . Aw *jeeze* but whit's the cook goin' tae say aboot this . . .?' spluttered Assistant Steward Baird through his coating of sludge; revealing nervous apprehension equalled only by that of the unhappy Bosun.

Ordinary Seaman Grainger didn't say anything at all; simply standing there with the hose now directed harmlessly outboard. But Grainger's reactions were mixed, flitting between satisfaction in gaining ultimate victory and the unlikelihood of his finding another ship after he'd been bounced all the way down the gangway in Leith.

Someone from the deckwash gang shut down the hydrant with the slightest trace of reluctance. A hush — a very temporary hush — fell across the boat deck of the Motor Vessel *Auriga* as men stole from near and far to gaze with wondering eyes into the galley store room, and view the culinary catastrophe resulting from those starry-eyed dips into the dream factory of Olga the Finn.

But they smiled, and even sniggered about it later, when well out of earshot of Chief Officer Temple. Both Grainger and Hughie Baird were earnestly assured that each had undoubtedly got the better of the other. Hell, but Slimy Simmieson the middle watch greaser had even shaken Hughie warmly by the hand and congratulated him on gi'in' yon bastard Grainger his first proper bath in weeks by turnin' that hose onnim . . . until Slimy caught the pink-scrubbed look on Bairdy's face and shuffled hurriedly out of range in muttering confusion.

It had been a good time, a memorable time, up on the boat deck on that last normal morning; and might have given source to countless future anecdotes in countless bars the world over. The crew of *Auriga* were grateful to Grainger and Baird and the fabulous Olga.

But they shouldn't have been. Had they known what had been spawned in that flooded provision room, then the *Auriga*, during the coming night, would have shivered to the screams of thirty-six lost men awaking out of thirty-six tormented nightmares.

As they first felt the menace of The Madness.

The Chief Cook never laughed when he went to look at it. But the Chief Cook never laughed at anything really, so no one could tell precisely how annoyed he was when he discovered Grainger had added salt water to all his recipes at once.

Well, apart from the way he held his meat cleaver anyway. And shook it wistfully.

'I'll blotty keel 'im!' he raged in Swedish displeasure; precisely echoing Grainger's earlier sentiments. 'He won't get nothin' to eat on this sheep ever again!'

Chief Steward Sullivan eyed Chief Cook Holmquist morosely. In usual circumstances he found it hard to conceal his impatience with the Chief Cook's Scandinavian gloom, but this time he had to admit that Holmquist's glower was justified. The *Auriga* had most certainly steamed into the middle of a crisis — a catering disaster of the first magnitude.

'S'far as I can see, Sven, we're all goin' to be in the same boat in a manner of speaking. None of the dry stores *are* any more . . . we got dehydrated peas swelling up like ping-pong balls already; the cornflakes an' crispies look as though they've been marinated f'r a week and them dried potato packs over there'd make a good wallpaper paste but that's about all . . .'

Two figures blanked out the light from the door and grimly surveyed the shambles. 'Damn!' the Chief Steward thought, 'I got enough aggro without Temple and the Old Man chivvying me . . .'

'Morning, Mister Sullivan . . . Morning, Chief Cook. Trouble in store, eh?'

'Damn again,' Sullivan continued to reflect. 'He's making a joke. He's always worse when he starts off makin' jokes.'

He smiled weakly; just enough to let the Captain see he appreciated the humour but not so much that the Old Man would think he was taking things too lightly.

'It's not good news,' he admitted with a slight lack of originality.

'It's a blotty criminal thing,' Holmquist opined. 'This waste . . . this vandalism. Blotty criminal, Captin!'

'It was a flash of temper. Not intended, Chef; just a sailor's overreaction to provocation from Baird,' Temple interjected smoothly, anxious to defend the integrity of his deck department.

'Your lad Grainger did hit Hughie Baird first, David,' the Chief Steward corrected hurriedly, trying to appear reasonable while still turning the tables in favour of the catering branch. 'My boy was a victim of circumstance . . .'

'Aye,' intervened the Captain dryly. 'Well let's concentrate on the effects rather than the cause for now, shall we?'

'I know one of 'em,' Sullivan gloomed. 'That catering superintendent in Leith's a right bastard when it comes to spoiled stores.'

'I mean,' the Old Man continued heavily, 'the question of feeding everyone adequately until we finish the trip.'

'Zey won't get no cornflakes,' the Chef predicted with a touch of sadistic satisfaction. 'No bran; no wheaties. So there's no way they're going to get a proper balanced diet. No blotty way!'

'We will be in dock in twenty-four hours,' Captain Mowat reminded the Swede with commendable restraint. 'They'll probably survive without any roughage till then, by the grace of God. Anyway, I meant main courses . . . How are we for potatoes, Mister Sullivan?'

'We aren't. Our order never arrived aboard before we left Helsinki. I keep tellin' the Company them Finnish agents are bloody useless when it comes to vittling . . .'

'*I* never have problems getting deck supplies and replacements,' the Mate observed acidly. 'The stuff's always waiting when we go alongside . . . but then *I* radio my requirements in good time, of course.'

It wasn't usual for Temple to be so childish, but the smell of congealing bacon and eggs from the galley was driving the *Auriga*'s Chief Officer to a state of savagery.

'Yeah? But maybe *you* don't care about the quality, Mate. Look at the kind of seamen you're prepared to sign on. That Communist Grainger an' his antics. One thing f'r sure — if I had got my bags've potatoes they'da had more bloody brains than your Grai...'

'All *RIGHT*!' the Captain intervened, much more tartly this time. 'Nobody will starve because he can't get a plate of chips for the whole day. You carry powdered potato for emergencies, don't you, Chief?'

'Not any longer I don't,' the Steward retorted uncaringly, still brooding over Temple's remarks. They were all the flamin' same, the deck department. Always stuck together like bats in a cave when it came to defending their precious executive status; quick to slide out from under an' leave the engineering an' catering branches to take the can. AND the Old Man was one of the same breed. 'All I got now is half a ton of tater-flavoured sludge under me feet, sir.'

'Then Mister Holmquist can bake a little extra bread to soak up the gravy. Can't you, Holmquist?'

'*Hah*,' replied Chief Cook Holmquist with devastating contempt.

'And what,' demanded the Captain, drawing upon every last reserve of tolerance, 'does the Chef mean by "*Hah*", Mister Sullivan?'

Sullivan shuffled uneasily.

'It's the flour as well, sir. I'm, er, paddling in it.'

He tried not to see the smirk of satisfaction on Temple's superior features as the Old Man's patience finally disintegrated.

'Godammit, there must be *something* you can do to provide thirty-six lunches and thirty-six main meals ...'

'. . . with enough carbohydrate content to make them at least pointedly.

. . . with enough carbohydrate content to make them at least palatable, Sullivan. This tomfoolery can't make all that much difference. What did you have planned for lunch today, for instance?'

'Steak pie, sir,' Sullivan gloomed. 'With lashings of pastry and mashed potato.'

'Not now, you don't,' the Chief Cook put in, stubbing the toe of his boot into the sodden, deflated flour. 'Now I make jus' the steak. Stewed. I will serve it in soup plates.'

Even the Old Man's eyes, undeflected by wind, ice or tempest, flinched momentarily at the prospect, but Charles Mowat of the *Auriga* could be brave *in extremis*.

'And what,' he demanded with only the slightest pause, 'did you propose as a finisher, Mister Sullivan? As the sweet?'

Sullivan drew a deep breath.

'Bread pudding,' he whispered. 'Sir.'

The Captain turned away with a countenance most terrible to look upon. Only when he had skidded his way to the open door did he turn and speak again. Very deliberately.

'I have a Chief Steward and an Assistant Steward in my crew, Mister Sullivan. Their duties include both those of planning the dietary needs of their fellow seafarers and of ensuring that those needs are presented in a balanced and appetising manner . . .'

'Yessir,' said Chief Steward Sullivan uneasily.

'I also have a Chief Cook, Mister Holmquist. And *he* has a Second Cook to assist *him* . . .'

'Ya, Captin,' acknowledged Chief Cook Holmquist with a deceptive flash of caution.

'. . . and *their* duties are to prepare the aforesaid food in such a manner as previously described. Am I correct, gentlemen?'

The *Auriga* rolled slightly under the wash of an outward-bounder heading for the Skaw. It was acknowledgement enough. Captain Mowat stepped out on to the boat deck before swinging for his final devastating broadside.

'I shall now be forced to concoct a report to the Owners on the causes of this stupid affair. I still, however, look forward with keen anticipation to a most varied menu for the remainder of this voyage, gentlemen. I trust that your collective ingenuity will not necessitate my . . . ah . . . extending my written criticisms to *your* activities.'

The Chief Steward and the Chief Cook stared after his departing figure in stony silence. Bosun Peak would have said there weren't many captains like Mowat left, either. Most of *them* had been killed off in the war, too.

Some of 'em by their own bloody sailors.

'*I* still need my breakfast,' Chief Officer Temple reminded them waspishly. The Chief Steward turned slowly.

'What *you* need, Dave Temple, is . . .'

And then he described Chief Officer Temple's requirements in the most intimate and colourful detail. Even Chief Cook Holmquist gazed at his departmental head in ungrudging admiration before moving discreetly out of earshot.

'Ya, well, while you officers is chatting I go to see what stores I got left in the galley . . .'

He was actually grinning. For the first time since he'd signed aboard a British sheep, Sven Holmquist was grinning.

While Holmquist had only been aboard *Auriga* for four months, Third Mate Garvie had been in her for nearly three years, and for him it was time for a change.

The first two years had been O.K. He'd joined her when she was a brand new ship and he was a brand new Third with a brand new ticket; initially they'd been very happy together. But Sandy Garvie was an ambitious lad and waiting a little impatiently for company promotion. Apart from that the *Auriga* herself was slipping into too much of a routine; twelve months ago she'd been taken off general cargo running and chartered out in her original design role as a newsprint carrier, and since then Garvie had spent every hour at sea between eight and twelve, day and night, driving a predetermined furrow across the North Sea, through the Skagerrak, down the Kattegat, up the Baltic and into Helsinki Harbour.

Unless, of course, they were going the other way; back to Leith. Then it was *down* the Baltic, up the Kattegat, round Skagen an' into the Skag . . .

He took a quick look round after the Old Man and Temple had disappeared into the galley store, noting automatically *Auriga*'s position in relation to other traffic. One of the big Stena Line ferries had just slid down their starboard side on what was an even more rigidly prescribed routine run, Newcastle to Gothenberg and return. A new Russian freighter hammering to catch up from three miles astern, decks probably crammed with export-only Moskavitches or Ladas or other heavily subsidised symbols of the Communist good life. Several Danish fishing boats inshore to port, pastel blue and immaculate with their permanently-rigged red plastic trisails. An oil rig supply ship southbound; a snowy yacht canvas cutting the line of the horizon ahead . . . no give-way action yet required. The *Auriga* was free to proceed without worry.

He leaned on the rail and stared expressionlessly out over the long foredeck. From the bridge the ship looked much bigger than she really was; all vessels with their deckhousings located right aft did that. It was only when you were manoeuvring into harbour and suddenly remembered your stern, to find, when you swung, that it wasn't there, that the thought struck home. The *Auriga* didn't have the currently popular bulbous bow either. Her hull had been constructed to Lloyd's Ice Class I requirements; designed to cut through and withstand the sometimes frightening pressures of the Baltic winter freeze.

Three main holds and a small forward cargo compartment provided Third Officer Garvie's constant foreground view; all one hundred and odd metres ahead of him. MacGregor piggyback hydraulic hatch covers; Norwinch mooring equipment; two yellow painted and stork-like Liebherr electro-hydraulic cranes to replace the conventional forest of derricks and cargo-handling gear: she was a well fitted and massively strong vessel, the *Auriga*. But boring. Bloody boring when you'd been staring at her figure for three carbon-copy years.

'What d'you think'll happen to Grainger now, sir?' a voice said from behind. There was a slight note of excited awe in it. Garvie turned and saw Cadet Simpson sneaking a quick glance aft down the boat deck, waiting for the Old Man's reappearance. There was a glistening clutch of soapsuds clinging to the top of Simpson's head. He'd been cleaning the wheelhouse windows and tended to be a bit over-enthusiastic.

The Third Mate shrugged. 'Probably be keel-hauled. Then set adrift in the longboat, if I know the Old Man. After he's hanged him from the highest yardarm.'

Simpson frowned. 'But we don't have a longboa ... Oh I see what you mean. The Captain is a bit ... er ...'

'Yeah, he is. You finished those stability problems yet?'

Every cadet with the company was given a voyage task for off-watch study. The mates were expected to assist where help was needed, which it usually was, because most cadets were further ahead in their knowledge of how to chip rusty scuppers and wash windows. The ships had changed over the last hundred years, but a deck officer's apprenticeship hadn't. Not all that much.

'Sort of,' Simpson confirmed uncomfortably.

'Bring 'em down to me after lunch,' Garvie said wearily, 'but not too long after. I'm planning a quiet zizz in my bunk as my routine for today.'

'Yessir,' the cadet nodded. 'What about Willie's?'

Willie Kennedy was the other *Auriga* cadet. Thick as two short planks in Garvie's jaundiced opinion — not at all the stuff they used to make apprentices of when *he* was one. Nearly three years ago.

'What about Willie's what?' the Third Mate prompted fatalistically.

'He's . . . ah, having difficulty with his metacentric heights, sir.'

'Well you gotter admit he's a funny shape,' Garvie sniggered. Simpson didn't laugh; even the soap bubbles hardly wobbled at all.

'Oh, bring Kennedy down with you,' the Third Mate growled in resignation. 'Bring the Bosun an' the ship's cat. Bring everybody an' we'll have a bloody party . . .'

'We don't *have* a ship's cat, sir,' Simpson volunteered blankly.

'Get on with the windows, Simpson,' pleaded Third Officer Garvie.

It was nine o'clock in the morning.

Twenty-three hours to go before the *Auriga* picked up the Forth pilot off Inchkeith.

Three and a half hours before lunch would be served.

Chapter Two

The remainder of that last unremarkable morning passed — for those members of the *Auriga*'s complement not directly involved with the catering department — in much the same manner as countless earlier mornings at sea.

Only for the events which were to come, did that period hold any special significance. Because had The Madness possessed physical form, that would have been the period in which it first stirred.

Had it possessed a face, then it might well have smiled. In anticipation of its release.

For some crewmen, their arrival alongside in Leith would mean a welcome break from routine; for the majority simply a continuation of the daily grind.

Captain Charles Mowat would be handing over to the relief master who would take the ship coastwise U.K. for reloading outward. Then plain Charles Mowat would board his train at Edinburgh Waverley station and, for the succeeding ten days, become husband, rose-pruner and reader of the lesson in the little Sussex village church where he worshipped. He would have to catch a later train now, in all probability, thanks to the additional paper work necessitated by the nubile machinations of Olga the Finn.

Chief Officer Temple was staying with the ship. His leave wasn't due until next time round. It didn't matter a great deal; Mrs Jennifer Temple had left him in favour of the more attentive company of an East Lothian District Council official some six months previously. It wasn't that her local authority paramour had proved a better lover than David, or even a less argumentative consort when breakfast failed to meet the standard required, but at least he did come home every night and didn't share his affections between her and a ten-thousand-ton mistress.

Chief Engineer Eric Webster would be staying with the *Auriga* on this occasion. He should have been journeying down to Liverpool with gifts for a legion of little Websters, but one of the main engine air-start compressors was suspect. Chief Webster was a conscientious man who'd never learned to delegate worry, so Second Enginer Beckman was gleefully being shunted off home instead.

Second Officer Yancy was going, never to return to *Auriga*. He would add his third stripe before heading straight for Turnhouse Airport and Singapore to take over as mate of their sister ship *Aries*. He would go with mixed feelings; disappointment at foregoing a keenly anticipated ten days in bed with Mrs Yancy balanced against unexpected promotion. But Ted Nevison, recently deceased Chief Officer of *Aries*, hadn't really meant to get himself run over by a bus load of Malay schoolkids and inconvenience everybody.

Third Officer Garvie was gloomily staying aboard to watch

7874 rolls of newsprint going over the wall. It was an experience which lost all novelty after the first couple of thousand had cleared the holds, but he could alleviate the monotony by accepting the fun-filled challenge of sorting out young Kennedy's metacentric heights. And there was always the hopeful possibility that the *Aries'* Second Mate might be stricken by some ten-ton Oriental juggernaut as well.

Bosun Peak would be staying; but Peak never left the *Auriga* voluntarily. He was as much part of the ship as the funnel, for all his lugubrious disaffection with modern sailormen. Donkeyman Trott always reckoned the only way they'd get Peaky off've the boat wus inna canvas suit, an' him with 'is mouth shut f'r the first time ever . . .

. . . it was a pity, Donkeyman Trott making a joke like that.

Slimy Simmieson the middle watch greaser was off for ten days — taking his missis to *Majorca,* f'r crying out loud — and so was Radio Officer MacNally. Not that R. O. MacNally was going to Majorca, of course. No. All he planned was to catch a bus along to Granton and just happen to drop in on a certain voluptuous lady he knew. *Her* husband also happened to be a radio officer pal of MacNally's, only *his* ship was still at the end of an eight-week queue waiting to offload cement in Lagos, Nigeria.

Which all went to prove it wasn't only Helsinki which had an Olga.

Engineers Bench and Jennings were designated to spend just as long as was needed over the innards of the starting compressor, mainly holding the spanners for Chief Webster like oil-dappled theatre nurses. Bench didn't mind; he was young enough still to feel the romance of the sea, but Third Jennings never had, so all he wanted to do was get back to Paisley and find a job in a garage or some other more stable place of work. Certainly one where the foreman didn't wear four gold rings and have a perverted sense of duty.

There were others aboard who would stay aboard. Seaman Chikwanda, who never wanted to go back to Uganda again, and young Seaman Guy whose mother had died four months ago and who couldn't bear the thought of going home without finding her waiting. And Greaser Behrens, who determinedly headed for home

22

every time the ship docked, but was always returned within two hours by an irritated policeman in a state of ultimate inebriation. Behrens, that was; not the policeman.

Apprentice Simpson was going home to see his new-born baby sister for the first time; as well as his still faintly disbelieving Mum and his disenchanted Dad. Able Seaman Reid would be hurrying down to Grimsby to view his new three piece suite and his brand new quadrophonic hi-fi set and his gleaming, up-to-the-minute family freezer — and to ask his wife which bailiff had seized her last voyage purchases of a colour television console, a mahogany dining table with six chairs and a washing machine because she hadn't bloody paid f'r THEM yet!

And Ordinary Seaman Grainger . . .? Well he didn't have any specific plans during that last ordinary morning aboard the *Auriga*. Before all the terrible things began to happen.

But you can't really deliberate on your future actions, can you? Not when your past ones are just about to catch up with you.

They'd already overtaken Assistant Steward Baird.

Like the other members of the catering branch he spent the morning helping restore order out of chaos and, coincidentally, accomplishing the impossible by way of balanced nutrition.

Hughie had been given the first of those most delicate culinary assignments — Sullivan presented *him* with the bucket and shovel — as well as the smug assistance of Second Cook Monaghan, who managed to suggest a positively tangible air of reproach for the deplorable conduct of them what shoulda know'd better . . . meaning Hughie Baird, of course, who to Terry Monaghan's constant chagrin, sported one thin much coveted gold stripe. When he wasn't mucking out store rooms anyway.

Meanwhile their respective superiors tackled the more demanding mission of search and rescue — the tracking down of all remaining supplies of carbohydrate and associated products on the *Auriga*. For Chief Cook Holmquist it presented a challenge; for Chief Steward Sullivan, who had by now allowed his concern to get out of all proportion, a nightmare obsessed by the ever-nearing spectre of the Company Catering Superintendent awaiting him in Leith.

By nine thirty a.m. the situation was becoming desperate. So far the vegetable room had yielded a plethora of root vegetables, a rather more handsome quantity of tomatoes and mushrooms and a pitiful, wizened sick bed of previously discarded potatoes. Only two fresh loaves and a handful of morning rolls had survived the breakfast onslaught in the galley, while the gleaming, stainless-steel emptiness of the tiny bakery to starboard testified more to Holmquist's Scandinavian hygiene than to Sullivan's prospects of one day attaining a company pension.

The Chief Steward poured himself a cup of black coffee and flopped into a chair, sipping dispiritedly. 'I'm going to get the chop,' he gloomed with almost morbid satisfaction. 'I tell you, Sven, it's me for the chop and Mrs Sullivan doomed to finish her life without any of the little luxuries a chief steward's salary can provide.'

Holmquist shrugged grudgingly. 'It was not your fault. What that blotty mad sailor done was not your fault.'

'Neither is it the Old Man's if the mate goes bananas on the coast an' piles us up deliberately . . . but he still loses 'is ticket. It's all a question of responsibility, Chef. The burden of command.'

'The Captin has only threatened you if the meals are not good, not with bread and everyt'ing, ya?'

Holmquist picked up the two loaves and waved them triumphantly. 'Here we have the Captin's lunch, the Captin's dinner . . . and plenty lef' for toast at his breakfas'.'

Baird squelched in from the store room and said moodily, 'Whit do ye want me tae do wi' . . .'

There were smears of congealed potato flour down both sides of his chin. It made him look like a clown but Sullivan didn't laugh. 'Get on with cleanin' up the mess you an' your pal made. Don't bother me . . . *That* won't kid the Old Man, Chef. 'E's going to ask first thing about what the rest of the crew are eatin'. Mowat's fair. Except with stewards.'

'*I* need a smoke,' Baird complained aggressively. 'An' you still havnae said what you want done wi' . . .'

'Not in my galley, you don't.' Holmquist growled, devoid of sympathy. 'I don' have no one smoking cigarettes in my galley, Hughie Baird.'

'An' you can't go out on deck either,' Sullivan added remorselessly. 'You tramp that muck out on the boat deck an' Dave Temple'll have your guts for lifeboat falls.'

'Look, I didn't sign on as a bluidy navvy,' Baird complained.

'They didn't design the vittling store as a booby house f'r nutters like you an' Grainger to banjo each other in, either,' Sullivan retorted. 'So bugger off an' shovel, Assistant Steward Baird.'

'The crew won't make no complaints about being short of bread for this one day,' reasoned Holmquist, pointedly ignoring the still resentfully hovering Hughie.

'Them?' the Chief Steward laughed bitterly. 'Them boys'd complain if we cut the rind off their bacon, they would. Them babies dressed up as sailors'd be straight round to the union if we so much as skimmed the skin off've their rice pudding ...'

'You still havnae told me whit you want me tae do wi' ...' Baird persisted irritably.

'Dump it. You ruined it — you *dump* it, laddie. Now.'

'The crew, they don' complain on Swedish sheeps,' the Chief Cook stated loftily.

'Yeah? Well you Swedes, you eat anythin', don't you?' Sullivan growled with true British contempt for all things foreign. 'Fish bones, seal meat, reindeer ...'

'You t'ink we is blotty Eskimos?' Holmquist challenged him.

'Och the *hell* wi' it,' the Assistant Steward snarled, then raised his voice to call the store room. 'O.K., Monaghan — the boss here says to dump it. Yon bag o' flour in the locker ... jus' sling it ower the wall.'

'There's not much difference,' the Chief Steward defended himself. 'You all wear fur most've the time. An' it snows most've the time, doesn't it? And all you Scowegians is ... WHAT did you say, Hughie?'

Baird hesitated at the door with a surreptitious look of triumph. 'Och, nuthin'. I'm just tellin' Monaghan tae dump everythin' like you said. Sir.'

'*Flour*. You said flour, dammit.'

'It's all grey-coloured. Probably spoiled anyrod,' Baird elaborated with exquisite cruelty. 'I reckon you're right, Chief, an' that we should dum ...'

'I don't blame Grainger for tryin' to drown you,' the Chief Steward said, elbowing his assistant out of the way. 'Not any more I don't. So just shut up, an' show me.'

Bosun Peak, like Chief Steward Sullivan, spent a great part of that last morning worrying about the consequences of the galley store affair. Though Peak's concern was over his admittedly somewhat apathetic attempt at prevention — as opposed to Sullivan's much-feared persecution over the result — both men were allowing the matter to assume a psychological significance out of all proportion to its true importance.

Ships are like that, though. Ships and oil rigs and monasteries; environments where little aggravations can develop into big tensions, minor irritations into major provocations — which was why Ordinary Seaman Grainger had played at fire engines with Hughie Baird in the first place, come to that. Because the longer he brooded over Olga the more beautiful, the more desirable, the more coveted she had become.

So while Sullivan composed himself for crucifixion by the Company Catering Superintendent, Peaky prepared himself to spend the remainder of his life as a destitute failure in a seaman's hostel . . . and nobody else aboard the *Auriga* gave the matter any more than a passing thought.

To Captain Mowat — a seadog who barked automatically but bit seldom — it was a fleeting irritation. His report to the Owners — that condemnatory document looming so large in the Chief Steward's thoughts — would make no reference to the incident other than as accidental damage occasioned during deckwashing duties. And Mowat would have been perfectly prepared to eat whatever was put before him for the next twenty-four hours, whether liquid, slop or crust. He'd spent thirty-two days on a liferaft in the Indian Ocean during the war, and watched sixteen of his companions die through lack of food and water. Captain Charles Mowat had never again complained seriously about the quality of his diet.

For Chief Officer Temple it was simply another disciplinary nuisance aggravated, certainly, by the inexcusable infringement of his breakfast routine. But life at sea was becoming more and more overtly democratic, and young ratings like Grainger less concerned for the traditional majesty of maritime authority, while the corresponding new breed of Chief Officers such as Temple were learning to bend with the trade union winds. As far as Grainger's future was concerned, Temple merely planned to tear him off a strip and forget the whole thing – but he wasn't going to tell the hot-headed seaman too soon. After lunch would do; and let the kid sweat a little first.

Ironically, even if Temple had had any authority over Chief Steward Sullivan, which he hadn't, or any reason to try to cause friction between the Chief and the Old Man – which again he hadn't, because Dave Temple normally got on well with his catering opposite number unless the toast was burned or the marmalade too runny – then worries about tomorrow's breakfast would not have been a decisive factor anyway. *Auriga* was due to go on stand-by at 0745 in preparation for picking up the Inchkeith pilot, and that was enough to sabotage any prospect of a civilised meal anyway.

And Grainger – the basic cause of it all? Well he was discovering, during the course of that last morning, just what the expression 'Industrial Victimisation' really meant, because Bosun Peak had started him off with the soul-destroying task of squeegeeing down about forty acres of deckhousing. Then, as Peak's self-inflicted worries increased, he'd switched Grainger to oiling the wire ropes of the forr'ad cargo crane; up to his grubby elbows in black stinking grease. And finally, when Peaky's concern for his own future had escalated to positive vindictiveness towards those responsible, Ordinary Seaman Grainger found himself clambering into the Stygian blackness of the rust-dank cable locker with a chipping hammer in one hand, a tin of red oxide paint in the other, a nightmare afternoon yawning endlessly ahead of him and a fervent hope that – even if Temple didn't fire him like a rocket out've a line-throwing gun – he'd never, ever have to sail aboard another ship on another sea again.

As Bosun Peak observed morosely, yet with a certain satisfaction, to Donkeyman Trott, 'I tell yer, Trotty, there's more ways of skinnin' a ship's cat than by tellin' it it's been a naughty pussy ...'

'What d'you think?' Chief Steward Sullivan asked anxiously.

Holmquist stirred his hand in the galvanised bin and allowed the contents to trickle back. 'How long you had this? I don' remember it coming on the sheep since I been cook.'

'Not all that long . . .'

'Six months onyway,' Hughie Baird interjected with a touch of spite. 'You only got it up at Kotka because the Old Man wus on that health food kick; nutrients and fibre wi' everything.'

The way he said it implied that Sullivan had bought the stuff so as to ingratiate himself by capitalising on a temporary whim of the Captain's. Which had been true. The Chief Steward glared at his understudy defensively.

'I didn't need Mowat to tell me brown bread's good for people . . .'

'It's no' brown, it's grey,' Baird persisted dogmatically. 'Like I said — it's gone bad.'

'It is rye flour,' the Chief Cook pronounced, deigning to afford Baird a patronising eye.

'If you was a real professional then you would know rye flour is a grey colour, Hughie Baird. When it is baked, then it becomes more brown . . . in Sweden we make spiced cakes and crispbread with rye.'

'See?' Sullivan snapped with satisfaction, but his junior was still simmering over being given a shovel instead of sympathy after the unwarranted attack by Grainger.

'It disnae alter the fact that it's been aboard a long time. You even forgot about it yersel' . . . look at the way it's all congealed around the sides of the bag. Ah wouldnae gie yon to a dog if it wis me.'

'Dog? What're you talking about dogs for, laddie?' Sullivan retorting with matching bloody-mindedness. 'What's dogs got to do with sailors on a ship . . .? It's all right in the middle anyway. See?'

He carefully scraped with a circular motion. The outer edges of the flour had formed into a dark, almost purplish-black shell inside the sack, but the rest of it avalanched into the hollow he'd made in a dry, free-running stream. Anxiously he glanced at his watch — it was half past nine and lunchtime was getting ever nearer.

'Nothing wrong with it,' he confirmed irritably.

Holmquist leaned over and inspected the flour again. He didn't really like what he saw — especially the way it had darkened, presumably through contact with the damp sea air — but he didn't like the brash young Assistant Steward either, and felt grudgingly bound to support Chief Sullivan. He shrugged.

'Should be O.K. But not for steak pie. I can't make steak pie pastry wit' rye flour.'

'An' you cannae eat stew with spiced cake,' Baird argued mercilessly. 'Even if the flour *hasnae* gone bad — which it has — you cannae gie them stew wi' cake, can you?'

Sullivan flapped his hands in ever-increasing frustration. He was getting bloody fed up with bloody snippy kids and bloody unimaginative Scowegian chefs an' bloody unreasonable bloody ship's captains.

'There's . . . well . . . hundreds of things we can give 'em apart from steak pie, dammit. You're both talkin' like we only *had* steak pie aboard. You both gotter *fixation* about steak pie . . .'

'All right — what else?' Baird demanded. 'What else can we give 'em that's savoury, disnae need pastry an' can be eaten without potatoes, then?'

'Call me sir,' the Chief Steward warned him, attempting to ward off the attack. 'You remember I'm "Sir", Assistant Steward Baird, an' don't get too stroppy.'

'What else — sir?' Hughie pressed, quite unabashed.

'*I* don't know; not off-hand. But there must be something we c'n do.'

'How about sandwiches?' offered Second Cook Monaghan tentatively, entering the debate with the diffidence appropriate to a junior rate.

Sullivan and Baird turned on him contemptuously; united for the first time.

'Sandwiches?' the Chief Steward snarled. 'Sandwiches are f'r picnics, sonny. And church socials. I don't feed *my* ships on sandwiches . . .'

'*Sandwiches* . . .?' the Assistant Steward echoed, emphasising the gulf which one thin gold stripe formed between him and a Second Cook. 'Ah wouldnae gie a dog a sandwich . . .'

'Yessir. Sorry, sir,' Monaghan acknowledged with due humility. Then added, 'Of course you'll appreciate, sir, I was thinking of . . . ohhh, say *Sandwiches Alsaciens*. Rye bread spread with horse-radish butter under a garnish of Strasbourg sausage . . . but you'll know all about that already, sir. An' about *Sandwiches du Bookmaker*. Buttered, laid with half-inch grilled steak an' spread, naturally, with English mustard . . . an' them *Sandwiches Antibois*, o' course. Chopped hard boiled eggs, capers, gherkins . . . all presented on a bed've tarragon butter.'

'Well, yeah; well . . .' Chief Steward Sullivan muttered uneasily, staring at the Second Chef in ill-concealed astonishment. He had forgotten that young Monaghan commenced his culinary career in the kitchens of Claridges, before life at sea, and the extra money that went with it had beckoned.

'Yon's just fancy shoreside food,' Baird interrupted anxiously, seeing his advantage slipping away. 'Ah wouldnae gie stuff like yon tae a do . . .'

'Shut UP!' Sullivan snarled furiously. Young Monaghan smiled discreetly to himself — it wasn't only Grainger who had a fervent desire to take Hughie bloody Baird down a peg or two.

Then Sven Holmquist, already secretly elated by his protege's triumph, added the *coup de grâce*.

'Ya, they would be good, Chief Steward. Good for a lunch . . . and later, for dinner tonight, I will make Scandinavian table for everybody. Swedish *Vitkalssoppa* to start. Then Norwegian *Fiskbullar* — fish balls *med* rye cake for accompaniment and as the main course, *Danske Smørrebrød*. The open sandwiches of Denmark; toppings of prawn, salami, sliced cold pork, fried bacon with apple and onion rings . . . maybe I even see if I got enough stores to make the *Anasjovisoga*; the anchovy eye, you call it? Wit' the raw egg yolks an' the fine chopped onion . . .'

'Christ!' Hughie Baird muttered, adopting an over-theatrical expression of revulsion.

'Well, let's get on with it then,' Sullivan urged, concealing his relief with a briskness he didn't really feel. Maybe it would work out after all; maybe the Old Man would even appreciate eating Scowegian for a day.

Maybe he'd even put in a *good* bit about Sullivan in his report . . .

Maybe the Company Catering Superintendent would have a *smile* on his face . . .?

'Oh, and Hughie,' the Chief Steward added, all nice and friendly,

30

suddenly hopeful for the first time since the *Auriga* had suffered her galley store flush-out.

'Aye?' snapped Hughie, still smarting with disgruntlement.

'Get bloody shovelling again, Hughie,' suggested Chief Steward Sullivan.

Pleasurably.

Chief Cook Holmquist and Second Cook Monaghan began to prepare the daily menu rather later than usual on that last day. It was nearly ten o'clock by the time they commenced the first task — mixing the rye flour to the correct consistency in the bakery which was pleasantly warm; ideal for proving dough in the limited period available.

Young Monaghan noted, once again, that some of the noxious black grains had unavoidably infiltrated the fresh central core of the flour bin as he emptied it. He didn't mention it to either Sullivan or Holmquist, though. There'd been enough trouble in the galley already that morning.

By the time lunch was ready to serve, the *Auriga* had less than twenty hours left before she picked up the Inchkeith pilot in the Firth of Forth.

Some of her crew had even less time than that.

Chapter Three

Chief Cook Holmquist first saw the cat at twenty to one, just as the initial selection of sandwiches was ready, their rye casings still delightfully warm and exuding an aroma guaranteed to tempt the most recalcitrant palate.

It was a black cat, mostly, with brown ears and a bit of white around the paws and the tip of its long furry tail. It was crouching, large as life, on the crew mess servery, and eating with a funny, jerky enthusiasm suggesting a long and arduous fast.

Wolfing its food, in fact. Only you can't really say that about cats.

'Bogger OFF!' Holmquist roared in outraged reflex. 'Blotty cat, you bogger off NOW . . .'

The pan lid he threw planed like an erratic discus, swung off course and demolished a pile of aluminium dish covers with deafening precision. They collapsed; the cat took off with an accompanying screech and half a rye *Sandwich à la Tartare* still firmly clutched in its jaws; the *Auriga's* Chief Cook launched a running kick which missed the animal altogether, putting a permanent dent in the fridge door and his right boot instead, while the most unlikely cat shot through the galley door, out on to the boat deck, then finally disappeared on the end of a fading howl.

'BLOTTY CAT!' Holmquist bellowed after it, hopping wildly while trying to rub his foot and shake his fist at the same time.

'Blotty what?' enquired Chief Steward Sullivan mildly, having entered the galley in search of a reason for the commotion but not with any particular urgency — ship's galleys do tend to echo with the sounds of breaking dishes on occasions, though more often when the seas are running thirty feet high and approaching from directly abeam.

'Blotty CAT!' the Chief Cook repeated in one-legged fury.

'I thought you said "cat" f'r a minute,' Sullivan said, rubbing his ear. 'It's funny how you think a bloke's sayin' somethi . . .'

'There is a cat on this sheep,' Holmquist snarled. 'A blotty cat, Chief Steward, what was eating my sandwiches and stinking out my galley.'

'But we don't *have* a cat aboard,' Sullivan persisted. 'Not with the rabies prevention regulations in British ports, an' the quarantine, and the trouble an' fines they slap on you if it gets ashore unnoticed . . .'

'It was a blotty *cat*, I tell you. You sink I see cats on sheeps when there ain't no sheep's cats around . . .?'

'Er, well . . .' the Chief Steward muttered doubtfully, a little confused by now about precisely which species of animal the Chef was claiming to have seen. Second Cook Monaghan bumbled through from the bakery under a second tray of sandwiches and a grey dusting of rye flour.

'You see a cat?' Sullivan asked him diffidently. 'Here in the galley?'

'A what, Chief?'

'A cat. The opposite of a dog.'

Monaghan looked blank. 'But we don't *have* a ca . . .'

'Blotty British sheep!' the Chief Cook blazed uncontrollably. 'Is a lunatic asylum . . . Is a blotty floating *crazy* house!'

. . . and that was a terrible thing to say, too. Under the circumstances.

With The Madness now already abroad and undetected.

No one else aboard the *Auriga* saw the black cat with the brown ears and the white tip to its tail. Or not right then, anyway. Though Chief Steward Sullivan did have to admit that something rather odd must have happened to four of Monaghan's sandwiches, in that they'd disappeared from the tray for no apparent reason. Being a practical man, Sullivan was perfectly prepared to accept a cat as being a more likely reason for their disappearance than, say, some magical phenomenon.

Unless Hughie Baird had nicked 'em, of course. Only he was still shovelling out the galley store . . .

Strange, really. Trying to imagine a stowaway cat.

Lunchtime aboard the *Auriga* turned out to be an event which provoked mixed reactions. It proved a moment of triumph for Chief Steward Sullivan; an unexpected acknowledgement from the Chief Cook of his assistant's culinary resourcefulness — mixed with a superior 'You wait an' see what I do tonight when this sheep eat proper Scandinavian': a period of chagrin tempered by hungry desire on the part of Hughie Baird, and a time of general appreciation from all other members of the crew from the Captain downwards.

On behalf of the ratings' mess, Greaser Simmieson expressed satisfaction more succinctly than most. He waved his fourth rye *Sandwich Dijonais* — created by young Monaghan with love, sliced hard boiled egg, parsley, ham, delicate seasoning and merely the slightest hint of *moutarde de Dijon* — while announcing dreamily, 'I tell you, lads; these egg an' bacon sannies is ace grub, an' that's a fact . . .'

The only lower deck man who didn't nod agreement between bites was Ordinary Seaman Grainger, but his chipping hammer

arm was too painful, and everything tasted of bloody dust anyway. And there was still the afternoon in the cable locker to
occupy his mind as an imminently pending penance.

In the officers' saloon on the boat deck, starboard side, the
consensus of approval followed a similar, if somewhat less extrava-
gant pattern.

'Nice change,' commented Chief Engineer Webster to no one in
particular. And reached for a fourth sandwich.

'All right, these,' echoed Second Officer Yancy, enjoying his
temporary relief from the afternoon watch on the bridge.

'Nice bread . . . wholemeal is it?' mused Fourth Engineer Bench
to Third Jennings. Jennings didn't actually reply — he would still
have preferred a cheeseburger in a home-town Paisley Wimpy bar
— but at least he munched with apparent enthusiasm.

Third Mate Garvie didn't say anything either, in his case largely
because he wasn't there. He was back on the bridge relieving 2/O
Yancy as the late lunch had upset everybody's watch times. But
he'd enjoyed his as much as anyone; all five sandwiches and three
cups of tea and two baked apples with syrup.

Even Chief Officer Temple muttered a grudging, 'At least they're
different.' Then he fixed the Chief Steward with a pointed stare,
and added, '*Some* compensation for the breakfast, I s'ppose.'

'Yeah, well, I . . . ah . . . got young Monaghan to knock 'em up,'
Sullivan put in modestly. 'After I'd told him how to do 'em, of
course.'

His eyes shifted to the head of the deck officers' table and locked
on to those of his Captain. Mowat frowned momentarily, then interpreted the tense appeal in his senior catering executive's gaze, and
smiled inwardly.

'Excellent; thoroughly enjoyable. I knew I could rely on your
ingenuity, Mister Sullivan.'

'Thank you, sir,' acknowledged Chief Steward Sullivan with
dead-pan shamelessness. 'And you want to see what I'm planning
for tonight's meal . . . I thought up the idea of everyone eatin'
Scandinavian.'

It was nearly three o'clock on that last afternoon in the North Sea
by the time young Monaghan had filled the dishwasher racks,

tidied up the bakery, set the big oven to the temperature required for the Chief Cook's forthcoming rye crispbread, scoured the serving trays, swept the deck and rinsed out the wiping-down cloths in preparation for the assault on dinner.

'You have to not waste time, Terry,' urged Holmquist from the galley table, where he'd been absorbing his third coffee in sombre reflection. 'You got to do the officers' tea an' the crew room smoko, then you got to open them tins of anchovy and lay out the beef for the *Kottbullar* an' fillet them herring . . .'

'Yes, Chef,' said Monaghan who was far too meek and not particularly bright sometimes.

'I got all the thinking to do,' gloomed Chief Cook Holmquist wearily. 'I dunno why I got other peoples to pretend to help in the galley.'

It took a conscious effort; to lift the coffee pot for the fourth time.

While it may have appeared inconceivable to *Auriga*'s catering and supply department — immersed as they were in logistic impossibilities — the remainder of the ship's complement spent that final afternoon at sea in performing perfectly normal, routine tasks.

And if a few slightly odd things *did* happen . . . well, nobody gave them more than a passing thought.

Not at the time, anyway.

At three p.m. Second Engineer Beckman noted the last of the hourly readings in the engineroom log, placed it carefully in its rack and leaned back in his swivel chair.

He'd eaten far too much at lunch; even the air-conditioned freshness of the port side control room wasn't enough to prevent a stealthy languor from fuzzing the edges of his brain. But a ship's engineer didn't have to remain alert nowadays for the first signs of mechanical ailment — the *Auriga* had been built in accordance with Lloyd's requirements for manual supervision of the engineroom for only eight hours per day; it was all there in front of him on three large panels, all monitored and analysed through the Decca ISIS system and the Negretti and Zamba instrumentation; all displays of exhaust gas and turbo-charger temps, main and auxiliary engine temps, lube oil, fuel oil, fresh water, sea water, ambient, internal, external . . . anything too hot or too cold or too erratic or too sluggish triggered either a bell or a klaxon or a buzzer or a bloody illuminated and strident alarm of some kind. And only then did the ship's engineers engineer . . .

Beckman suddenly felt a splurge of happiness as he remembered his unexpected leave, starting tomorrow. Ella and the kids didn't even know yet — they weren't looking forward to his return until next month — but then they didn't understand about things like recalcitrant air compressors and do-everything-yourself Chiefs. He began to toy with the idea of not phoning when the ship docked; of just catching the first train down to Hull an' surprising them all.

The heavy-weather locks were off the swivel chair. Beckman's slothfulness disappeared under the adrenalin of excitement and he spun himself like a suddenly elated child, whirling round and round in the middle of that sound-proofed electronic wonder box.

He had to sit for quite a long time after the chair had stopped spinning. Much longer than he would have expected in fact, even after such an ill-advised display of juvenile hilarity; but the giddiness seemed to last for ages, and the disorientation. He even felt sick for a few minutes and his head was pounding furiously.

Beckman didn't think any more of it after he'd recovered.

Christ but he was tired, though. He'd have to cut down on these midday meals of Sullivan's.

Odd. How a little spin could affect a bloke who'd regularly been thrown around every ocean in the world . . .

Second Mate Yancy prepared to enter his three o'clock dead reckoning position on the chart and idly drummed his pencil on the table.

They were well into the North Sea by now; past Hanstholm Light and the north-west coast of Denmark and clear of the glut of traffic which tended to converge there on various tracks into the Skagerrak.

The brass dividers glinted as he picked them out of the rack, caught by the rectangular beam of sunlight scribing slow arcs from the starboard chartroom window. There was only the merest hint of a southerly swell; the *Auriga* wasn't rolling so much as performing a leisurely and occasional curtsey, acknowledging the fact that she was suspended fifteen fathoms above the earth proper by that most powerful and unstable of all mediums, the sea.

Because the sea could destroy her, Yancy knew that as well as any seaman. It wasn't a matter for debate; it was a fact of maritime life. All ships, whether large or small, only existed by the grace of the sea; just as all sailors only lived for as long as the sea permitted them to. Not that Second Officer Yancy brooded over the possibility of the sea killing him, of course. But then he'd never really given his own mortality a thought; not even when he was about to fly to Singapore simply because of the death of another man who . . . well, who hadn't — just as Yancy hadn't — seriously considered the prospect of his dying in advance of his natural span.

Yet even that was ironic. For if Ted Nevison, late Chief Officer of the *Aries*, ever *had* briefly reflected on any premature departure from this mortal coil, then being a seaman — and thus most at risk from the sea — it was unlikely that he would ever have anticipated his final breath being expelled under the wheels of a Malayan bus.

Certainly not any more likely than that Bill Yancy would have envisaged the prospect of his being afflicted by the monstrous agony which, by three o'clock on that sunny afternoon, already prowled the *Auriga*'s compartments in search of its first victim.

But then no man — whether seaman or landsman or even condemned man — could surely conceive of dying from a thing like The Madness. For The Madness, by its very nature, presents an utterly inconceivable form of death . . .

. . . so Second Officer Yancy was simply working up his position at three p.m. on that sunny afternoon, and not considering dying at all. In fact the greatest concern he had at that time was whether or not he would manage to keep his bleary eyes open when they called him for the Inchkeith pilot stand-by. He was glad he was going to be a Chief Officer soon — the Second Mate's watch from midnight to four knocked the hell out've a bloke's stamina, especially when it was aggravated by an early morning call to duty.

Marking a neat line across their track with the 2B pencil to indicate his D.R. position he leaned across the chart and frowned at the Decca Navigator console. The *Auriga*'s Captain was very much of the old school — his watchkeeping officers did their sums the good, traditional way first and only *then* checked with the aid of solid-state, micro-circuit wizardry. It was the same when the North Sea fog clamped down so tight that even the bows were lost to a peering eye. Aboard the *Auriga* one officer kept his head buried in the hood of the steaming radar — and the other stuck his ear out of the window and listened.

It was only after Yancy had finished in the chartroom and was stepping out over the coaming to the starboard bridge wing that he stumbled. It took him rather a long moment to regain his balance, muttering a mild curse at the way ships rolled at the most unexpected times. Then he looked at the gentle sea, and realised that the *Auriga* couldn't have tilted in such an unladylike manner, certainly not enough to throw as experienced a seaman as he was into temporary instability.

Second Officer Yancy frowned in mystification, just as Second Engineer Beckman was currently doing a long way below him in the engine control room, and for much the same reason.

Then promptly forgot about the incident. Just as Beckman did.

By three thirty Chief Officer David Temple had completed his defects list and end-of-voyage stores demand for onward transmission to the Leith agents. Still half an hour to go before he relieved 2/O Yancy for the four to eight, but Temple was in a restless mood; not content to sit back where many would and wait for his call at one bell. He was well aware of the friction that could be caused by the succeeding watchkeeper being as little as one minute late for the handover. That minute seemed a very long time when a bloke had already pounded the restricted area of a ship's bridge for four interminable hours — and like those other minor aggravations swelling to major conflicts in any close society. Even an unintentional delay in acknowledging 'I have the watch' could convert previously placid relationships into powder kegs of resentment.

He straightened the papers on the ship's office desk, wet his finger and absently rubbed a clear wood scratch where a carelessly stowed coffee cup had shattered during a winter gale more than five months before — and which he'd been absently and religiously darkening with spittle almost daily ever since — then picked up his uniform cap and, after switching out the light, carefully locked the door behind him. It was only after he'd walked past the empty officers' lounge and climbed the starboard ladder to the next deck that he remembered the awful and continuing penance of Ordinary Seaman Grainger, still presumably incarcerated in the rusted crypt of the cable locker under the patronage of an unforgiving Bosun Peak. Temple hesitated briefly — a tendency towards mercy prompted partly by common humanity and partly by a desire not to push his relationship with the Seamen's Union further than the stage of a wink and an understanding nod — until he recalled the too-late offering of shatter-crisp bacon and concrete-blob egg, unaccompanied by toast of any colour or consistency, which had formed his criminally vandalised breakfast — whereupon Chief Officer Temple's mouth hardened to an uncompromising slit.

Apart from which, the daywork men stood down at four o'clock anyway, and thirty more minutes in the cable locker for Grainger was as nothing compared to Temple's gastronomic deprivation. Shrugging he continued to climb the next ladder to the captain's deck, and thence to the bridge.

Yancy turned his head but didn't lever himself away from the rail where he'd been leaning. 'You're early,' he remarked. 'Or is it my birthday?'

Temple felt vaguely irritated, taking the Second Officer's greeting as ungracious and not humorous as had been intended. Instead of smiling he impulsively waved the handful of papers he was carrying and walked past into the wheelhouse.

'Don't put your hat on. I'm going in to see Sparks with these first. I'll be with you in good time.'

'That's O.K.,' Yancy called after him pointedly. 'You still got twenty-six an' a half minutes.'

He pushed himself from his slouching stance though, and stared hard around the line of the horizon as if acknowledging Temple's disapproval. He wouldn't wear an equal number of gold rings until after they'd docked tomorrow, and there was still a wide gulf between a first and second mate on most British ships.

MacNally the Wireless Officer wasn't lounging so much as practising a state of catalepsy. He'd even got his *feet* on the bloody table, which meant the only change from normal was that his nose wasn't buried in one of his apparently endless supply of science fiction paperbacks. Temple knocked perfunctorily and stepped across the coaming into the radio room abaft the bridge. MacNally opened one eye and fixed the new arrival with a Cyclopean stare.

'How do, pardner.'

'Oh,' Temple said heavily, affecting a look of surprise. 'I didn't realise I was moseyin' into the Bull Brand bloody Saloon.'

'Talking of bulls,' MacNally mused, 'I was just dreaming of a certain lady I'm meeting in Granton tomorrow night. Wo*wie!*'

'Yes,' Dave Temple snapped shortly, thinking of that certain lady's husband, currently floating on twelve thousand tons of cement off Lagos. If MacNally reckoned he was a bull, then that made the lady a first class . . .

'And what can the wonderful world of highly complex electronics do for an honest, able seaman such as yourself, Mate?' the R.O. asked expansively. Temple grinned, it was hard to resist MacNally's invariable good humour.

'Do you, perchance, have any method of contacting shore?'

MacNally looked thoughtful. 'Semaphore? Carrier pigeon . . .? Or I could light a tar barrel on top've the wheelhouse . . .'

The *Auriga*'s Mate dutifully obliged as straight man.

'How about using your radio?'

Sparks opened the other eye, following Temple's pointing finger with exaggerated care. He stared at the battery of grey nylon-coated consoles and switches and dials with gradually dawning disbelief.

'You mean that's a radio?' he burbled ecstatically. 'You are actually telling me I gotta *radio* in here, Chief Officer? To send . . . well . . . messages an' things . . .?'

Temple found the game was beginning to pall. He slid the papers under MacNally's nose while the R.O. debated. 'So that's why they keep sendin' me my wages every week. 'Cause I gotta *radio* to use . . .'

'I want a link call to the Leith agents,' the Mate said shortly. 'Now, MacNally. And please shut up.'

'I can't, can I? Not if I'm supposed to be calling Stonehaven.'

But Sparks was already triggering the pressel of the M.F. transmitter handset. He winked at Temple and began speaking in a professionally modulated tone. 'Stonehaven Radio, Stonehaven

Radio; this is Mike Lima Delta Tango *Auriga* Link call, please . . .
Stonehaven Radio, Stonehav . . .'

Suddenly, unexpectedly, he replaced the handset and began massaging his wrist instead. Then he flexed the fingers of his right hand doubtfully. He was frowning.

'What's wrong?' Temple said suspiciously.

But MacNally wasn't joking. Or it didn't seem as if he was, anyway.

'My fingers . . . I dunno. They're tingling.'

The medium frequency receiver crackled. 'Ship calling Stonehaven Radio; say again your call sign . . . over.'

'Pins and needles?' the mate queried unsympathetically. 'Well we both know what causes *that*, superstud.'

He was thinking about the lady in Granton again, but MacNally didn't respond, while the frown was still there. Almost a wince.

'Shit!' muttered the Radio Operator, and grabbed for the handset again. 'Stonehaven Radio; this is Mike Lima Delta Tango *Auriga*. I say again; this is Mike Lima Delta . . .'

It took fourteen minutes for Temple to complete the radio telephone deck stores request. By the time he handed the set back to MacNally it was close to his scheduled change of watch. Yancy would be padding the boards like a caged lion.

He said 'Thanks' as he got to the door, but uncharacteristically MacNally didn't reply. Temple turned briefly, curiously, before he left.

The *Auriga*'s radio operator was uneasily massaging his wrists again; both of them now. And flexing his fingers.

He was still frowning, too.

Five o'clock that last afternoon found Captain Charles Mowat reading his Bible. It wasn't a particularly unusual thing for him to do; most days around that time the Captain would pick up his well-thumbed copy of the Lord's word and read a while. It wasn't a measure of the intensity of Mowat's religious zeal. No, Charles Mowat studied the Bible because it was a thoroughly good read and, to his way of thinking, completely justified the best-seller status which the world afforded it. Plot; characters; action; violence — it was without equal.

And if one built up a little credit account with Heaven at the same time, then So Be It! Even if one didn't, Mowat wouldn't have felt any resentment, or that he had wasted his literary appreciation. He had embraced God during those thirty-two days adrift in the Indian Ocean — for *some*thing all-powerful must have kept a sixteen-year-old and not particularly strong lad alive while so many resolute and more able companions had died horribly — and he certainly didn't grudge the Lord a few minutes per day of grateful co-operation in return.

There was a knock at the day room door. Mowat called, 'Come in' and Chief Webster stuck his slightly florid face around the edge.

'I just seen a cat, Charlie.'

'A what?'

'A *cat*. A pussy ca . . .'

'Bloody hell!' said the Captain. But Mowat didn't make a fetish of his religion.

Webster trundled in and flopped heavily on the settee. 'Lord but I'm tired . . . it was a black cat. Or a brown one. Going full ahead past the alleyway door.'

Mowat laid the Bible aside in resignation.

'The Customs won't like it.'

'The Customs don't like anything . . .'

Eric Webster never had forgiven H.M. Customs and Excise for the day, many years before, when as a very young and cocky fourth engineer he'd spent a large part of one voyage soldering round metal tins of duty-free cigarettes end to end in the form of a pipe; then had placed them within a maze of engineroom piping, and carefully lagged and painted and thereby camouflaged what ultimately represented a substantial capital investment in amateur smuggling for a poorly paid youngster . . . only to watch with muffled discomfiture as the very first Customs officer to board performed a perfunctory search below; offered him a friendly cigarette; said chattily, 'We all know that the chances of me finding anything in this jungle are pretty remote, eh son?'; then promptly fell backwards as the 'pipe' he was leaning against abruptly gave way . . .

'Bloody Customs!' muttered Chief Engineer Webster in dark recollection.

'I'll have to report it. The Prevention of Rabies Act ... We should try and catch it before we get in.'

'*Hah*,' snorted the Chief sardonically, imagining the decks and compartments of the *Auriga* echoing with the shouts and running footsteps of men frenziedly pursuing an elusive phantom. But it was still only five o'clock in the afternoon, and Eric Webster's vision merely cynical anticipation and not a ghastly premonition.

'You quite sure you don't want to go home tomorrow?' the Captain asked, changing the subject. 'Beckman's perfectly capable of overhauling that compressor himself, you know.'

'If he wasn't he wouldn't be my second,' Webster retorted. 'But there's other things to check, Charlie. I want to take a look at the fresh water generator, maybe even poke around with the alternator P.T.O. . . . Hell, I'm goin' to forget what a spanner feels like soon.'

'You still need a rest. Everybody does.'

'I've got seven kids. And Aggie. A week at home an' I'd have to come back aboard for the rest . . . Anything wrong?'

The Old Man looked up vaguely; he'd been sort of stretching both arms and rotating the wrists at the same time. There was an expression of mystification on his face.

'Mmmmm? No. No, it's just my hands have gone to sleep. Tingling; cold too, like they get when you make a snowball.'

'You're getting old, Charlie,' the Chief smirked superiorly, then found himself stretching convulsively, hugely, as well.

'Y'know, I *am* tired, at that.'

'You're getting old, Eric,' said the Captain. Triumphantly.

During that final afternoon of the *Auriga*'s comparatively brief existence several other members of her crew had become aware of minor physical irritations; largely unremarked and either shrugged off or even totally ignored.

Able Seaman Reid, for instance, who was married to a houseful of expensive new furniture and who spent as much time while on leave with the Grimsby bailiffs as he did with an unrepentant Mrs Reid — he suddenly began to itch all over, and was still scratching furiously after two showers and a complete change of underclothing.

Then there was Greaser Behrens, determined as never before to

43

head straight for home and religiously avoid every hostelry between Leith and Carlisle no matter what temptation was afforded. 'Ter jus' have a half pint an' maybe wan wee whisky . . .' He discovered his resolve was being gravely undermined by a sensation of coldness; of the sort of lowering of body temperature which could only be rectified by the self-administration of a large medicinal dose of Lamb's Navy rum. Or Vodka? Reinforced by a modest — and singular, of course — draught of the Guinness that every advertisement assured was good for him.

Apprentice Simpson didn't feel at all well, and incurred Third Officer Garvie's sardonic displeasure by being sick all over Cadet Kennedy's metacentric heights during their abruptly curtailed teach-in in the 3/O's cabin. Donkeyman Trott became very quiet about five o'clock that afternoon but didn't tell anybody, not even Bosun Peak, that his introspection was because he sensed a peculiar constriction in his chest and it worried him a lot; both his brothers having died suddenly within the past two years from heart attacks.

Third Engineer Jennings had stumbled twice for no apparent reason when washing his shoreside shirts and socks, while Slimy Simmieson had actually fallen six feet, fortunately without serious injury, from the top of the *David Brown D-series* reduction gear casing where he'd been completing his end-of-watch cleaning. A mystified and shaken Simmieson had claimed, 'Yon whole bloody thing shimmied sideways so it did, an' that's a fact', but an unsympathetic Second Engineer Beckman reckoned the accident occurred because Slimy was a careless bastard even when he was concentrating, and *that* only happened once a bloody year . . .

A general lassitude also affected many of the *Auriga's* complement; especially the off-watch personnel. Those who habitually dozed away their in-between hours found themselves even more ready than usual to stretch out on their berths, while the more active — notably Seaman Chikwanda from Uganda, normally a body-building fanatic with a torso as black and beautiful as a piece of sculptured ebonite; and Fourth Engineer Bench who spent every spare moment in turning, filing and assembling a 1/25th scale model of an 1866 tandem compound steam engine — even they couldn't resist the temptation of putting their feet up before dinner for once.

In fact the only man aboard the *Auriga* who didn't feel any discomfort or dizziness or slothfulness during that last afternoon was young Seaman Guy, recently bereaved of his mother.

And that was truly ironic. For Derek Guy had finally made a carefully considered decision regarding an act he intended to perform that very night.

He was going to commit suicide. In a most elaborate and memorable manner.

Chapter Four

So, ultimately, came the time for Chef Holmquist's special dinner on that eve of the *Auriga*'s dying; with the sun still a benevolent wink in the reddening sky and the crustacean silhouettes of the Ekofisk rigs clambering a little threateningly above the misted horizon over to port.

Yet not one of the *Auriga*'s thirty-six crewmen felt at all threatened, not even then; except Donkeyman Trott possibly, still worrying over the ever-tightening constriction in his chest.

This stealthy onset of The Madness formed the very essence of its attack; for The Madness was an ancient affliction, and consequently very wise. For over two thousand recorded years it had lain largely dormant, making only brief yet appallingly lethal entries on the catalogue of man's suffering; yet each time it had struck, scribes had vied with each other, and written with shaking hands and blanched faces of the unspeakable foulness of its onslaught. Each time, when its monstrous appetite for misery had temporarily been sated, so it had withdrawn from the limelight of history.

And waited. As it had done for the unwitting Assyrians over six hundred years before the birth of Christ; and for the Parsees some three hundred years later. To the people of what was eventually to become France The Madness first came in the year 857 A.D., but then returned with ever increasing rapacity six times in the 10th century alone; seven times within the succeeding hundred years; a further ten forays during the 12th century . . . and then it had squirmed across medieval Europe, tormenting and excreting death in its wake as it fell upon the 16th-century citizens of Sweden, and the 17th-century innocents of Russia and Germany and . . .

But then, strangely, The Madness had slept. Oh, occasionally it had re-awakened — as in England in the Year Of Our Lord 1762 where it consumed a man, his wife and all of their six children and caused their reason to snap and their bodies to rot even while they were still alive. And in England again very much later — quite uncomfortably later for the peace of mind of contemporary man. And yet again to an unsuspecting France more concerned by then with the pollution of its residents by exhaust fumes from internal combustion engines, and with the Algerian problem, and whether or not Paris should construct a second major airport.

Then again The Madness had gone to ground; skulking and resting briefly once again. Until the nineteen eighties. Until, in fact, a nubile young charmer called Olga unwittingly caused a hose to be directed into the store room of the Motor Vessel *Auriga* . . .

Nineteen-year-old Seaman Derek Guy had prepared fastidiously for his impending self-destruction. Long before dinner was actually served in the crew mess he'd changed into his best shore-going jeans with the death's head brass-buckled belt from Hamburg, and the black T-shirt with the personalised spangle motif revealing that he was a punk rock music fan — purchased after a considerable struggle with his conscience from one of the boutiques lining Amsterdam's litter-strewn Kalverstraat. That particular struggle had been caused by an equally tempting, if slightly more expensive alternative; namely that of purchasing the services of one of the professional ladies displayed in yet another of that same city's busiest shopping centres — the windows in the red light canal street running just to port of the Damrak, steering up towards Dam Square.

But Derek's Mum was still alive then, and he knew how much the suspicion of his having done a thing like that would have hurt her.

He'd even washed his hair before dinner, and shaved what sporadic fuzzle of beard there was to shave, because he reckoned they'd probably inspect his corpse pretty closely an' . . . well . . . a bloke din't want to look a scruff *all* 'is life, did 'e? Especially not when 'e was dead.

Ironically, Derek Guy probably felt the least threatened person aboard the *Auriga* on that last evening at sea; apart from seeming to be the healthiest. Maybe that was because his time of vulnerability was nearly over. He'd never known his father — whose name had been Wrzaszcyk anyway, and whose paternal ambitions had not been stirred by twenty minutes of illicit passion with a casually picked-up Miss Guy — and consequently his whole stable world had revolved around Mum. Then he had gone to sea without quite knowing why, and Miss Guy's heart had been broken for the second time, and so she had died . . . and Derek had understood, too late, the reason for her death. And discovered, also far too late, that he had loved her very much indeed and couldn't bear the thought of not having anyone to go home to.

Which was why he'd decided to kill himself. Death seemed so uncomplicated, so much less harrowing than life. Apart from which young Seaman Guy had always been pretty bloody stupid as well.

He'd postponed his suicide. Originally planned for late afternoon, he'd reluctantly delayed it for a little longer; until after dinner that evening.

Why . . .? Because he really enjoyed eating Scandinavian, o' course. An' couldn't bear the thought of missing out.

Assistant Steward Baird, who'd been one of the joint catalysts of all the trouble in the first place, was in a furious mood by the time dinner was ready.

All day — all bloody *day* he'd been shovellin' an' washin' and cleanin' out the store room; apart from a quick bite at half a dozen o' Dopey Monaghan's fancy shoreside sandwiches, anyway. And Chief Steward Fatso had only relented when it wis too bluidy late tae do anythin' other than rush down to his cabin, shower and change into his white shirt with the epaulettes, then belt back up tae the galley just in time tae help serve Blockheid Holmquist's even more poofy an' fancy Scowegian dinner.

An' after all *that*, they three moth brains had combined tae pour soup all down the front of his number one gear . . .

It was strange, really. The way in which Assistant Steward

Hughie Baird had managed to get himself basted in uncomfortably hot Swedish cabbage soup. Rather unsettling, in fact. And not only for Hughie Baird.

'How can I,' the Chef had demanded waspishly, 'make the creation of the *Svampsas*, Terry, if you keeps leanin' over the hot plate every time I stirs the mushrooms?'

'I dunno, Chef,' said Monaghan, already trying, with the posture of a ballet dancer, to ladle soup into individual plates and avoid precisely such a complaint.

'Oh, lift the bloody pot on to the preparation table,' the Chief Steward growled, hovering on the periphery of that culinary frenzy. 'Portion it out from there.'

'The Old Man's down in the saloon now,' Hughie Baird warned as he came into the galley, looking harassed and resentful. 'An' Chief Webster. An' the Third Mate; agitatin' to get back up an' relieve Mister Temple. *An'* the Second's down, an' Benchy an' . . .'

'Shut up an' give Monaghan a hand with the soup,' Sullivan snapped urgently. All day long he'd clutched at the reprieve offered by tonight's meal. Apprehension at Mowat's reaction to any sign of inadequacy within his department had steadily escalated to obsessive proportions — and the prospect of everything being lost through inefficiency in the final stage was unthinkable. A Captain kept waiting for his dinner could be a vindictive report-writer indeed.

There was a sharp sizzle from the hot plate and everybody glared at Monaghan. The ladle had caught in the spun-aluminium rim. Soup still trickled down the side of the huge pot and bubbled into dehydrated foulness around the base.

'Christ but you're only wasting *time*,' Sullivan agitated. 'Lift it over here an' get outa the Chef's road, laddie.'

'British sheeps,' Holmquist gloomed predictably. 'They got no idea how to run a galley. Move yourself, Terry; I got to add the sherry damn quick . . .'

But young Monaghan didn't move at all. He simply stood there with the tipped-over ladle still dribbling Swedish *Vitkalssoppa* on to the stove and his face as white as Holmquist's hat. Every few seconds his arm seemed to twitch involuntarily to the accompaniment of yet another steam cloud.

Nobody noticed, engrossed as they were with their own private problems.

'There'll no *be* any fancy soup soon,' predicted Hughie Baird with ill-concealed spite; then added *sotto voce*, 'Not that anybody's goin' tae be too disappointed about that, mind.'

'My mushrooms is frizzling. I don' serve no mushroom sauce made wit' frizzled mushrooms, I warn you, Chief Stewart.'

'Come ON, Monaghan ...'

Still pale and with a curious look of desperation, almost of panic, in his eyes, the Second Cook gave a sudden, convulsive jerk as if trying to free the ladle — only there seemed no strength to his arm so that, instead of his utensil clearing the pot's rim, the whole container teetered crazily with its contents surging and leaping in a creamy, butter-yellowed tidal wave.

'WATCH IT, DAMMIT!'

Chief Sullivan seized Monaghan while Hughie Baird grabbed unthinkingly for the pot. The three of them stumbled; the pot slid sideways — and the tidal wave of *Vitkalssoppa* stayed precisely where it was. Most of it took a vertical course towards the hot plate, exploded into further gouts of steam, and continued aft until met by the barrier of Hughie Baird's midriff. Not much actually made it to the deck.

'Ohhhhh ye bastard!' howled a suddenly very active Assistant Steward, plucking with frenzied hands at the sodden shirt front clinging like a hot poultice to his skin.

'Mind my mushrooms, stupit boy,' roared a single-minded Chief Cook. Compassion towards his juniors had never been one of Holmquist's traits.

'The soup. Save the rest've the bloody soup!' the Chief Steward was pleading, with a matching lack of concern for Baird's agony. Already his mind was calculating, battling yet again with impending ruin — please to God there would still be enough for the officers; an' surely there wasn't a crew mess in the whole've the British merchant navy that wouldn't acclaim a substitute of tinned tomato ...

Terry Monaghan had sagged, strangely silent and unnoticed, on to the Chief Cook's chair; an act which he would never have dared to commit at any other time. His face remained as

49

white as the *Auriga*'s deckhousing, while his eyes held a look of . . . fear.

The initial rigor seemed to be subsiding, but his right arm still jerked spasmodically. As if someone or something was over-riding the locomotory impulses transmitted from his brain . . .

Forward of the galley and on the same deck Bosun Peak finished washing his hands and carefully hung his towel over the heated rail. Glancing automatically in the mirror he noted the thin, lugubrious features which stared back at him, and frowned. The image frowned back as if in commiseration and it occurred to Peak that mirrors were curious, unreliable things; while *he* knew he was a lean, rugged, pretty handsome feller, all the mirrors he'd ever inspected reflected a stranger with a sharp nose and a gloom-compressed slit of a mouth, and eyes that revealed nothing but weary acceptance of life's perpetual adversity.

Mind you, the mirror wasn't so far out; not this time. Not with a couple of adversities like Grainger and Temple to brood over. It was obvious that Seaman Grainger had spilled that red oxide paint as a deliberate act of defiance; no way did Peak fall for the kid's yarn that he'd suddenly gone all dizzy on the ladder from the cable locker. 'Couldn't hold on, Bose, an' had to let go of somethin'.' Only he couldn't prove it for certain, and there'd been a funny expression in Grainger's eyes while he was cleaning up the mess — a sort of wild, unsettling glint which had warned Peak not to push sarcasm too far. Gone for ever were the good old days when the master of a British ship was God, an' the Bosun stood at His right hand sharin' a marline spike with a real bucko mate . . . which brought his thoughts to his other current adversity — the pending wrath of Mister High an' Mighty Temple! But then it had never occurred to Peaky that the *Auriga*'s Mate had already dismissed his senior petty officer's part in the morning's deckwashing fiasco as an inevitable element of life in today's merchant navy.

Which accounted for the excess of gloom reflected by the mirror; even allowing for the fact that it *was* a scurrilous distortion of reality.

Nervous anticipation made him swallow; the prominent Adam's apple bobbing convulsively. Then he hesitated, frowned even more severely than before, and swallowed again. Yes, dammit, there was something there; something not quite right in his throat. He swallowed a third time, and a fourth. The obstruction seemed to go away, leaving a vague sense of discomfort which only reinforced his natural aspect of woe. Now he was developing a bloody cold, or 'flu or somethin', on top of everythin' else . . .

Reaching for his tumbler in which he kept his dentures overnight he rinsed it and sipped experimentally. Naturally the irritation didn't completely disappear — things never did get better for Peak — so he slammed the glass back into its stowage, fought his way through the curtain across his cabin door, and headed aft towards the crew's mess room. He wasn't hungry — if he had been it would've been for proper British vittles like sausage'n mash or mince an' chips with mushy peas — and rumour had it the whole ship was eating Scowegian tonight, which probably meant dried fish and reindeer fritters an' them sturgeon's roe things that looked like tadpole spawn balanced on fairy-sized bits o' toast; but they said 'Feed a cold and starve a fever', and Peaky was nothing if not an avid follower of dogma, relevant or irrelevant.

On the way past the Donkeyman's cabin he banged on the closed door, but there was no answering hail. Trotty was probably along in the mess already.

Bosun Peak shrugged and carried on his way. By the time he reached the crew's mess his throat was niggling him again, and he was preoccupied with his speculations on when, and how, disciplinary Nemesis would strike after this morning . . .

. . . so he never noticed that Donkeyman Trott wasn't there after all. Or enquired if anybody had seen the old reprobate recently.

Which they hadn't.

David Temple, still keeping watch on the *Auriga*'s bridge, wasn't aware of the Second Cook's inexplicable behaviour with the soup ladle and the consequent delay in serving another meal on that penultimate day. Even if he had been, it wouldn't have concerned him unduly; no dinner could ever inspire in him the same reverence as a properly presented English breakfast. Apart from which, he held the watch until 2000 whatever happened, so the timing of his short chow relief wasn't too critical.

There was another factor contributing to the Mate's contentment. It was a magnificent evening; exceptional for the North Sea, with the wind a balmy southerly airstream caressing the port side of the ship, and the sun a fading smile in the sky igniting a thousand fiery wavelets along the take-off wake of the odd seabird flapping wildly to vacate the ship's hydraulically determined track across that burnished surface.

It was the kind of night when a seaman could give thanks for being a seaman, and maybe come to terms with the sacrifices demanded by his calling. Though in David Temple's case it had been Jennifer who had finally and tearfully presented the ultimatum — either the ship, or her.

She was a lovely ship, the *Auriga* . . .

He leaned back into the corner of the starboard wing, elbows propped against the teak rail, and wryly surveyed his chosen option. Why had he substituted the erratic trace of a Seagraph III echo sounder for the beat of a woman's heart; or the angular coldness of Chadburn telegraph and Decca radar for the soft curves of breast and shoulder and thigh? Whatever had possessed him to set the remote efficiency of a total-flooding CO_2 fire-fighting system against the softly whispered words which quench a woman's fears, or a Gringe smoke detector against a truly loving husband's perception of the tremulous early warnings of a wife's distress?

He didn't know, though on certain nights such as this he began, just began to understand. Probably he never would completely for the sea, like The Madness which was already at work unbeknown to Chief Officer Temple, was an equally insidious captor of the minds of men exposed to its assault.

He lit a cigarette. The smoke, barely varying from its exhaled form, drifted slowly outboard in emulation of the blue exhaust projected from *Auriga*'s rectangular-sectioned funnel abaft the bridge. Abruptly a banging, wooden noise focused his attention back into the wheelhouse again; A.B. Reid, the stand-by Quartermaster, was tidying out the ply-compartmented signal locker, kneeling low and peering ferociously as he rattled and clattered a hand brush into the rear of each section. Around him radiated a multi-coloured fan of international code flags and Temple noted absently that the most frequently used ones — the yellow Q, and the G and H pilot indicators — huddled smoke-grimed and dull beside their pristine brethren. It reminded him in passing that they'd be required again early tomorrow as the ship entered the Firth of Forth . . .

Had The Madness possessed a sense of humour, it might have been smiling broadly at that moment; savouring the bizarre irony of Temple's reflection. For the yellow 'Q' flag was the Pratique request for inward clearance; it declares to the world that *My vessel is healthy* . . . and the 'H' — *I have a pilot on board* . . . Well, perhaps The Madness was also capable of a terrible foresight?

It was odd, the way young Reid kept breaking off from what he was doing and scratching feverishly instead. Temple pushed himself away from the bridge rail and began to walk towards the Quartermaster, intending to ask what was wrong. He'd always been sympathetic towards Reid, possibly because they had something in common; only in the case of Reid's wife there hadn't been a convenient East Lothian District Council official to offer amorous consolation. She just kept spend, spend, spending money the poor sod couldn't possibly hope to earn as her particular form of solace against loneliness.

Until Radio Operator MacNally claimed his attention suddenly, banging his cabin door as he stepped into the narrow transverse alleyway linking his quarters with the radio room on the port side of the bridge deck. The R.O. still wore that faintly puzzled expression he'd first adopted during his earlier attack of . . . cramp, was it? Those pins and needles he'd complained of. Temple opened his mouth to ask if they'd gone away but Sparks forestalled him. As usual.

'I was lookin' for you. Who likes milk on this ship, Mate?'

Temple blinked. 'Milk?'

'Milk,' MacNally confirmed. But there wasn't any fire to it. Almost as if MacNally was forcing himself to be ebullient. 'The white stuff that squirts out've cows.'

'Cows?'

'Animals. With horns an' a leg at each corner . . .'

'What the *hell* are you going on about, MacNally?'

'Every afternoon I get tea, right? An' because I spend hours longer than anyone else aboard in doing my duty, my mission of mercy . . .'

53

'Oh aye?' Temple prodded sardonically, thinking about the feet on the radio desk and the sci-fi paperbacks invariably scattered like confetti within MacNally's shack.

'Hours an' *hours* longer,' MacNally emphasised. 'And because I do that, they bring me a special pot on a tray from the galley to save me mingling with scruffy deck people, and *engineers* . . . wash my mouth out that I should have to use the word . . .'

'Either shut up, MacNally,' the Mate said wearily, and not for the first time, 'or get to the point. What about milk?'

'It's gone; *that's* the point, Mate. Some prowling bastard has stolen my milk — the milk I didn't actually use, and which I left in the jug, on the tray, beside the empty teapot, in my cabi . . .'

Temple had a quick look around the horizon, checking there was nothing in sight, and stepped into the alleyway running abaft the chartroom. 'Let's see,' he said fatalistically. MacNally opened his cabin door again and stood back with a proprietary air.

'Enter, Sherlock Holmes,' he gestured with a sweep of his hand. 'It's not so much the milk that matters; that would've gone back to the galley anyway . . . It's the mess the bastard left that gets on my wick. See?'

Temple saw. And felt strangely uneasy.

The tray still lay on the shelf beside the Radio Officer's bunk, but virtually every article on it had been scattered with an apparently deliberate disregard for the consequences. The teapot had been forced to the raised edge of the tray where it now teetered dangerously; sugar lumps were slowly breaking down in the milk residue left from the overturned jug; the white china cup lay shattered on the deck and MacNally's pillow and bedspread were smeared with a brown sticky substance.

'Chocolate,' the Operator explained angrily. 'The bastard took the spare choc biscuits as well.'

The Mate chewed his lower lip, pensively pushing the teapot back into the middle of the tray while conscious of growing concern. In some ways it was a small incident; but again this was a ship, a captive community, and any contempt for acceptable standards of behaviour by one of its members — such as this theft, no matter how petty, allied to a blatant invasion of privacy — could create ill feeling and mistrust out of all proportion to a similar act ashore.

'Anything else missing?' he queried grimly. MacNally shrugged. 'Not as far as I know. There's British and Finnish small change in the ashtray there; that hasn't been touched. And the drawers seem O.K.'

The V.H.F. exten... speaker from the radio room suddenly crackled. 'Char... Transport, this is *Oil Supplier* . . .'; one of the specialist Nally vessels calling the Ekofisk rigs, now a long way astern had evaporated completely by now.

I suppose I'd better go for dinner. If some bastard hasn't stolen it already.'

Temple noticed the Operator was now flexing his fingers almost constantly, and occasionally massaging the muscles of his forearms without seemingly being aware of it. The gesture made him think of Reid's incessant scratching through in the wheelhouse, but there was the mystery of the milk to take precedence. Then something else caught his eye.

He asked, 'You carry anything wet out of the cabin, did you; say, dripping with spilt milk?'

MacNally followed his eyes. There was a curiously regular line of whitish splodges leading from the bunk to the open door. They faded as they progressed.

'Nope — But someone has.'

'Or some*thing* . . .' the Mate muttered doubtfully, kneeling to inspect the trail more closely and feeling, as he did so, faintly ridiculous. This time Sparks didn't make any facetious remarks about magnifying glasses or meerschaum pipes. The milky traces did seem to bear a certain regularity, a pattern.

'An animal?' Temple frowned. 'A dog, maybe. Or a cat?'

There was no answer and he glanced up quizzically. MacNally was massaging his arms again and looking worried.

'You *sure* you're feeling all right, Mac?'

The Operator started; as if his mind had been a long way awa 'Right . . . ? Yeah. Yeah,' it's jus' these pins an' needles back aga Did you say a dog, Dave?'

'Or a cat. I dunno.'

'But you don't get cats aboard ships. Not now. Not wit rabies regulations.'

'Maybe the cat hasn't seen 'em,' Temple said dryly. 'Or

it's a Finnish cat and can't read English. Anyway, either we've got a stowaway animal on board, or a bloody small-minded thief. . . .'

Suddenly he remembered he'd been absent from the bridge for over five minutes. The *Auriga* had been travelling virtually blind across the last one and a quarter min. of sea. He stood up quickly.

'Got to go topside. Look, leave it and I'll see y

As he left the Radio Operator's cabin MacN at chow.'
moved. He wore that curious, detached expression a ill hadn't
normal circumstances Temple might have voiced his co under
little more forcefully, but every seaman's instinct drove him ba
to the bridge.

Even then his disquiet wasn't really lessened for, despite the fact that his eyes were hurriedly scanning the horizon ahead as soon as he entered the wheelhouse, he couldn't help noticing that Able Seaman Reid was still engrossed with *his* particular obsession too. Scratching, in his case. It might only have been imagination, but didn't there seem to be a mechanical, almost desperate quality to the young sailor's actions? A kind of repetitive, vaguely trance-like sequence of movement . . .?

That was the moment when — despite his puzzlement over the vandalised tea tray, allied to his disenchantment over the precautions he would be forced to institute if there really was a stray unquarantined animal loose — Chief Officer David Temple sensed e first, still unspecific warning that something was not quite right.

That something strange, rather unsettling, was beginning to en to the *Auriga*.

e wasn't fully aware of it at the time, David Temple had ubconsciously linked the inexplicable discomfort in acNally's hands and wrists with the curious physical ered by Duty Quartermaster Reid. Temple was the first *uriga* to recognise, even unwittingly, that whatever rtaking the ship, it was of a collective nature.

be alone in his unease for much longer. The just over one hour. By the time it was com members of that closely-knit maritime com cause for anxiety as they realised that not s beginning to feel an increasing concern

'Anything else missing?' he queried grimly. MacNally shrugged.

'Not as far as I know. There's British and Finnish small change in the ashtray there; that hasn't been touched. And the drawers seem O.K.'

The V.H.F. extension speaker from the radio room suddenly crackled. 'Charlie Transport, this is *Oil Supplier* . . .'; one of the specialist supply vessels calling the Ekofisk rigs, now a long way astern. MacNally switched it off and shrugged again. His enforced bounce had evaporated completely by now.

'I suppose I'd better go for dinner. If some bastard hasn't stolen it already.'

Temple noticed the Operator was now flexing his fingers almost constantly, and occasionally massaging the muscles of his forearms without seemingly being aware of it. The gesture made him think of Reid's incessant scratching through in the wheelhouse, but there was the mystery of the milk to take precedence. Then something else caught his eye.

He asked, 'You carry anything wet out of the cabin, did you; say, dripping with spilt milk?'

MacNally followed his eyes. There was a curiously regular line of whitish splodges leading from the bunk to the open door. They faded as they progressed.

'Nope — But someone has.'

'Or some*thing* . . .' the Mate muttered doubtfully, kneeling to inspect the trail more closely and feeling, as he did so, faintly ridiculous. This time Sparks didn't make any facetious remarks about magnifying glasses or meerschaum pipes. The milky traces did seem to bear a certain regularity, a pattern.

'An animal?' Temple frowned. 'A dog, maybe. Or a cat?'

There was no answer and he glanced up quizzically. MacNally was massaging his arms again and looking worried.

'You *sure* you're feeling all right, Mac?'

The Operator started; as if his mind had been a long way away. 'Right . . . ? Yeah. Yeah,' it's jus' these pins an' needles back again. Did you say a dog, Dave?'

'Or a cat. I dunno.'

'But you don't get cats aboard ships. Not now. Not with the rabies regulations.'

'Maybe the cat hasn't seen 'em,' Temple said dryly. 'Or maybe it's a Finnish cat and can't read English. Anyway, either we've got a stowaway animal on board, or a bloody small-minded thief. . . .'

Suddenly he remembered he'd been absent from the bridge for over five minutes. The *Auriga* had been travelling virtually blind across the last one and a quarter miles of sea. He stood up quickly.

'Got to go topside. Look, leave it and I'll see you later at chow.'

As he left the Radio Operator's cabin MacNally still hadn't moved. He wore that curious, detached expression again. Under normal circumstances Temple might have voiced his concern a little more forcefully, but every seaman's instinct drove him back to the bridge.

Even then his disquiet wasn't really lessened for, despite the fact that his eyes were hurriedly scanning the horizon ahead as soon as he entered the wheelhouse, he couldn't help noticing that Able Seaman Reid was still engrossed with *his* particular obsession too. Scratching, in his case. It might only have been imagination, but didn't there seem to be a mechanical, almost desperate quality to the young sailor's actions? A kind of repetitive, vaguely trance-like sequence of movement . . .?

That was the moment when — despite his puzzlement over the vandalised tea tray, allied to his disenchantment over the precautions he would be forced to institute if there really was a stray unquarantined animal loose — Chief Officer David Temple sensed the first, still unspecific warning that something was not quite right.

That something strange, rather unsettling, was beginning to happen to the *Auriga*.

While he wasn't fully aware of it at the time, David Temple had already subconsciously linked the inexplicable discomfort in Operator MacNally's hands and wrists with the curious physical irritation suffered by Duty Quartermaster Reid. Temple was the first man aboard *Auriga* to recognise, even unwittingly, that whatever affliction *was* overtaking the ship, it was of a collective nature.

He would not be alone in his unease for much longer. The evening meal lasted just over one hour. By the time it was completed several other members of that closely-knit maritime community were to be given cause for anxiety as they realised that not only were they themselves beginning to feel an increasing concern for their own state of health, but also the same rather odd characteristic was apparently developing in those around them.

Chief Engineer Webster, for instance. He'd never been able to shake off that unwelcome lethargy first evinced in the Captain's day room earlier. Maybe it was the unusually close atmosphere in the officers' saloon, aggravated no doubt by the additional delay in actually serving dinner through what was bound to have been another of Sullivan's screw-ups, but Webster found he was fast sinking into a state of utter fatigue. It was as though his mind was outside his body and looking down, hypnotised, unable to concentrate on forcing the fleshy shell of Eric Webster to move, nod, acknowledge the desultory conversation around it.

He was floating; vague; yet his brain was crystal clear in recording and analysing the object of his fixed attention. He was watching – no, staring at with an undeviating intensity – the tips of the fingers on the Captain's right hand as they toyed idly, a little impatiently, with his place setting on the adjacent table.

They were white. For almost the length of his neatly trimmed nails the fingers of the Captain's right hand had turned a pallid, bleached-corpse white . . .

Second Engineer Beckman – whose euphoria at the prospect of unexpected home leave had been just a little shaken in the engine control room – when the chair had stopped spinning but his brain hadn't – had never really felt one hundred per cent since then; not even after a deep yet strangely unsatisfying pre-dinner sleep disturbed, as it had been, by dreams he couldn't quite remember but had nevertheless wakened from with staring, terrified eyes and a pillow drenched with sweat. Now Beckman sat pensively at the foot of the engineers' table and wondered why his feet suddenly seemed so cold.

Second Mate Yancy's hands were cold as well. That fact, in itself, was enough to cause him a certain surprise considering the mildness of the evening and the way he'd been feeling earlier. When Dave Temple had relieved him from the bridge at four p.m. he'd been far too warm, yet now he was conscious of an occasional shiver despite the comparatively higher temperature in the saloon. Yancy's concern at that stage had certainly begun to focus on his state of health, but only in the mildly agitated manner of one threatened with losing an opportunity dearly coveted, and through

57

a mere whim of fate at that — for if *he* couldn't fly out to Singapore tomorrow morning, then the company would send someone else as relief Mate of *Aries*. And Second Officer Yancy would still be Second Officer Yancy for a long time to come.

He didn't feel hungry which, in itself, was a worrying symptom after a four-hour watch in the fresh air, but he decided he would force a good meal down anyway. They said 'Feed a cold and starve a fever . . .'

When Radio Operator MacNally finally arrived late in the saloon to find everybody still unattended, several of the *Auriga*'s officers watched expectantly for the inevitable MacNally sarcasm directed, not for the first time, towards Sullivan's catering department. Only on this occasion Sparks didn't say a word; just sat down quietly and fiddled a bit with his knife and fork. Third Engineer Jennings noticed then that the R.O.'s hands were trembling spasmodically but Jennings didn't risk remarking on it for Sparks, challenged in verbal combat, was an awe-inspiring adversary indeed. Apart from which Jennings had a headache himself an' just wished to Christ he could go home and go to bed.

Every bloody night for the rest of his life.

There was one more participant in that strangely subdued gathering who, by dinner time, had become uneasily preoccupied with his well-being. Furthermore he, out of all those present, was developing what were undoubtedly the most macabre symptoms to date.

Third Mate Garvie's *ears* had begun to feel cold, of all unlikely things; especially considering the hot-house environment of the saloon. Another worry too kept niggling him — a tendon or a muscle or whatever had started jumping tremulously along the left side of his chin causing, or at least Garvie so imagined, a ferocious nervous tic to appear every few seconds.

He was wrong as it happened. The muscular facial spasms were still barely perceptible and, anyway, had any critical observer been assessing Sandy Garvie all that closely they would probably have been struck by a further, rather more gruesome manifestation unsuspected, as yet, even by Garvie himself.

Fifteen minutes before, while hurrying to wash for dinner and with the imminent need to relieve Chief Officer Temple foremost in his mind, Sandy had carelessly pulled the top button from his only clean shirt. Feverishly he'd rummaged for a safety pin, pushed it through the neckband to secure the collar, and continued to don his black uniform necktie.

He still wore the tie, and the shirt. It still looked very smart and clean.

But just below the points of the collar, largely concealed by the knotted tie, seeped a small but gradually spreading stain of bright red blood. For when the young Mate had hastily inserted that safety pin during his moment of sartorial crisis, he'd forced the point of it clean through a carelessly pinched fold of skin and flesh at the base of his throat.

Yet even now, fifteen minutes later, Third Officer Garvie still didn't feel the slightest pain. Or realise that anything was wrong.

In the crew mess the situation was much the same; several men were absorbed with their own particular ailments, but no one felt ill enough to do more than pass it off with a philosophical shrug. What could a bloke do anyway? The *Auriga* didn't carry a doctor to consult about minor irritations — anything serious and the only recourse was a Pan Medic radio call for shore advice, which you didn't get when you only felt tired, or itchy, or your legs were beginning to feel a little odd. Anyway, early tomorrow would see Scotland on the bow and every medical facility available for the asking. Not that the headache wouldn't have passed over by then after a couple of aspirins; and the oddly trembling hands settled again after a good night's kip ... but funny about the legs, all the same. An' the steadily increasing cramp pains in the guts.

They all ate dinner, jaded or not. Most seamen have felt seasick at one time or another, and you can't feel much worse than that. The one thing you do learn is to keep eating; keep your strength up even if every mouthful takes a superhuman effort of will. Nobody felt *that* sick, anyway. Apart from which the Chef had really excelled himself. What with the pork balls done in prune and apple sauce, and the stewed lamb an' cabbage accompanied by lashings of that rye bread smothered in butter to give a soak-up to the gravy ... the Swedish baked omelette all pink with frozen shrimps; toasted rye alongside that, o' course. Followed by rye sweetcakes, an' the cheese — on rye, needless to say. And finally, Sven Holmquist's ultimate offering ... *Bondepige med slör* was the Danish name; *Peasant Girl with a Veil* in English — puréed apple and layered crumbs fried in brown sugar and butter, topped with chocolate, crowned with whipped cream . . .

Crumbs made, once again, from the rye flour salvaged out of the flooded store room.

Tasty, all the same. A bit dry, but very tasty. And the extra roughage wouldn't do those previously unsettled digestions any harm either, come to that.

Rye bread, eh? Must remember to tell the wife about that . . .

The last meal ever to be served aboard *Auriga* was being cleared away by eight o'clock that evening.

And by that time The Madness, too, was firmly entrenched.

It had precisely twelve hours in which to take command before sanity, and the Inchkeith pilot, attempted to board in the morning.

Chapter Five

The Donkeyman's cabin door was still firmly shut when Peak gloomed his way back to his own berth after the meal was over. Of course it had been much as expected — a total bloody disaster what wi' them eggs mucked about with fish stuff, an' a decent bit o' pork spoiled by prune jam or whatever. Well, prune jam on *meat*, f'r Chrissakes . . .

The Bosun frowned. It suddenly struck him that Trotty hadn't been along to the mess for dinner. Peak couldn't remember Trott missing out on a chow session in over twenty years; not apart from that Nagasaki episode, anyway, when they'd both drunk so much rot-gut rice wine that he'd been laid up f'r three days and Trotty had lost his sight for twenty-four hours and hadn't been able to face up to even a cup o' tea for the fear of permanent blindness. But Trott always had been a worrier; convinced his ticker was dodgy since his brothers parted their cables so early in life . . . Come to that, Peak reflected, Trotty *had* been a bit quiet the last time he'd seen him down on the afterdeck. But that was a long time ago, over an hour before the dinner was ready.

He thumped on the closed door and growled, 'C'mon then. Let's 'ave yer.'

There was no answer.

'Trotty?' called the Bosun. 'You in there, mate?'

Still no answer; only the low hum of the air conditioning blower across the alleyway and the noisy clatter of dishes being cleared in the crew mess. A.B. Reid came past, heading back up to the bridge to complete what little remained of his watch and Peak said 'Seen the Donkeyman anywhere, lad?'

Reid shrugged. 'Nope. He wasn't in the mess when I was.'

Peak noticed the youngster was scratching all the time he spoke. 'What're you scratchin' for?' he asked ill-temperedly.

Reid scratched again. 'Because I'm itchy, Bose.'

'Ahhh,' said the Bosun sagely, 'I wouldn't never have thought of a reason like that . . . Where would 'e be, d'you reckon?'

'Trotty?'

'I wasn't thinking about the President of the United States.'

'*He's* not on board, is he . . .?'

Peak glowered suspiciously at the younger man. Reid scratched his backside and said defensively, 'Tried his cabin, Bose? Trott's, I mean.'

Peak thumped the door again, not deigning to reply. Reid looked at his watch anxiously. 'I'm due back up topside. Mister Garvie's already gone up there to relieve Mister Temple.'

'No answer,' Peak muttered fatalistically; life was always like that in his experience; you kept on knockin', but there was never no one there. It was just as well he was a contented man by nature.

'Locked, is it?'

The Bosun tried the handle. The door swung open and then closed again with a click as the ship rolled gently to port.

'No,' Peak said, somewhat unnecessarily.

'Can I *go* now, Bose?' Reid persisted. 'I dunno where the Donkeyman is. Oh, sod this bloody itching.'

'You want to put some ointment onnit,' Peak advised, establishing policy without actually detailing what kind of ointment he was thinking about. 'An' I'll tell you something else, lad —

you'd better get a move on, I don't 'ave no time for sailormen late in relieving the watch.'

Reid went. He didn't say anything because he didn't dare to. He just went. Scratching.

'A bit o' friendly chivvying,' Peaky reflected with profound self-satisfaction. 'A happy-go-lucky Father-figure like me, these youngsters need. To cheer·'em up a bit . . .'

He opened the door again, and stepped a little hesitantly into Trotty's cabin. It was very dark after the brightly lit alleyway — the curtains had been drawn over the single scuttle — and it took Bosun Peak's old eyes a few seconds to adjust.

'Trotty?' he repeated and was surprised to find his voice had modulated to an unintentionally tentative whisper. Maybe that was because he could have sworn he caught a glimpse of something white slipping — or was it more sort of sliding? — around the base of the door frame and disappearing into the alleyway. Something . . . well . . . that couldn't have been in the Donkeyman's cabin in the first place.

Something like an animal, f'r instance.

Which was quite daft, seeing they didn't have any animals aboard *Auri* . . .

Then he stopped speculating; for that was the moment when the darkness finally relinquished its censorship of detail, and when Bosun Peak abruptly forgot all about half-imagined creatures, whether they slipped, slithered or even wriggled impossibly across the periphery of his consciousness. Forgot about everything else too, for that matter, other than the steadily creeping prickle of trepidation below the nape of his scrawny neck.

As the silhouette occupying Donkeyman Trott's bunk slowly materialised through the unaccustomed gloom.

Yet another illusion was beginning to disintegrate rapidly by then — the already tenuous myth of comradely solidarity within the ranks of the catering department.

Even the element of black comedy which usually glossed over times of particular stress was wearing a bit thin by the time Hughie Baird finally returned to the galley, bearing an expression of total mutiny and a pile of dirty dishes balanced precariously in both hands and on the crook of his left arm. The clatter they made as he jettisoned them beside the dishwasher further underlined his resentment.

'Ah'm no' stackin' these in yon machine as well, an' that's for sure. No' when *he's* done nothin' all the meal time.'

'He' was amplified by a jerk of the head towards where young Monaghan still wilted in the Chief Cook's chair — a temerity not entirely overlooked by Holmquist either. In fact the awesome Swede appeared more outraged by Terry's contempt for propriety than his withdrawal of labour since the spilled soup episode.

'And I only create wit my pots and my pans, Chief Stewart; not waste my energies on the cleaning. I am the architect, ya? Not the naval labourer!'

'Navvy's,' Sullivan corrected with a distant look in his eyes; but he was still uneasy about the reception which not only the Captain but all the officers had seemingly afforded what should have proved a highly successful Scandinavian offering. They had been far too thoughtful as they filed from the saloon after eating, almost as if *deliberately* avoiding compliments. Or did that suggest they might have been criticisms?

'. . . it's navvies are labourers, Chef. Not navals,' he supplemented absently. Holmquist drew himself up and frowned severely.

'Is this a sheep or is it not a sheep, hah?'

'Ohhhh *shit*, he's off again,' Sullivan groaned. He made one last attempt to force a conciliatory smile.

''Course it's a shee . . . ship. Yeah.'

The irascible Swede gathered himself for the intellectual kill. 'Then why, Chief Stewart; *why* am I not correct to say *naval* . . . ?'

Fortunately Terry Monaghan chose that moment to utter a low moan which, apart from reminding the others of his existence, also diverted the tension building between his sparring superiors. They turned as one to stare at the lad, even though the interest still tended to be more waspish than concerned.

'I say he's havin' you on,' the Assistant Steward diagnosed mercilessly. But Hughie Baird's stomach was still stinging and pink where the soup had burned him, and his best white shirt with the ego-boosting epaulettes was probably ruined beyond repair. Another thing — the *Auriga*'s Assistant Steward had begun to feel a little peaky himself during the last frenetic half hour; not ill, but definitely off-colour. Probably through being ordered back to

shovellin' out the flooded store room after all they fancy rye sandwiches he'd eaten for lunch . . . yet *Holmquist* had the gall to moan
about bein' a bloody navvy . . .

'I reckon Monaghan's swingin' the lead, Chief. Sat sittin' there
for the past hour while we wis doin' all the graft. So *ah'm* no' going
tae stack the dishwasher if he's . . .'

'I'll only tell you once — shut it, Hughie!'

Sullivan's voice bore an unfamiliar note of menace, and Hughie
Baird suddenly remembered it wasn't only shoreside catering
superintendents who could write the sort of conduct report that lost
a man his job. There was something else, too, about the Chief
Steward's expression which indicated that the petty bickering was
over; that something perhaps a little abnormal was happening in
the galley of the Motor Vessel *Auriga*.

The boy in the chair didn't even seem aware of them as they
moved closer and really looked at him for the first time since his
withdrawal from the fray.

His eyes appeared glazed yet they were staring; almost haunted.
He was breathing in a funny, spasmodic way while, every few
seconds, the arms hanging so limply by his sides gave an odd,
tremulous little jerk before the bowed shoulders sagged once again
in an attitude of utter exhaustion. They were symptoms which,
even taken by themselves, were more than enough to convince the
most jaded cynic that there was something very wrong with the
Auriga's Second Cook.

Only they weren't the only symptoms. For there was one further
manifestation of a more horrific nature to be observed now. A feature
which caused each of the three onlookers to recoil slightly; to
swallow and step back an involuntary pace.

And that was the steady trickle of saliva drooling from the
corner of Terry Monaghan's slack mouth, suspended there and
glistening in the light. A thin cord of mucus growing ever longer as
they stared.

Like the first idiot-oozing of a shrivelling brain.

Third Engineer Jennings and Fourth Engineer Bench had decided
to enter the change-of-watch log readings together; Jennings
because his headache was matching the pain of his homesickness
and he needed something to take his mind off both, and young

Bench because he was still feeling unusually tired — so much so he couldn't even generate his otherwise invariable enthusiasm for the shiny challenge of that part-assembled mini-steam engine — and reckoned he probably needed a change of pace; forgo being a modelling hermit for once and make a sociable gesture.

Not that Wimpy Jennings offered the ultimate in sophisticated discourse, mind you. His conversations tended to wander into rapturous monologues eulogising the delights of being permanently shorebound — supper in a certain chain of enfranchised coffee bars an' then goin' home f'r the night; a few pints with regular pals in the local boozer, then goin' home f'r the night; dancing down the local disco with a bird . . . then goin' back to *her* place f'r the night. Well, Jennings wasn't all *that* obsessed with sleeping in his own bed. Not to the extent of being stupid about it.

As soon as they closed the engine control room door behind them the clamour of the fourteen-cylinder *Pielstick* cut to a muted rumble. The Third wiped his hand across his aching brow and muttered, 'Thank Christ! That'd gie a stone statue a headache, yon noise . . . You enter the figures, Benchy; I'll shout them out. O.K.?'

When he took his hand from his forehead he noticed the back of it was shiny with sweat, the hairs sticking together in little black whorls. That worried Jennings, who was beginning to feel really lousy by then. The air-conditioned environment of the control room tended to be on the dry side if anything; certainly not humid enough to cause perspiration. Furthermore his eyes seemed to be playing him up, too — some of the instrumentation appearing fuzzy, slightly out of focus . . . Mind you, what could a bloke expect, spending eighty per cent of his time in a steel box that never stayed still for two consecutive minutes? Shipboard life just wasn't natural, not like living an' working ashore in a civilised place like Paisley. If human beings had been meant to go to sea then they'da been born with stabilisers for stomachs an' gyroscopically-controlled brains . . .

'Shaft revs — one twe . . . there's a pencil there, kid. Rolled under the rack, see?'

Fourth Engineer Bench nodded and slowly stretched out his hand. It did strike Jennings then that there was a rather excessive expression of concentration on his companion's face but he was too busy screwing up his own eyes to comment, trying as he was to focus on those bloody instruments.

'Shaft — one twenty-nine. Main alternator — one two zero ze . . . Here, you O.K., Benchy? Hey, Benchy . . .?'

'I can't . . .' the youngster muttered. 'Oh Christ, Jennings, I can't . . .'

Jennings stared at the Fourth, forgetting his own headache; forgetting pretty well everything at that moment as he took in the strain, the white lips, the trembling hand gripping the little pencil and sensing, at the same time, the rising panic apparent in the other man's eyes.

'Can't what, Benchy? What can't you do, kid?'

The *Auriga*'s Fourth Engineer half turned towards him. The fingers clutching the pencil were white now, and shaking with tension. There was sweat on Bench's brow too, every bit as shiny as on Jennings'.

'I can't lift it, Wimpy. The — the fucking pencil . . . it's so heavy I can't bloody *lift* it!'

Seaman Derek Guy stood combing his hair in his cabin, blissfully unaware of the various, ominously coincidental happenings currently taking place within the confines of *Auriga*. 'Blissful' probably was the most appropriate adjective to describe his mood — well, hadn't he just completed a fabulous meal? Hadn't the radio just confirmed that his team, in fact the *only* football team — Liverpool — were once again poised to smash their star-studded way through to the coming season's League Cup? Wasn't it true there would be no more nights of lying awake in his bunk and thinking, pining, for the Mum he'd never appreciated until it was too late? Hell, wasn't it the end of rousing out on deck on a wind-swept bloody early morning, along with the rest of the bleary-eyed daywork crowd, to hose an' scrub an' listen to that miserable git of a Bosun carrying on about how things was in the old days when sailors was proper sailors . . . stupid bastards!

Maybe it wasn't all good on reflection — that news about The Team. It took the edge off what he proposed to do shortly. God knew that since he went to sea he'd got little enough chance to watch Liverpool play . . . no, create pure synchronised magic was a better expression, the way the lads rippled an' weaved through the opposition defences . . . but once he was dead, well, that would be that, wouldn't it? It seemed almost like being a traitor, in a way. Lettin' the team down; to kill himself just when they deserved support . . .

He shrugged and promptly forgot about Liverpool Football Club, concentrating, instead, on squeezing an adolescent spot beside his nose. Like he said, you gotter look smart if you're dead; *every*body'll be starin' at you . . .

. . . but The Madness couldn't expect to have things all its own way, not even aboard a vulnerable prey like the *Auriga*. When it came up against someone as mixed up and pitiful as young Derek Guy, anything which affected *his* mental processes was like gilding an already unbalanced lily.

Conscientiously he picked the stray hairs from his comb and dropped them into the waste basket. Mum had always insisted he do that, leave the comb as you found it. Then he slid his small suitcase from its stowage under the bunk and opened the lid.

Everything was there, all prepared and ready; all the aids he would need for his impending self-destruction. A length of nylon rope with a proper hangman's knot in it; a large, see-through plastic bag; a bottle of dilute hydrochloric acid, thoughtfully purchased in Helsinki; another bottle containing five hundred aspirins; a broad roll of Elastoplast . . . and a cut-throat razor. The old-fashioned kind, with a black bone handle and a little, brass-inset motif. The very, very sharp kind.

He lifted the razor out of the case and tentatively opened it. The hollow ground blade sparkled and shone with a bluish sheen, and natural caution told Derek to handle it very carefully. It was the kind of razor a bloke could cut himself on.

Someone started banging on someone's door further along the alleyway but he ignored them, settling down on his bunk and admiring the razor. It gave him a warm, almost a tingling feeling inside; a sort of secret excitement. There was no hurry. He'd probably be dead for quite a while and he wanted to savour the prospect; to anticipate what was to be, all said an' done, a once-in-a-lifetime experience.

He found it difficult to concentrate, though. He couldn't help wondering if he'd done the right thing in wearing his black T-shirt. It would be cold on deck once the sun went down, and Mum always used to tell him about wrapping up well. You could catch a lousy chill, not being properly dressed for the North Sea.

He started to think about Liverpool F.C. again. And to worry in case that bloke on the radio had been wrong about their chances for the Cup . . .

When Radio Operator MacNally returned to his cabin, having virtually ignored everybody else during dinner, he went straight to his bathroom cabinet and rummaged around for something — anything — to quell the sudden nausea swamping him.

Apart from shaving gear there wasn't much in there, MacNally normally sporting the rude health of a stud bull; so all he finished up with was a long plastic tube of giant size indigestion tablets — about twenty of them. He'd bought those a year ago to help in a heated battle with Sullivan over what had constituted, to MacNally's mind, an excess of fried foods in *Auriga*'s diet. For a full week following the clash MacNally, to the escalating fury of the Chief Steward and the unconcealed delight of the other officers, had ostentatiously counted out two tablets before every meal and noisily, pointedly, sucked them as he swept from the saloon.

It had been a close contest. By the time Sullivan grudgingly agreed to increase the casserole and grill content in future menus, Radio Operator MacNally's bowels had seized up like concrete-filled nylon stockings. It had been another long week before he'd been able to sit on the toilet without adopting a blue-tinged expression of strain.

Then he did a strange thing; the sort of action he'd taken in the past when trying by devious stratagems to confound his enemies. Only this time there was one chilling difference. There was no humour in MacNally's eyes as he climbed, still fully dressed, into his bunk and lay back in the mess left by his anonymous visitor. Apparently there was no awareness, either, as cold tea and the dregs of spilled milk soaked into his uniform trousers. He simply lay there with one arm folded behind his head and the other clutching the plastic tube of tablets, holding them high above him, gazing at them with an earnest and undeviating intensity.

Every so often the raised arm did tremble slightly while just occasionally his chest expanded; rising fractionally before shuddering as though clawing for breath. But those movements, combined with the tears which steadily trickled from the corners of his eyes, remained the only indications that Radio Operator MacNally was alive.

By the time David Temple arrived back on the bridge he'd completely lost whatever good humour his earlier reflections had created. For one thing he'd just been virtually barracked into finishing an already late dinner in an even greater hurry, driven from the saloon by the racket that intolerable and far-too-stroppy Second Steward Baird made while clearing tables after the first sitting. That aggravation alone forced the Mate to clench a resolute jaw all the way to the upper deck, willing himself not to strain domestic harmony yet further by inviting the second eyeball-to-eyeball confrontation of the day with Chief Steward Sullivan regarding his bloody slack, bloody useless bloody department . . .

. . . and talking of domestic harmony in relation to galley personnel — there was even more they had to answer for. The belated meal service had eventually caused a domino effect of delay in reliefs, upsetting routine and meaning the four to eight watchkeepers now had to forgo Holmquist's admittedly tempting sweet course in order to gallop straight back to the bridge to hand the formal care of the *Auriga* until midnight over to their successors — which meant Sandy Garvie anyway, in Temple's case, and *he* was already up there.

It was untidy. It was unseamanlike. It was enough to make a Chief Officer like David Temple, fastidious in his clutch on the old-fashioned values, fit to spit marline spikes . . .

Or perhaps the inadequacies of Chief Steward Sullivan were only an excuse for Temple's outward displeasure; a tangible expression of annoyance masking the deeper concern buried in his subconscious.

For in reality he was much more worried by the happenings of that day. By the odd incident involving Sparks' vandalised tea tray, for instance. Could some unsuspected animal really have been the cause? If so, then why had no one else aboard reported seeing it? Or had it been the work of some unbalanced crew member after all; someone simmering with resentment, say, after a verbal collision with the redoubtable MacNally . . .? If it had been, then David Temple, while he couldn't condone it, could certainly understand it.

Perhaps the most unsettling worry of all was presented by the ever-growing enigma he still couldn't put his finger on — that feeling of something ominous about to happen; of something insidious and unidentifiable, already upsetting the well-being of the *Auriga*'s crew . . .

He strode moodily through the wheelhouse and into the chartroom just as the stay-bright imitation-brass plastic clock on the bulkhead struck eight bells — yet another quartz-crystal activated and fully automated symptom of maritime 'progress' in itself.

It was also the precise moment when Bosun Peak's watering eyes finally managed to penetrate the gloom of his missing shipmate's cabin and when Radio Operator MacNally first lay staring in his unaccounted-for mess; while Fourth Engineer Bench was still discovering that an ordinary pencil had suddenly become as heavy as a railway engine. And while the shocked silence in the galley, caused by the hideously drooling aspect of young Terry Monaghan, was becoming so strained you could almost taste the disbelief of it.

Temple was vaguely aware, as he stepped through the chartroom door, of the Old Man's simultaneous arrival on the bridge; climbing the starboard ladder perhaps a little less briskly than was his usual habit during that post-dinner phase of the evening.

Then a confusion of apparently unrelated incidents made him conscious, for the first time, of some crisis much more specific than mere conjecture. The first was the manner in which Third Officer Garvie turned from the chart table at his approach — almost guiltily, yet with a smile which was both defiant and somehow unsettlingly evil.

The second was the shout from below decks; a cry of anguish which must have chilled the blood of all who detected it. The lament of a soul rendered heedless by shock and grief.

It was then that David Temple also registered the blood fouling the base of Third Mate Garvie's throat.

Chapter Six

No member of a ship's crew, whether First Mate or Deck Boy, Greaser or even — to a lesser extent — Chief Engineer, feels completely at ease in the presence of the Master. There is always an awareness, no matter how relaxed the manner of the Captain, of the need to maintain an air of competence; to demonstrate the efficiency and aplomb with which one carries out one's shipboard duties.

In many cases the contemporary Master does not seek or wish it. He doesn't have to; for over three thousand years the sea has fostered an acceptance that he, and he alone, possesses the qualities of a demi-God; that he, and only he, is the supreme authority both under law and in the eyes of the greatest Deity of all. It tends to make him a solitary man but also unique. Consequently it affords an aura of mystique to all but the most inept of Captains, whether they like it or not. It acts as a constant goad to his subordinates during periods of routine; a splint to stiffen their resolve in moments of crisis. It is a great responsibility.

Charles Mowat carried it with a dignity equal to any, and with a conviction greater than most. And why shouldn't he? For in his case that sovereignty was a fact of maritime life . . .

Which was probably why, when terrible things began to happen to the *Auriga*, they were received at first with calm fortitude — merely because the Captain *was* on the bridge. 'Take it easy, lads. God's already in His Heaven!' But then again, none of those present could ever have realised that the eight electronic bells marked not only the beginning of the blackest night but also the end of normality. That they were poised on the brink of a monstrous insanity which would neutralise all previous values as if they'd never existed . . .

It was now twenty hundred hours British Summer Time.

'Come on, Trotty,' Peak said, lowering his head and peering like an uncertain bull into the gloom. 'C'mon, let's 'ave yer, mate . . .'

But the shape at the head of the bunk didn't move; didn't let out a sound.

'Trotty?'

Still nothing. No response at all.

The Bosun moved one faltering step closer, holding the door wide to allow the reflected glow from the alleyway to creep into the cabin. For some inexplicable reason he hesitated to switch on the cabin light itself. Perhaps Bosun Peak was already cold with the fear of what he might see — what he somehow sensed he would see once every possible excuse for delay had vanished.

'Trotty . . .?'

The figure really was huddled; sort of hunched up and pulled back into the corner as if . . . as if trying to retreat, to escape from something. Peak swallowed, conscious as he did so of the same discomfort in his throat he'd felt earlier, but now there was some-thing else — a pounding allied to a liquid rushing, pulsating in his ears. It took him a few more seconds to realise he was listening to the sounds of his own heart, to the physical manifestation of a terrible apprehension . . .

. . . he switched the light on.

'Trotty, mate . . . Awwwww *Christ,* TROTTYYYYYY!'

And that was the moment when Bosun Peak began to cry. For the first time in fifty years he began to cry like a child . . .

'Monaghan . . .?'

The eyes stared back at them, vacant and dull. None of the three gaping men were even aware of the muffled sounds of Bosun Peak's distress from further forward on the same deck, but that was because the galley was presenting its own private brand of nightmare.

The sliver of mucus from young Monaghan's slack jaw touched the Chief Cook's table and began to spread, glinting and radiating outwards.

'What do we dae . . .?' Hughie Baird whispered, all trace of cyni-cism shattered by the apparition which already bore only a faint resemblance to Second Cook Monaghan. 'Ohhhh Jeeze but whit do we *dae,* Mister Sullivan?'

It would be unfair to criticise those watchers for their utter helplessness. Had a hardened medical man well experienced in the routine and not-so-routine of general practice suddenly been confronted by such a rapid deterioration in the human condition, even he might well have been excused an initial period of shocked impotence; an inability to reconcile Monaghan's suffering with what could, at best, only remain as a dim recollection gleaned in student days of afflictions rare and bizarre.

While *Auriga*'s crew were merely seamen; they had no concept of The Madness. They couldn't even be expected to know that such a living foulness could exist, for The Madness, despite the combined resources of specialised research and pathological expertise, still manages to maintain a low profile; invite minimal priority even after two thousand years of assault on humanity. In modern times it is a statistically irrelevant aberration compared with the major causes of man's torment and, as such, commands little of medicine's interest. It is not important.

Unless, of course, you just happen to *be* that tiny, agonised statistic; choking for help under the smother of greater priorities. Because then, with the vitriol already in your veins and the dementia consuming your brain, you will scream aloud to God for the presence of someone − anyone − who is familiar with the ways of The Madness.

But He probably wouldn't hear you. Not from an island of diagnostic ignorance like, say, a ship at sea . . .

'. . . whit are we going tae DO?' Hughie Baird babbled, fast moving towards a state of revolted hysteria. Chief Steward Sullivan flapped his hands helplessly.

'He . . . he's not well. Terry's not well . . .'

'Oh f'r *fuck's* sake!'

Sullivan took a deep breath, fighting to get a grip on himself. 'Call the Captain. Hughie, you go an' get the Captain *jaldi*. Or Temple − anyone dammit . . . Chef! Gimme a hand with him . . .'

But Holmquist didn't budge. Not one inch. He simply stood there gazing at his assistant. A runnel of sweat trickled unheeded down one side of his florid cheek and formed a droplet under the fleshy chin. It looked like a crystal stalactite; an embryonic twin to the mucoid-skein of Monaghan's imbecility.

'I'm not going to touch him. You cannot make me to touch him, Chief Stewart,' he muttered doggedly.

73

Baird stopped halfway through the door; Sullivan stared, one tentative hand frozen above Terry's bowed shoulder.

'Say again,' the older man echoed. 'Say again what you just said, Holmquist.'

There was a long silence interrupted only by the subterranean beat of the *Pielstick* and the erratic half-breaths of Terry Monaghan. The big Swede dropped his eyes.

'Get the Captain, Hughie,' Sullivan said quietly, unexpectedly. 'Go on, son. We'll look after him.'

Assistant Steward Baird hesitated only a few seconds longer, blinking dazedly at the tableau in the galley and especially at the rather surprising and new-found stature of Chief Steward Sullivan then Terry moaned again, a strangled gurgling plea for breath, and the fear mingling with excitement took him running into the alleyway on a fading shout of urgency. Sullivan picked up a clean dishtowel and gently began to wipe Terry's chin; his other hand steadying the boy's shoulder, squeezing it reassuringly.

'O.K., Terry. You'll be O.K. I promise you, son.'

He looked up at Holmquist, conscious as he did so of a great pride swelling within him at his own uncharacteristic composure. Chief Steward Sullivan had always been an inadequate man, unhappily aware of his need to camouflage ineptitude under a screen of hyper-efficiency — which, to everyone else, simply revealed itself in undiluted panic. Yet now he was coping. Better than that, he was gaining strength from the apparent weakness of others.

'Why won't you touch him, Sven?'

The Chief Cook shuffled; it was the first time Sullivan had ever seen him react with anything but uncompromising aggression. It made him feel even more in control.

'Why not?' he said again, just as calmly.

'I am cook. Maybe if Terry got some catching disease I pass it on to the rest of the crew. I got my responsibilities, Chief Stewart.'

Sullivan looked at him expressionlessly, then down at the pitiful creature in the chair.

'Yeah,' he echoed dryly. 'You got to remember your responsibilities, Chief Cook. For a moment I wondered if you was afraid of catching it yourself ... Funny ... how wrong you can be about people.'

He didn't push Holmquist any harder, but that was largely because Chief Steward Sullivan didn't know precisely what to do with the kid anyway.

The Captain would, though. That's what Captains were for.

'It's only a *pencil*, f'r . . .'

Jennings suddenly frowned at the Fourth Engineer, then started to grin in grudging appreciation. He wasn't feeling particularly like grinning — that bloody headache seemed to be getting worse all the time, and now he was cold; imagine sweating, yet feeling cold in the same instant — but the look on Benchy's face was really something. The kid should've been an actor . . . Wimpy *Jennings* should've been an actor for that matter. Actor's didn't have to go on bloody ships.

Yeah, O.K., so joke over. Now — main alternator revs; wun two zero zero . . .'

'I'm not *kidding*, Jennings!'

The plastic brass clock on the control room bulkhead began to chime eight bells. The *Auriga's* Third Engineer found himself listening to it, counting the double rings with a concentration born almost of desperation; as if clinging to the familiar in a world suddenly shadowed by things he didn't understand. Frightening things.

'It's a *pencil*. You gotter be havin' me on, Benchy. Pick it up PLEASE!'

Bench began to go bug-eyed, the tendons in his arm and neck bunching hugely under the strain. Jennings saw but couldn't comprehend the purple flush suffusing the kid's features. The clock finished ringing and the ensuing silence cocooned them, broken only by the throb of the main engine behind the sound-proofed casing and the hum of the blowers, and the harsher rasping of Bench's breathing.

Something blew in Jennings' mind and he lunged for the pencil, snatching Bench's locked wrist with one hand, registering the steely claw of the Fourth's fingers with the other. Maybe it was a reflex, maybe just sheer terror, but Bench immediately shrieked and lashed out with his left; an angled blow skidding awkwardly off Jennings' temple. Jennings started to shout, plead, 'Pick it up;

oh pick it UP you bastaaaard . . .' while boring into his assailant, shoulders hunched and head down for protection.

The pencil spun out of range, cannoned off the engineroom log before skittering over the edge of the desk. It didn't sound very heavy as it hit the deck. Certainly not as heavy as a railway engine.

Bench suddenly went limp and started to cry; great shuddering sobs of near exhaustion. Cautiously Jennings drew away and felt the pain in his head swamp back worse than ever; aggravated by the blow it now seemed his whole brain was loose, toppling to one side within his cranium.

He began to moan softly, not because he was trying to attract sympathy or divert Bench's attention but because he couldn't help it. The extraneous sounds of the ship for the next few seconds were punctuated only by the Third's misery and the stertorous pump of the Fourth Engineer's run-away lungs.

Only after his breathing quietened did Bench grind the palms of his hands against his eyes, for all the world like a little boy fighting for dignity after a tearful tantrum. But there was still an expression of bewildered apprehension about him.

'I'm scared, Wimpy,' he muttered. 'Christ but I'm scared. That pencil, it was like it was welded to the table, so help me.'

Jennings was shivering and white as a ghost. He looked even worse than Bench, but he stopped groaning and bent down with difficulty, holding his head stiff-necked to lessen the pain. It still exploded inside his skull though, coloured lights slowly sliding down against the black retina until they finally disappeared; like a parachute distress flare swallowed by a night sea.

'Take it from me,' he gritted. 'Take the bloody thing an' see what happens.'

The other youngster stared at his extended palm; the pencil looked so innocuous and exactly like a . . . well, a pencil, really. He couldn't help noticing that Jennings' hand was shaking and that there was a curious pallor to the tips of the upturned fingers, as if the blood was draining out of them. Tentatively he reached out with his own hand, then the unreasoning fear overwhelmed him again and he snatched it away sharply.

'I can't, I won't . . .'

Jennings' voice held the tension of a wire stretched to breaking point. He brought his other arm up slowly. There was a fist on the end of it bunched tight as a python's hug. Third Engineer Jennings was one of the biggest men aboard the *Auriga*.

'Take . . . yon . . . fucking . . . PENCIL!'

Another kind of fear made Bench reach out a second time. The Madness had only stroked him; it hadn't made him suicidal. Or not then, anyway. He picked up the pencil.

Between finger and thumb.

'It's not heavy at all,' he whispered wonderingly. And that wonderment in itself demonstrated one of the many ways of The Madness; its ability to create a delusion so intense, so bizarre, that the victim wasn't surprised at the fantasy, only at the return of normality.

Jennings began to feel nauseated as well as headachy and cold and sweaty and trembly. He half-sat, half-fell into the swivel chair and said, 'Christ man but what's happenin' to us?'

'We should tell the Chief,' Benchy urged, every bit as shaken.

The Third shrugged weakly. All that mattered to him right then was the fact that he could be home in Paisley in a little over twelve hours — especially if he simply walked straight off the ship as soon as they got in.

'So what can Webster do? He's no' a doctor, is he?'

Maybe it was Bench's answer that made Jennings stare again in revitalised concern, or maybe it was the look in the youngster's eyes — that burning, slightly excited glint of imbalance. Whatever it was, Jennings suddenly realised that the *Auriga*'s Fourth Engineer wasn't really better; that the thing which had taken control of his mind was still there, gnawing and distorting logic.

When Bench said, perfectly reasonably, 'He could keep the pencil safe, couldn't he? There's scientists ashore'll be dying to examine a pencil like that, Wimpy. One that can suddenly weigh as heavy as . . . as a railway engine.'

Seaman Chikwanda lay in his bunk staring up at the deckhead. His bedlight was on even though it was still broad daylight outside, but he'd discovered after his return from dinner that the altitude and direction of the setting sun in relation to the *Auriga*'s course caused an annoying flash through the porthole every time the ship rolled. He'd still been feeling unaccountably tired so he'd drawn the curtain — and then hadn't been able to sleep anyway because of the unsettling images flitting through his mind.

They'd begun to form some time ago, during the late afternoon when Chikwanda would normally have been working with the weights. He'd been aggrieved then, about the weights and his un-accustomed lack of enthusiasm; there were many occasions, very many occasions in the North Sea, when the motion of the ship made it too risky to undertake even the basic weight-lifting schedule essential to any body-building programme, yet today — with the sea hardly more than a succession of gentle undulations — he'd been unable to summon the energy to tackle them. He hadn't even managed more than a few minutes of general exercise; less than a couple of dozen press-ups had left him face down and gasping like a dying crocodile, which was a jolly damn nuisance altogether. A jolly damn blessed nuisance in fact, and most hurtful to one's pride; being forced to lie down when one could be building muscle.

And it was then they had returned. The images he had thought were finally forgotten.

It had been at the birth of Uganda's torment; during the early days of Idi Amin's regime when the people had believed he was good, and only a few were beginning to fear. Kampala University was still undergoing a ferment of academic excitement at the apparent dawning of an era in which Uganda would become a centre for the sciences, the arts, all things which made a country great.

That euphoria had been just as pronounced within the less erudite departments of the university; among the younger lec-turers concerned with their students' physical attainments, such as junior athletic coach Chikwanda, and that perhaps made it all the more difficult to understand when the long-anticipated logistics of learning never arrived; when reference books and laboratory supplies unaccountably disappeared, and government-promised gymnasium equipment simply didn't turn up.

So the students, encouraged a little by their impatient mentors and the example set by their fellows in the European seats of academic freedom, arranged a 'demonstration'. It was a good-natured demonstration, a cheerful gathering of girls and boys concerned only that the General should hear of their difficulties, and issue a paternal spur to his education ministry suppliers.

Then the soldiers came. Uniformed soldiers. They took thirty of the students away in covered lorries. Quite a few of them were found the following day in the jungle outside Kampala. The boys had been castrated; disembowelled; bayonetted; shot. The girls had been raped; crucified; spitted on bamboo poles; mastectomised by human teeth . . . not many of them had been lucky enough simply to have been shot.

One of the girls had been Chikwanda's fiancée. He had loved her very much. He had revealed his grief too openly, too publicly; the soldiers had visited the university once more . . . but Chikwanda had fled. For many months afterwards he had awakened in the night with staring eyes and the fear-sweat of reprisal varnishing his black skin, for the vengeance of Amin had a long arm.

Until, eventually, Idi Amin too had been forced to run. And the nightmares had ceased, and ex-athletic coach Chikwanda had become a British seaman, because he had no country, no allegiance. The one thing he had never been able to dismiss from his memory was the fact that those soldiers, the animal soldiers who had violated the thing he loved the most, had also been Ugandans.

He didn't want to be a Ugandan any more . . .

At eight bells in the evening watch on that last night of the *Auriga*'s existence Able Seaman Chikwanda lay in his bunk, and stared up at the deckhead, and saw a tiny spider. And remembered death, and violence, and the smell of his own fear.

Then, as he watched, the little spider above him seemed to grow bigger. And bigger still. And its body became fat and leathery-black, palpitating and sidling slowly across the periphery of his vision; a swelling, creeping hideosity poised to strike.

Whereupon the spider looked down at Chikwanda and, because The Madness was spreading in the sailor's mind, he saw it had the head of Idi Amin. And the General-spider smiled at him with round cheeks and jolly bug eyes . . . only Chikwanda could also make out the fangs, and the green slime welcome of that arachnid maw — and the promise of its horror.

Gradually it began to descend, claw legs already hooked in anticipation; revolving slowly above his face.

Lying rigid as a frozen corpse Chikwanda began to whimper, and to lose control over bladder and bowels.

Greaser Behrens found himself thinking about insects too, during that eight bells period in the North Sea when quite a lot of people were engaged in their first traumatic introduction to awful things. Though in Sammy Behrens' case the insects were only part of a more general speculation on the causes of tactile sensation or — as he so succinctly put it to Slimy Simmieson in the crew's recreation room — 'I gotter crawly feeling all over me skin, mate. What c'n make a bloke's skin feel crawly when there isn't nothin' to see?'

'Crabs,' suggested Slimy, idly leafing through a four-month-old copy of *Sea Breezes*. 'You probably got crabs, pal. Squirmin' an' crawlin' an' breedin' like rabbits.'

'I'd know if I'd got *rabbits*,' Behrens muttered, slightly missing the point. 'An' it's only dirty people get crabs. Crabs are parasites; you got to be really dirty to get parasites.'

'That's right,' his oppo confirmed. 'So you probably got crabs like I said.'

'I've had a shower,' Sammy defended himself.

'I've 'ad measles,' Slimy countered. 'About the same time as I had a teddy bear an' a rattle.'

'I din't know you'd lost 'em,' Greaser Behrens growled. 'Anyway you only get crabs around your private parts. I gottem . . . I got whatever it is all over.'

'*Private* parts . . .' Simmieson jeered. 'So *that's* what yer calls 'em is it, vicar?'

'No need to be so fucking crude,' retorted Behrens with shameless hypocrisy.

'*Private* parts,' repeated Simmieson with relish. 'You didn't keep 'em so private that night in Kotka, did yer? An' you didn't keep 'em so private when we picked up them two scrubbers down Leith Walk las' trip, did yer . . .?'

'Christ I could do with a drink,' Sammy muttered in an abrupt change of tack. He wasn't being defensive now; just sincere. Simmieson eyed him with furtive concern — Behrens was a struggling alcoholic and Slimy, behind all the banter, was his mate. Too many times in the past had he watched Sammy Behrens being poured back aboard when he should've been halfway home on leave; too many times had he seen the wild, frightened stare in eyes glimpsing the first horrors of delirium tremens . . .

'No you don't,' he said firmly. 'You been off the booze five weeks now, pal, an' you ain't goin' to spoil no record. We made a deal.'

'Just one can,' Behrens pleaded. 'Half a can. A . . . a lager, even. Now I ain't goin' to go berserk onna bloody *lager*, am I?'

'And I ain't goin' to take the missis all the way to Majorca knowin' you already started back on the juice before I even left, dummy. So forget it.'

'I'm cold,' Behrens said pathetically. 'And I'm crawly all over, Slimy . . .'

But Simmieson's eyes were obdurately fixed on the magazine before him and Behrens knew argument was futile.

What he didn't know was that Slimy Simmieson, too, was feeling terribly cold. And that he was getting sick and dizzy again, just like he'd felt earlier, in the *Auriga*'s engineroom, when he'd fallen off the gearbox casing for no apparent reason.

Despite the sudden shout from below decks David Temple still found himself staring blankly at the bloodstain seeping from under Third Mate Garvie's collar. It wasn't the blood that held him, so much as Garvie's apparent lack of concern over the fact that he *was* bleeding. Any wound, however minor, which could cause that mess had to be painful, certainly uncomfortable, so why was the youngster so unperturbed about it?

Or was that the real reason for Temple's unease at the appearance of the Third Mate? Garvie's initial expression on seeing him had changed to a perfectly normal smile of welcome, but there had been something else there at first — something disturbing. Something chilling even, despite only that fleeting impression of it . . .

'What the hell's wrong with your neck?' Temple snapped, angry with his own reaction; angry that he knew some more urgent crisis was developing below but that for some reason he felt compelled to ignore it until Garvie had spoken.

'Neck, sir?' Garvie said innocently.

'Oh come on, Garvie — you know damn well what I mean.'

The shout came again, closer this time. Garvie tried to squint downwards, under his chin, but only succeeded in contorting his facial muscles in comical, cheek-straining gloom. He fumbled

81

under the knot of his tie with his fingers instead. When he looked at them the tips were red; sticky red.

He said, 'Oh!' in a surprised voice. Temple nearly snarled in frustration.

'*Oh?*' Whaddyou mean — OH?'

'It's blood,' Garvie muttered blankly.

'Where from?'

'Me, sir?' Garvie hazarded vaguely, a little timid at his senior's reaction.

Urgent footsteps began to clatter up the internal stairway to the bridge while the Old Man's irritation echoed through from the wheelhouse. 'Where *is* everybody? Mister Temple . . . Garvie! Dammit, but am I running a madhouse out here . . .?'

Which was an exquisite irony considering . . . Temple slammed the chart table in thwarted surrender; yelled 'Look in the mirror for God's sake, laddie', and hurried through the door muttering, 'Coming! Coming f'r cryin' out loud . . .' It was only a defence, only weak bluster to conceal the real apprehension growing within him.

'Everybody' obviously meant, to Captain Mowat's way of thinking, the *Auriga*'s deck officers. Cadet Kennedy's over-generous figure could already be detected on watch, discreetly keeping out of the way in the far corner of the port bridge wing. Mulholland, the relieving eight to twelve Quartermaster, stood looking in disgust at the still-to-be-re-stowed contents of the flag locker abandoned earlier by Reid while A.B. Reid himself was arriving at the head of the port ladder, scratching continuously and saying plaintively, '*I'm* here, sir, I got sent for a late meal an' I been loookin' for ointment an' then the bloo . . . the Bosun, sir, was needing a hand with the Donkeyman's cab . . .'

'. . . and who's doing all the shouting?' continued the Old Man, his flow of petulance barely interrupted by Temple's appearance. As breakfast symbolised a hallowed moment of the day for Chief Officer Temple, so did his evening sojourn on the bridge traditionally represent a cherished period of tranquillity for *Auriga*'s Master. It was a good time, a quiet time; a time when he felt close to the ship, and even closer to God.

It was a bad time for anyone daring to disturb Charles Mowat's reflections. But bad times are relative; can only be measured against the yardstick of normality — either the Old Man was in a paternal mood or in a bloody foul mood — so when Assistant Steward Baird finally burst upon *Auriga*'s bridge blurting 'Monaghan! Terry Monaghan's awfy sick ...' there was still no way of knowing they were about to enter the worst time of all.

Certainly the unexpectedly tolerant manner in which the Captain received that violation of his nocturnal communion; the controlled nod he directed towards David Temple as authority to go down and investigate; did nothing more to aggravate the understandable concern shown by those present. Even Temple, already more aware of strange things occurring aboard the ship than anyone else, was briefly reassured by the composure of his Master as he followed Baird's clattering footsteps back down the route to the galley.

At five past eight on that last night there was still no sense of impending catastrophe; no premonition that every last man in *Auriga* was in terrible danger.

Apart from any awareness young Monaghan may have had perhaps, secretly perceived through some dim window in his shrouded mind. And by Seaman Chikwanda, still staring gob-eyed at the loathsomeness above him.

And by Bosun Peak, of course, who had, by then, looked upon the ultimate work of The Madness; and so learned precisely what it could do to a man.

Chapter Seven

Peak was leaning against the alleyway bulkhead as Temple and Baird hurried towards him. Neither particularly registered his attitude, he was simply there as an obstacle to be circumnavigated. Hughie Baird shoved past unseeingly, worried sick with the need to get back to Monaghan; David Temple just tugged Peak's sleeve and said urgently, 'Galley, Bose, Monaghan's had an attack or something ...'

He was ten yards past before he realised Peak wasn't following;

wasn't even making an effort to stir himself. Stopping, he turned, frowned back to the exasperation of the over-excited Hughie Baird.

'Come on, sir! He's awfully sick . . .'

'Peak? Come on, Peak!'

The Bosun still didn't budge; just lifted his head a fraction and drew a deep, shuddering breath. Something sparkled on his cheek, a fleeting diamond under the deckhead glare, and if Temple hadn't known Peaky better he might have sworn it was a tear.

'He's dead . . .' the ancient mariner muttered and then sort of hugged himself, clasping his arms tight around his chest as if suddenly cold. ''E's dead I tell you,' he repeated in a whisper.

'He cannae be,' Baird blurted out, ashen-faced with the shock. 'Terry cannae be *dead*. No' as quick as that . . .'

The way he said it made it more of an appeal. Temple felt his previous foreboding returning but this time it had an edge to it; sharp-honed by a fearful certainty.

'Who's dead, Bose? *Who's* dead for Christ's sake?'

Peak opened his mouth but then the thin face dissolved again in grief. His eyes said enough, though; their liquid gaze fixed hypnotically on the open door opposite . . . The *Auriga*'s Chief Officer began to run towards it, all pretension to dignity overwhelmed by that mute confirmation of some awful occurrence. Desperately he clutched for the anchor of the door frame, pivoted under that headlong rush, cannoned against the further post . . . and halted.

Stunned.

The corpse of Donkeyman Trott was sitting — no, cowering in the corner formed by the head of his bunk; pulled back and shrivelled like some wizened monkey-figure frozen in mid-terror. A stiffening, huddled untidiness of arrested death . . .

He must have been changing for dinner when . . . *it* happened. His working gear still lay strewn beside the bunk while his best trousers — the ones Trotty had only worn for twenty-odd years — were hitched halfway up white matchstick legs, now drawn hard to his scrawny chest. Otherwise he was simply wearing a vest; a yellowed, dirty vest with a frayed tear under one spindly arm. It seemed so unfair. Donkeyman Trott had always been a scruffy, unedifying little man in life, attracting lasting friendship only from the equally colourless Bosun Peak, yet somehow they had managed to maintain a precarious dignity, the two of them, even though owing more to advancing years than to personalities. Yet now Trotty's dignity had been stripped by death; demeaned as he was by the embarrassment of his puny nakedness.

'Awwww *Jesus*!' Baird's tremulous whisper came from behind. 'Aw Jesus, sir, but look at his eyes . . .'

They were huge. Staring. Even dull-glazed as they were under the patina of approaching mortification they seemed to hold Temple, as if it were he, and not the ghastly thing which must have occurred earlier, that was responsible for their condition. They were still pathetic, still disbelieving; still reflecting an unimaginable horror . . .

Abruptly Peak shouldered Temple aside, blundering past and into the cabin itself. Bending down, the old seaman seized the lower edge of the coverlet, tenderly turning it upwards and backwards to conceal his friend's humiliation. Now Trotty only looked as if he were sitting up in bed; quite normal in a way, if it hadn't been for the raised arms clasped elbows together, palms outwards as if to ward off some anonymous threat. And that bloody awful terror distorting his suffused features . . .

'You're not to stare at 'im,' Peak half sobbed, half shouted. 'I'll see to 'im. I'll do everything f'r 'im, Mister. But you ain't goin' to look at 'im like that no longer.'

David Temple looked at the Bosun instead and saw, mixed in with the grief and the sadness, a terrible anger. And knew he had to be very, very careful.

'We've got to know how,' he said, clawing for control. 'We've got to find out how he died.'

Peak stood on guard a moment longer and the Mate noticed, without thinking any more about it then, that the prominent Adam's apple was constantly working, as if trying to swallow. Then Peak sagged slightly and stood aside.

'His heart,' he muttered. 'Trotty always 'ad a dodgy ticker.'

Temple cautiously entered the cabin, forcing himself to approach the bunk and look down at Donkeyman Trott. The eyes still seemed to stare back at him. He knew he was supposed to do something; draw the lids down to close them like they did on films when a celluloid hero died, but Trotty hadn't really been a hero, and this wasn't a film. He couldn't bring himself to do it.

Hughie Baird stirred in the alleyway. 'What about Monaghan? We've got tae get back tae Monaghan, sir.'

Temple nodded, mesmerised by that blind accusation. There was still one action he had to take; not so much for Donkeyman Trott as for *Auriga*'s log. Hesitatingly he reached for one bony wrist, forcing back revulsion and concentrating instead on feeling for a pulse.

It struck him that he didn't really know where to find it. Oh, he'd idly counted his own heart beats before — it had been one of many ways of passing a boring period in school — but he'd never been all that sure what part of the wrist to hold; not until he'd actually located the throb of the artery itself. How did one find the negative factor of a dead man's life-stream? When did one relinquish what one already knew must be a fruitless quest?

It was then that he saw the scratches.

There were three of them, running close together and diagonally across Trott's left forearm. They hadn't been there long, the gleam of fresh blood caught the light in congealing hair-lines. He bent to see better. They continued clear across the underside of the left arm and then jumped the gap, reappearing faintly as fading abrasions in the skin of the right.

'Bosun?'

Peak shuffled to stand beside him. Temple gave up his search for the pulse and gestured gently. 'Did he have these the . . . last time you saw him?'

Peak frowned. The old eyes were still liquid but his face bore a more normal expression of gloom. He shrugged. 'No . . . I dunno. But it wus his heart killed 'im. He always said it would.'

'Sir,' the Assistant Steward's plaintive urgency was heard again. 'Please, sir, but there's Monaghan. An' there's nothing we can dae for the Donkeyman . . .'

Temple stirred, stood upright. He couldn't take his gaze from those scratches. They *were* recent and, furthermore, almost certainly made while the arms were locked together like that. Protectively. But to defend himself against what?

'The scratches,' Peak muttered so low Temple hardly caught it. 'They look like they wus done by an animal. By . . . a cat.'

Auriga's Chief Officer suddenly shivered. It was as if a cold wind had curled around the door and caressed him but he knew it wasn't that; not in this air-conditioned environmentally controlled steel box. No; it was because of the question that loomed larger in his mind as he looked at the fine lacerations — those incontrovertibly feline scratches — on the dead man's arms.

'Dear God,' he thought, 'but what kind of cat can become so powerful that it can kill a *man*?'

Which was the precise moment selected by Hughie Baird to put into words what Chief Officer David Temple had hardly dared to consider as an answer. Something only a distraught boy would actually say aloud on an isolated ship, far from land and help.

'The Donkeyman, sir. Ah've been lookin' at his eyes,' the Assistant Steward whispered tremulously. 'Och Jeeze, sir, but ... but ah'd *swear* yon poor wee bastard died of fright.'

Chief Engineer Webster was having trouble with his vision too. Oh, nothing as permanent as that suffered by Donkeyman Trott who would never see again; but still confusing for the Chief.

It wasn't so much a diminution of sight in Webster's case as a failure of co-ordination between eyes and brain. He was still perfectly able to see detail — in fact detail tended to be even more noticeable than usual in that little things like textures of paint and the colours of the evening sky seemed to generate a sense of wonderment never before experienced — but there was a perplexing inability to relate those visual experiences to reality; to draw any conclusion from observation. It was an extension to that phase of detached introspection felt earlier, during dinner in the officers' saloon.

It was probably most apparent when he walked, or maybe floated was a more apt description, back to his quarters. There was a door in a bulkhead, and a little white plate with brass screws bearing the legend *Chief Engineer* which he'd hardly been aware of before by virtue of its familiarity, yet this time he'd had to stare at it, and concentrate hard, and only then was he satisfied that it was the door to his own cabin.

Eventually he'd gone back to trying to finish his letter to Aggie in which he had to explain why an air compressor claimed higher priority over his leave time than she did. Or Cindy did; and Willie and Susie and Jerry an' little Tommy an' ...

... but he'd never managed to marshal his thoughts before there came an abrupt knock on the door followed almost immediately by the entry of Third Engineer Jennings with young Bench in tow, both looking a bit flustered.

'Come . . .' the Chief shouted about ten seconds too late.

'Can we see you, Chief?' Jennings appealed worriedly.

'. . . in,' finished the Chief doggedly, shoving his writing pad to one side. Whenever Wimpy Jennings paid a visit the subject of discussion was never in doubt. Eric Webster wasn't *that* far removed from reality.

'No, you *can't* go home to Paisley when we get in,' he began, attempting to forestall the inevitable request. 'An' your contract of service is with head office, Wimpy son, so there's no point in botherin' me with . . .'

'It isn't about that, Chief,' Jennings retorted, looking white and shaky. And it wasn't — Jennings had already decided he was going home with or without bloody permission anyway. But there were still twelve hours to go, and Jennings was getting more and more uneasy.

'Oh,' said the Chief, looking bewildered. Even if he'd been thinking with crystal clarity he'd still have felt at a loss; he'd never once spoken to Third Engineer Jennings before without Paisley dominating the conversation. He reflected 'Perhaps the ship's sinking instead? Or they've set my engineroom on fire. Somethin' *almost* as important as bloody Paisley.' But he couldn't generate any real concern.

'Can I sit down, Chief?' the Third muttered.

Webster stared resignedly at the abandoned writing pad and tried to think of some reason, any reason, to cut this unwelcome visit short. He was definitely feeling peculiar — his old stomach pains seemed to be coming back now; probably triggered by worry about little things a less responsible man would have ignored but which he, being Eric Webster, couldn't overlook. 'D'you really have to, lad?' he sighed, injecting a wistful note of discouragement.

It was only when he saw Jennings already sitting on his settee and looking at him a bit oddly that he realised it had taken him a full minute to respond. Bench must have noticed too, because the youngster shuffled in the doorway and asked, 'You all right, sir?'

'Nice lad, Bench,' reflected Chief Engineer Webster distantly. 'Still calls his superiors *sir*, and likes the sea; engineerin' daft and responsible with it . . .'

But it was an abstract rumination, vague and as if from a distance; just like his earlier contemplation of the Captain's fingers . . .

'Not marvellous,' the Chief conceded. 'You might as well sit down too, son.'

'Thank you, sir,' echoed Bench awkwardly. Already seated.

Webster leaned back and eyed his two juniors with a certain paternal impatience. Neither of them said anything, yet slowly, despite his remote preoccupation, the Chief found himself becoming more and more intrigued with the reason for their visit. Jennings looked flustered somehow; all upset and pretty peaky with it judging by his pallor and the way his hand trembled as he played with a pencil . . . while young Bench — he seemed almost the reverse. His attitude was one of pent-up excitement; a tense, almost overwrought air of having made some still-secret discovery, revealed not only in the way he perched rigidly on the very edge of the settee but by the sparkle of agitation in his eyes.

And the way, the rather odd way he kept staring at Jennings' hands. Or was it at the pencil in Jennings' hands . . . ?

'Well?' the Chief made the effort to ask eventually.

It was Jennings' turn to wriggle uncomfortably and look embarrassed.

'It's . . . this, Chief.'

Webster eyed the proffered object. 'It's a pencil,' he declared with complete authority.

'Yes, Chief. But Benchy here says it's . . . oh, Christ, but this is bloody stupid, so it is.'

'Are *you* feeling all right, son?' Webster interjected, with sudden concern. Jennings was looking really white now, and a bit distressed. The ship rolled slightly, only a gentle lurch but enough to make the Chief think absently that the sea must be getting up a little; one big swell meant there were others to follow.

'What about the pencil?' he added, encouraged by the prospect of early release from what seemed a rather pointless discussion. 'Then you get to bed, Wimpy. Bed's best when you're a bit low.'

'It's a special pencil, sir,' Bench abruptly put in, unable to contain his secret a moment longer. 'It . . . well, it's a very heavy pencil. Sometimes, anyway '

The Chief looked at him. 'What?'

'The pencil, sir. It was too heavy to lift earlier — like it weighed heavy as a . . . oh, a railway engine or something.'

This time the silence was even longer.

'Don't be silly, lad,' the Chief said. Finally.

'I'm not, sir. Honestly, down in the control room it was heavy as a . . .'

'Oh, give me the pencil,' Webster demanded wearily, holding out his hand. Wimpy Jennings didn't respond right away, just sat there looking white and unhappy and almost apologetic.

'Look, maybe we should go, eh? Ah'm holdin' the thing an' *ah'm* not having troub . . .'

'Give me the bloody pencil,' snapped the Chief shortly, determined now to get the whole damn farce over and done with and earn a bit of peace and quiet.

Jennings gave him the pencil. Bench stared at it during every millisecond of its transference.

'See?' the Third said dismissively.

'Please, sir, I think we should keep it. For examination,' Bench appealed. The way he said it brought all Wimpy Jennings' fears to a head, because this *was* the Chief Engineer's cabin, and no junior officer with Bench's seriousness would have dared to maintain a joke such as this in the presence of ultimate authority. And then there were Bench's eyes . . . eyes revealing an expression totally outside the conception of any prankster.

. . . and that was the moment when Wimpy Jennings finally accepted that Fourth Engineer Bench of the *Auriga* really had become insane.

'It *is* heavy, isn't it, sir?' Bench prompted anxiously while, for the first time, Jennings noticed something peculiar about the kid's mouth. He kept passing his tongue around his lips, and they were cracked and dry; starting to peel, almost to wither . . .

'Don't be bloody *silly*, son,' Webster said again, even more firmly this time, and Jennings felt unbelievably grateful for that voice of blessed reason. In fact he was so grateful that he began to

90

cry, which was a disturbing thing in itself and could never have happened if he'd still been home in Paisley.

Funny — about the tears. A bit . . . crazy, really.

'Don't be bloody silly,' the Chief snapped for a third time, holding the pencil and looking down at it with complete conviction. 'There's nothing heavy about this pencil, young Bench, an' that's a fact . . .'

Then his voice broke off. Wimpy Jennings gazed at the older man through a blur of tears and noted the changing expression on his face. And saw the odd manner in which Webster was now holding the pencil — with his hand over it; pressing down; and with his whole hand and arm trembling as though exerting an unbearable pressure . . .

'Oh, Christ!' Jennings heard himself praying through a nightmare of approaching terror. 'Ohhhh dear sweet Jesus *Christ*, please save me from them . . .'

'Jennings . . . Bench,' Chief Engineer Eric Webster croaked with the veins standing out against his straining neck. 'Help me, damn you! The pencil. . . . It's trying to get away, lads. It's tryin' to float clear up to the bloody sky . . .'

Derek Guy found himself getting more and more irritated as the noises in the crew alleyway continued. First there'd been banging on someone's door; then shouting, then Mister Temple's voice and running feet, then, strangely enough, that long silence which followed. That interminably long silence.

It was, in fact, the silence that finally made him move. The longer it lasted the more his curiosity overcame his annoyance at what should have been the most meaningful evening of his life being spoiled by people — including officers — who should've known better. And it *was* a special time? 'Course it was. Well how many would-be suicides gave themselves long enough really to think about it . . . to savour and plan, and just . . . well . . . jus' make a proper *event* of their self-destruction instead of doin' the first botched-up thing that came into their heads?

Pity about Liverpool F.C. . . . . It was niggling him, that was. Not to be there to encourage the lads . . .

He sighed and swung his feet over the edge of the bunk.

Standing up he waggled each leg in turn, shaking the creases out of his jeans with a proper appreciation of the solemnity of the coming occasion and the need for good appearance. Then, still being careful in case he cut himself, he placed the black-handled razor back in its box and locked the most important suitcase in the world before sliding it into its stowage.

There was a vague mutter of voices now, down the alley somewhere around the Donkeyman's berth. Hughie Baird's? Yeah, unfortunately one of them was Hughie Baird's. He didn't much go on Hughie Baird who was just a puffed-up little café hand with his one thin gold stripe an' his Glasgow accent.

Worse than anything else; worse even than ... than, well, *anything* was the fact that Hughie Baird was a *Celtic* supporter. Hell, they weren't English. They didn't even play *football*, come to that. What was it Baird called their game ... fitba' or somethin'?

One last critical glance in the mirror and Derek stepped out into the alley. Plenty of time to come back later; get prepared and up on deck when it got dark. Mustn't forget the suitcase. He smiled a little to himself at that. Imagine goin' all that way up to where he meant to kill himself, and then finding he'd forgotten the *suit*case.

It was a shame that he couldn't risk telling anyone a joke as funny as that ...

The noise had been coming from the Donkeyman's cabin. Hughie Baird was looking into it with his back turned towards Derek and, even from here, an odd tenseness evident in his stance. Derek hooked his thumbs into his new leather belt with elaborate casualness — mustn't let Baird notice anything special about his manner — and strolled nonchalantly towards the low mutter of conversation.

It was only when he came up behind Hughie Baird and looked into the Donkeyman's cabin and saw what was happening in there, that young Seaman Guy felt his whole world slipping sideways; all his so-fastidiously prepared plans under sudden threat ...

Chief Officer Temple noticed him first; standing behind Baird with that expression of total disbelief on his pastier-than-normal face, and his big round eyes and the way the boy shook his head from side to side as if unable to comprehend what had happened to Donkeyman Trott.

But it wasn't Derek Guy's physical reaction which caused David Temple's mouth to sag in ever-growing confusion; that could have been anticipated from any youth encountering a terrified corpse. It was the flood of venom which poured from Derek Guy's bloodless lips.

The way the awful child kept muttering, over and over again, 'Ohhhh the bastard! Oh the selfish old *bastard*! How could 'e do it to me? How could 'e *spoil* it like that f'r me?'

Outrage at the unjust caprices of fate wasn't felt solely by young Guy during those first traumatic minutes of the evening watch. Second Officer Yancy was probably the most deeply concerned. He now felt even more disoriented and giddy, while the chill in his hands had gradually spread to his other extremities leaving his feet, ears, even the tip of his nose numb and unfeeling. In fact Bill Yancy, trying desperately to relax in his cabin, was beginning to be frightened as well as resentful at the looming prospect of illness forcing him to stumble on what was, at best, an ever-narrowing promotion ladder. For the first time he was uneasy not simply at the short-term effect his strange illness might have on his career, but even more at what kind of affliction it was. The more he worried about it, the more agitated he became. The more agitated he became, the sicker and dizzier and plain bloody ill he felt . . .

He had to cling to the bunk for support as he swung his feet to the deck. He noticed how badly his hand was trembling as he opened the medicine cabinet door, and when he shook the bottle of aspirin into the palm of his other hand six or seven, instead of the intended two tablets, rolled out.

Yancy stared at them in frowning concentration, then — inexplicably, because he was perfectly aware of what he was doing and how silly it was — he crammed the whole handful into his mouth and began to chew with a mechanical, repetitive motion. His mouth was extraordinarily dry and every so often tiny crumbs of aspirin fell out and tumbled to the deck. He heaved a funny little sigh once during that time and a cloud of white dust sprayed from between his cracked lips.

They were good, though. Very effective. After he'd finished swallowing he didn't feel frightened any more; in fact he even caught sight of himself in the bathroom mirror and found he was smiling — white streaks all down the corners of his mouth and white dust all over his shirt front and he could still smile.

Second Officer Yancy tipped another half dozen aspirin tablets into the palm of his hand and began to chew again . . .

Second Engineer Beckman was another man disillusioned, as were Yancy and Seaman Derek Guy, by the cruel fickleness of the world. One deck below Yancy he, too, sat dispiritedly in his cabin and brooded over the prospect of staying aboard under doctor's orders in Leith instead of catching the train home for that bonus leave with Ella.

Like Bill Yancy's his mouth was terribly dry, but the earlier sensation of cold feet had given way to a burning pain in his stomach; a feeling of hyper-acidity you'd expect if you were suffering from a stomach ulcer or something. An' that would be typical, too — Chief Webster doing enough worrying for the whole engineering department of the *Auriga* yet him, Beckman, finishin' up with the bloody ulcer.

He decided dispiritedly to clean his teeth; see if it made his mouth any fresher, then, if his stomach still didn't feel easier, he'd go and ask if Sullivan had anything in the ship's medical stores that might help him.

He wobbled a bit as he stood up and reached for the toothpaste, and that made him think of Slimy Simmieson the middle watch greaser. Odd when you thought about it, the way Simmieson had just . . . well . . . fallen off the gearbox casing like that. If it'd been Behrens, now, he might have understood it. Behrens was always either half drunk or half bloody sober, but not Slimy, whatever Beckman pretended to think in public. Slimy was a steady man, and climbed around ships' engines like a sea-monkey . . .

Second Engineer Beckman stopped deliberating suddenly and blinked instead.

Without being aware of what he was doing he'd been squeezing the tube continuously. Now a spiralling white worm of toothpaste lay coiled in the basin like some flaccid maggot exhausted in its escape bid from the sanitary holding tanks.

Under normal circumstances Beckman would have been amused at himself, doing an absent-minded thing like that. He would

94

probably have remembered to tell Ella as a joke against himself; like she did when she related incidents of putting casseroles to cook in the spin dryer and that time when she put the hot water bottle outside the front door and the surprised family cat found itself tucked firmly up in bed. But Beckman didn't laugh on this occasion, not even a wry smile to himself.

Because he discovered that, even though he *knew* what he was doing to the toothpaste tube, he still couldn't stop. All he could do was stare at a remotely connected hand just squeezing, and squeezing, and squeezing.

One more member of the crew was sharing the same sense of outrage against life's adversities, and that was Ordinary Seaman Grainger.

Which was really justice when you thought about it, seeing Grainger had done more with his high-pressure flash of temper to invite the *Auriga* nightmare than anyone else aboard. But of course, to Grainger it simply represented another cruel twist of the knife of fortune. So much so that, when he heard the shouting and the running footsteps in the crew alleyway, he ignored them, just continuing to lie in his bunk glowering up at the deckhead with his hands behind his head, simmering furiously at everyone an' every-bloody-thing. And while he did so he felt more and more lousy, and more and more resentful towards that creepy little bastard Hughie Baird for the way he'd contaminated his — Grainger's — beloved Olga; and more and more bitter towards Po-faced Peak f'r sending him, sick as he was, down that bloody awful cable locker again after lunch. *And* towards Chief so-called-Officer Temple for the lack of understanding he'd shown regarding Grainger's perfectly justifiable act of self-defence this morning, and the Mate's subsequent indifference to his, Grainger's, victimi-sation under an antiquated system which revealed nothing less than total contempt f'r conditions of service clearly stipulated by Seamen's Union agreements . . .'

'Oh Gawd,' Grainger suddenly blurted aloud. 'I'm gonna be sick . . .'

Panicking, he swung his legs over the edge of the berth with the bile already sour in his throat. The wash basin was a long way away, almost hidden under a heap of rust-smeared working gear. Without any further warning Grainger felt the vomit surge clear into his mouth, the explosion tearing his guts apart even as he levered his abruptly contorted body out and down, feet scrabbling for the deck less than six inches below.

'Awwwww Chriiiiist,' he gibbered, with foulness spraying through agony-clenched teeth, hardly heeded now because of the shock of what was happening to him.

Perhaps that was because Ordinary Seaman Grainger couldn't seem to find that deck such a short way below him. In fact his brain, his senses, his whole disintegrating awareness told him he was falling, falling, falling into a pit of demented horror.

But that was only another of the many ways of The Madness.

And it had barely touched upon *Auriga* even then.

Chapter Eight

It was as if time had been condensed during those first few minutes of that last evening watch. Certainly there had been indications for some hours that a crisis *was* developing aboard the *Auriga*, but until then they had been widely separated; unnoticed by most and unconnected even by those of the ship's complement — such as Chief Officer Temple — who had been conscious that things were not entirely in order.

Until eight bells. When the blitzkrieg was finally launched.

In fact had The Madness possessed a humanoid counterpart, and had that counterpart been of a military character — say the supreme commander of some alien task force seeking a foothold on foreign soil — then by ten past eight it might have been very, very pleased with the results of its strategy.

Within minutes of its open declaration of war it had simultaneously struck at all four departments of the target's operating structure. Command, motive power, communication and logistic sections of *Auriga* had already been undermined, not only by the surprise of the assault but also through total ignorance of what *was* happening to them. Those two factors alone were enough to place the *Auriga* in jeopardy; for resistance to any form of threat, whether psychological, biological, toxicological or from little green monsters from outer space, can only be possible once that threat has been identified.

But as you could hardly expect a specialist in the ways of The Madness to be qualified to drive a ten-thousand-ton ship around the world; then neither could you reasonably demand that a sailor-man should be expert in the remoter fields of medical catastrophe. Even if they *did* appreciate the character of their affliction in the first place . . .

. . . while there was another facet of the coming nightmare which was outside the most fanciful imaginings of all those crewmen who were still robust and mentally alert, even though finding themselves faced by a horror never experienced before — and that was the Fifth Column nature of the malevolence among them. The clandestine phase of its assault was complete and The Madness had already infiltrated every last one of them to varying degrees, which meant that, as its power increased, so their own ability for rational counter-attack diminished accordingly.

More frightening still — they might never know which of their shipmates *had* suddenly become one of the possessed. Or not until it was too late.

By 2010 hours, British Summer Time, that particular awfulness had begun to develop.

It was revealing itself, for instance, on the *Auriga*'s bridge . . .

Third Officer Garvie hadn't followed Temple from the chartroom despite the disturbance caused by Hughie Baird's plea for help. In fact Sandy Garvie appeared almost bored as the urgent footsteps faded yet again in the direction of the galley and silence descended on the other side of the wheelhouse bulkhead.

He didn't even seem particularly concerned about the reason for the blood on his shirt, methodically continuing to enter the end-of-watch data in the deck log as if nothing special was happening aboard *Auriga*. Even his expression hadn't changed; he still bore that half-smiling look of a man at peace with the world and, furthermore, privy to a . . . well, a knowledge of something unsuspected by other, lesser souls.

Anyone familiar with the early stages of The Madness might well have been excused for feeling very nervous indeed from that particular moment, were they to be left alone in the presence of Third Officer Garvie.

Only after he'd closed the deck log and carefully replaced his pencil in the rack did the young Mate gaze pensively round for a mirror. There was one, a cheap one already showing black scalloped edges where the sea salt had undermined the silvering, and Sandy stared at his reflection for a long time before doing anything else.

Eventually he lifted his hand to his throat and experimentally gave the collar a little wriggle from side to side. The skin of his neck moved too, crinkling and sliding over its cartilagenous structure. Sandy smiled deprecatingly, amused at his own carelessness, before pulling the safety pin clear. While only a little more blood actually escaped from the tiny punctures, his shirt front was already in too much of a mess to justify the exaggerated care he then took in straightening his tie, tugging his reefer jacket into place and, finally, searching fastidiously for invisible specks of dust before leaving the chartroom.

Not once during all that time had Third Officer Garvie winced, or revealed the slightest trace of pain. But then Sandy Garvie wasn't displaying anything else either, come to that. When he did deign to stroll through the wheelhouse there seemed no animation of any kind about him; certainly not where it counted — in his eyes.

It wasn't an attitude shared by the *Auriga*'s Master who was waiting, arms clasped severely behind his back, on the starboard wing.

'I am disappointed that you didn't feel it incumbent on you to keep watch out here, Mister Garvie,' he snapped, in a direct reproach usually reserved for much more flagrant breaches of discipline. 'Considering you are well aware of the Chief Officer's absence from the bridge.'

Even as he spoke the Captain was conscious of his own guilt. Garvie was a good officer and perfectly justified in being in the chartroom, but Mowat was reacting to the ever-growing unease he felt within himself — generated not merely by the fact that some still-unexplained emergency was occurring below but also through increasing anxiety over his own health. The tingling in the

Captain's arms had now extended to his legs and, of even more concern, his mind seemed strangely confused; fuzzy somehow, and unable to concentrate.

'I'd heard your voice, sir. I did know you were here, up top,' Garvie countered meekly. 'And young Kennedy's on the other side, looking out.'

Mowat opened his mouth, then seemed to forget what he was going to retort and allowed it to close again with a snap. His eyes narrowed, fixed on Garvie's collar.

'You're bleeding. Do you know you're bleeding, Mister Garvie?'

The youngster's lips framed a brief smile. Had Mowat noticed he would have seen they were stuck together at the corners; dried, corrugated and pallid. But he didn't.

'Not now, sir,' the Third Mate pointed out tolerantly, 'or I don't think so, anyway. Not since I took the pin out.'

'Ah!' said the Captain as though that explained everything. But then he thought for a while and frowned hugely. 'Pin? What sort of pin?'

'A safety pin, sir. The one I stuck in my neck to hold my collar together.'

'Oh,' muttered *Auriga's* Master, only more faintly this time. He began to feel slightly ridiculous, because he sensed there was something odd about a man pinning his collar to his throat merely to look tidy, but he couldn't quite fathom what it was. Lord but his feet were getting colder and colder . . .

'. . . not deliberately of course, sir,' the Third Mate hastened to elaborate. 'I only jagged myself by accident. It's nothing.'

'I suppose not,' Captain Mowat conceded with an assurance he didn't feel but couldn't summon the mental effort to question further. Apart from which his thoughts were concentrated on what Temple might have to report on his return. 'But you should bathe it all the same, Garvie. With Dettol or something . . .'

So they stood there together on the bridge, the young man and the older man. Viewed from the port wing by Apprentice Kennedy and the two seamen they represented a calming influence to offset whatever crisis was mounting down in the galley. Anyway, *that* was probably nothing much either; knowing Hughie Baird's tendency to over-react.

Certainly no observer could have guessed that a frenzy as subtle as The Madness had just moved one significant step closer to taking command of the motor vessel *Auriga*. . . .

Hughie Baird, on the other hand, was fed-up tae the teeth with being subtle.

His concern over the condition of young Monaghan, and his frustration at being delayed any longer in returning with help, had already reached near-hysteria pitch, even before yon bluidy fairy scouser an' noted big mouth Liverpool Fitba' Club supporter Derek Guy appeared beside Trotty's death bed. When Guy launched into that unbelievable harangue of his which actually suggested that Trott had been actin' in his own selfish *interests* by partin' his cable in the way he did . . . well something just blew inside Assistant Steward Baird's skull. He fell upon Derek Guy with a resentment unmatched since his Scottish ancestors last had a square go at the English invaders at Bannockburn.

This time Bosun Peak didn't even try to separate them — but apart from being too engrossed in his private grief, Peak had been involved in one of Baird's hostilities already that day. He simply turned away, and blinked down at the tormented features of his friend, and didn't make the slightest effort to prevent a fresh gloss of tears from coursing down his cadaverous cheeks.

Temple, on the other hand, reacted savagely — over-reacted in fact as young Guy went down shrieking under a barrage of fists, making no attempt to defend himself. Temple found himself launched into the alleyway, grabbing Hughie Baird's shock of red hair in a blazing excess of rage, and smashing, smashing, smashing the young Steward's head against the deck with no gentlemanly restraint at all . . .

Though, on reflection, it was perfectly conceivable that the real Chief Officer David Temple *wasn't* committing such an untypical act when he sought to distribute whatever minimal brain Hughie Baird possessed all over the blue compo deck of the *Auriga*. Perhaps someone, or something else was doing it.

But therein lay the key to survival over the next twelve hours. The intriguing little guessing game presented by The Madness.

Trying to anticipate your sudden elevation to victim status;

before some other, perfectly normal shipmate did the same thing to you.

Chief Engineer Webster finally managed to pull the amazing pencil out of the sky and suddenly found it wasn't floating at all. Even when he placed it on his desk top and eyed it expectantly it didn't move; just lay there looking like ... well, a perfectly ordinary pencil with no ambitions towards levitation whatsoever.

'Goodness,' mused the Chief. 'My goodness but isn't that remarkable, lads?'

'I told you, sir,' Bench ventured with an air of complete vindication. *He* hadn't been surprised when the pencil floated like that. Any pencil that could become as heavy as a railway engine was equally capable of adopting a dual personality — balloon-like, or pretending it was a cloud.

'You're mad,' Wimpy Jennings whispered, tear-rimmed eyes big as saucers with the nightmare of it. 'Oh Christ, but you're *both* mad as each other!'

They turned to look at him. Webster's expression was full of concern. 'You aren't well,' the Chief said kindly. 'No more watch-keeping for you this trip, Wimpy my son, and that's an order.'

The desk writing lamp was on. Illuminating the underside of the Chief Engineer's face, with those thick eyebrows and receding hair line, it made him look satanic from where Jennings slumped; the embodiment of evil. The pressures inside the Third's skull suddenly grew unbearable and he began to whimper through the tears. Not even he knew whether the pain or the terror was the greater.

'Couple of aspirins and a good night's sleep. Can't beat it,' Webster pursued authoritatively. 'And don't worry, son ... we'll see the pencil's kept safe f'r the boffins to examine.'

'Ohhhh dear *God* . . .' Jennings pleaded. Fourth Engineer Bench laid his hand gently across the crying man's brow and Jennings wanted to pull away but found he couldn't. Benchy's touch felt so cold and clammy like ... like you'd expect from the caress of a corpse — but Wimpy Jennings was slipping fast now; there was a whirlpool suddenly, in the centre of the Chief's cabin, and already he could feel his senses spiralling round and round.

'He's a bit hot, sir,' he heard Bench say, in a tone which reeked of sympathy, except that Jennings knew it was all an act; a trick to lull and deceive him. Part of a plot hatched by fiends masquerading in familiar guise; a move in some grand strategy to prevent him from going home to . . . Paisley, was it? In Scotland?

'He's a bit of a problem, too,' Chief Engineer Webster added, with just the slightest trace of worry. 'That pencil's too important to risk Wimpy trying to destroy it before we get in.'

'Please,' Jennings sobbed through the mists closing around him. 'Please let me see the Captain.'

'See what I mean?' the Chief demanded cheerfully. 'He's going to do his best to sabotage the greatest scientific discovery since the propeller. And we daren't risk him doing that, dare we?'

'No, sir,' said Bench dutifully. 'Er . . . how could he do that, sir? Destroy it?'

'Mad,' Jennings' semi-conscious screamed. 'Both mad as hatters an' discussing their lunacy as casually as they would a cricket match.' But that was all he could do by then; shriek in silence.

'We've just witnessed a miracle, son,' Webster explained patiently. 'There's no denying that; it was a miracle. Yet for some reason or other Jennings refused to believe it . . . and that's where the danger lies, my boy. That's the Achilles' heel of miracles.'

'Not believing?'

'Exactly. Lack of faith, Bench. You can't expect a miracle to happen unless you have faith that it *will*, can you? Otherwise it wouldn't be a miracle in the first place.'

The oddest thing of all was that, even to the confused mind of Third Engineer Jennings, Chief Webster's elaborately reasoned dementia held incontestable logic. But that assumed that the pencil *was* a magic pencil in the first place; and it wasn't . . .

. . . was it?

'I think I see what you mean, sir. If Wimpy is allowed to cast doubt, then others may not believe. And if *they* don't believe . . .'

'. . . it might prevent it from ever happening again,' the Chief finished triumphantly. 'Lack of faith is a cancer, my boy. Even the slightest suspicion of ridicule at this stage might well prove disastrous.'

'Sir, it cannot be,' cried Fourth Engineer Bench, on a surge of theatrical anguish. 'Jennings must be restrained from committing such blasphemy; from sneering at this sign from Our Lord . . .'

The Madness was eating at Fourth Engineer Bench's brain by

then, you must remember. As it had already distorted his vision of reality to such an extent, it was hardly surprising that it also influenced the manner of his speech.

It hadn't affected Chief Webster's, though. He was as earthy as ever.

'Too bloody right he must,' he snapped, bending over the inert form of the Third Engineer. This time, surely, there could be no mistaking the sinister implication conveyed in his tone. 'I know exactly *how* we can stop him.'

Jennings opened his eyes with a last, superhuman effort of will, just in time to feel them lift him and begin to carry him through the door and out into the alleyway. He stared up, and saw the faces of monsters grinning down at him, and began to scream but only briefly. Then the whirlpool finally claimed him, and Wimpy Jennings passed into merciful oblivion.

Chief Engineer Webster glowered at Fourth Engineer Bench in hurt outrage.

'What was he struggling like that for?' he grumbled irritably. 'I only want to put 'im to bed. Then see the Captain . . .'

Well, you didn't think they were going to ditch Wimpy Jennings over the wall, did you? Or dissect him, and hide his various parts in the engineroom, just to stop him casting doubts on the supernatural abilities of a *pencil*?

Lord, no! For sometimes The Madness wasn't all violence and horror.

Sometimes it would simply endow a man with a mongrel cunning. Mind you — sometimes those could be the most dangerous times of all . . .

Greasers Simmieson and Behrens heard the rumpus outside the Donkeyman's cabin, yet still they ambled with a surprising lack of urgency to the door, pulling it open just in time to view an exhibition of pugilism scarcely matched in bar room brawls the world over. For a brief moment it was virtually impossible to see who was punching whom, and what was being violently done to whomsoever. The flash of gold braid was the only identifiable feature of the melee.

'Someone's wearin' Mister Temple's jacket,' Behrens hazarded eventually, entranced by the prospect of another break in the day's routine.

'Mister Temple's wearin' Mister Temple's jacket, stupid,' Slimy explained, having angled his head the right amount to recognise the upper layer of combatants. 'An' that's the Assistant Steward's skull 'e's doin' 'is best to put a flat end on.'

'But . . .'

Sammy Behrens frowned enormously for a bit, trying to work it out. Then he started again. 'But Mister Temple's an officer. Officers aren't allowed ter smash Hughie Baird's head in — are they?'

'Anyone's allowed ter smash Hughie Baird's 'ead in, far as I'm concerned,' Simmieson retorted with satisfaction. But Slimy didn't like Hughie Baird any more than Derek Guy did; though maybe that wasn't quite accurate now, seeing Guy's face was slowly going purplish-black as Baird's hands clung to his throat.

'Gawd, Sammy, come on!' Greaser Simmieson yelled as understanding finally dawned. 'This ain't no friendly. They're tryin' to kill each other!'

Young Guy never moved, not even after they'd pulled the Assistant Steward off him; just lay there huddled in a foetal bundle against the bulkhead and cried like a girl. None of those present could have guessed that disappointment formed as great a part of Derek Guy's misery as the shock of Baird's assault, and certainly none could have credited the reasoning behind it.

Hughie Baird, on the other hand, remained as verbally aggressive as ever despite his dismay at being attacked from so unexpected a quarter. Well, if Peaky had been the one tae banjo him, then that woulda been O.K. He'd have understood that, not resented it. Maybe if the Bosun had been a wee bit more ready wi' his fists this morning — beltin' intae Grainger of course, seein' it was yon bastard Grainger had started it — then they wouldn't have had the trouble they'd had with the vittling. But Temple! Supposed tae be an *officer*, no less. An' not only that, but the kind that let you know it; all posh an' talking like he'd got a plum in his mouth even wi' the Donkeyman stiff on his bunk an' Terry Monaghan sick as a . . .

Monaghan! Och *Jeeze* . . .

'Terry,' he exploded, suddenly frightened again. 'We've got tae get back tae the galley.'

Temple heard Slimy Simmieson mumble 'Aw, bloody *hell* . . .' in a thunderstruck voice and gathered he'd found Trott. Breathing heavily he tried to keep his tone level; to conceal the shock he felt at himself and the way he'd gone for Baird. What was it? What in God's name *was* happening aboard *Auriga*?

'Behrens! The Captain's on the bridge. Get him down here immediately. Simmieson . . .'

'His eyes. You seen the Donkeyman's *eyes*, Mister?'

'Shut it, Simmieson,' the Bosun's snarl came from the shadows. 'Stop talkin' about Trotty like 'e wasn't here no more.'

'Stay with Peak, Simmieson. Send the Captain to the galley soon as he arrives an' get Guy to his feet; check he's all right.'

'Bluidy wee poof!' Baird muttered with a last flash of fighting spirit.

'BAIRD!'

'Sir?' the Assistant Steward squeaked, jumping a foot in the air. The apprehension on his face afforded Temple a second of satisfaction. It didn't last, though. Not when he caught the glaze of Donkeyman Trott's dead stare, still locked on to him from inside that monastically furnished tomb.

'Come on,' he said dully. He'd meant to add something more; something cutting and censorious; but all of a sudden it didn't seem to matter. He began to run again. It struck him then that, no matter how much they hurried, the awful thing he was now certain had boarded them invariably seemed to be one step ahead.

One further unusual incident did take place during that frenetic opening stage of the evening watch, though under normal circumstances nobody would have attributed much significance to it.

It happened to Greaser Behrens, en route to pass Temple's request for the Captain to come down from the bridge and not long after he'd set off at a shambling run in a rather unfamiliar direction — upwards. Sammy was a natural troglodyte; an engineroom-dweller and not only that but one with a singular lack of curiosity about how the other half of the ship lived. Even though he'd been in *Auriga* for more than a year he'd never, in all that time, visited her bridge.

Oh, he'd *seen* it, mind you; on the few occasions when he'd been forced to go to the boat deck for abandon-ship drill as stipulated by the Department of Trade and Industry, or on the more frequent occasions when disenchanted policemen had left him lying on his keel on various wharves, staring blearily skywards while they persuaded the Chief Engineer to take him back . . . so he definitely knew *Auriga* had a bridge. A draughty exposed place right on top, forward of the funnel.

One thing Sammy *did* understand, however, was that you didn't approach it by way of the internal stairs. That route meant you would have to go through officers' accommodation which was out of bounds for all ratings. Apart from which, judging by the Mate's recent performance, meet one o' *them* by accident an' you was more likely to get your bloody head smashed in.

He stepped over the high coaming and out on deck, then started to hurry up the external ladder towards the next tier of accommodation. Then it happened. It was a beautiful evening, he noticed, with the sea a glassy swell and the horizon a haze of colour and only the distant fuzz of a solitary oil platform proving they weren't alone in the world . . . not that Greaser Behrens reflected along such lines at the best of times unless it was to admire the poetry of a good head of beer. Currently he was more absorbed with pondering over Trotty's abrupt demise and the upset it would cause — well, that an' them bloody insects or crabs or rabbits or whatever wus creepy-crawlin' all over his skin. Them an' the terrible thirst, excessive even in Sammy's experience, that was beginning to obsess his thoughts.

. . . then he met it, face to face as his head rose above the level of the next deck.

The cat!

It was a black sort of cat at first sight, with whiskers and brownish ears and four legs lookin' a bit like they'd been dipped in white paint at the ends; the paw ends. A — well, an ordinary sort of cat, really. Covered in fur.

The cat stared penetratingly at Behrens and Behrens blinked back. He knew it shouldn't be there on board the ship, not bound for a British port, it shouldn't, but he never meant to hurt it or even frighten it when he put his hand out and said, ''Ello, cat. Come to Uncle Sammy then . . .'

He never finished his invitation. The moment he spoke the cat arched its back; began to hiss, spit, open its mouth wide and terrifyingly with the throaty sibilation rising to a fang-exposed screech . . .

Behrens had time to see the needle claws unsheath; detect the previously unnoticed foam flecking the corners of the creature's maw — and it had launched itself towards him. But not against his protectively raised hand. No! Clean over that and springing straight for his face . . . for his bloody *eyes* f'r the love o' God!

He was lucky, being attacked on a steep ladder. As soon as he recoiled his foot slipped and his arm, spiralling frantically now for balance as much as protection, diverted the flying harpy-missile so all he felt was the brush of fur against his head and the lash of its tail. When he finally picked himself up at the bottom of the ladder it was gone. Disappeared, as if it had never existed.

But it *had* been there. He hadn't imagined it; seen a delusion as he sometimes did when he'd been ashore too long . . . for when the shaken Greaser put a hand to his stubbled cheek it came away sticky with some curiously mucous substance. At first he assumed it was blood but, when he plucked up the courage to examine it, he found it was only saliva. A kind of foamy saliva. Just like he'd glimpsed flecking the maw of that demented creature.

And that raised an even knottier question. For while the fact of having a stowaway animal on board was exceptional in itself, what, brooded Sammy Behrens in increasing apprehension — *what* in the name o' the Holy Father could have caused it to become so homicidally insane?

Had Greaser Behrens been called upon at that moment to ascribe a physical form to The Madness, he would have claimed that it looked like a cat. A perfectly ordinary cat too, apart from its behaviour.

But Seaman Chikwanda, isolated in his cabin two decks below, would have begged to differ. Or if Seaman Chikwanda had still possessed the power of rational speech he would.

For *his* personal introduction to The Madness was proceeding in a much more terrifying vein.

Chikwanda had never stirred during the whole of the time the swelling Amin-spider took to descend upon him.

Even when it was as big as a soup plate and suspended so close above his face that he could see the claw-like extremities opening and closing in anticipation, and detect that the creature's belly wasn't made of black leather at all but covered in fine silken hairs which constantly moved, rippling and swaying like a field of carbon-wheat brushed by the wind — even then Chikwanda could only whimper and stare in gob-eyed revulsion, and numbly await the touch of the ultimate ghastliness.

Then the most dreadful thing of all took place. The palpitating abdomen of the nightmare above seemingly erupted — split open like some pink and oozing flesh-flower to reveal the bone-white barbs of a finely tapered sting — and the sting suddenly snapped from its womb to angle downwards, shiny with mucous venom, directly at Chikwanda's arched and vulnerable throat.

He never screamed aloud, only silently within those compartments of the brain kept tightly locked by fortunate men. The strength which propelled him to the deck, smashing sideways and clean through the stout mahogany weather boards expressly designed to prevent such an event even in the worst the sea could offer, could have been generated only by the quintessence of fear.

He never felt the lacerations to his shoulders and calves, nor the blood which mixed freely with his own waste to leave a viscid trail as he scrabbled towards the furthest corner of the cabin. He never blinked, never moved again for a long time after he'd reached it, his back pressing against the bulkhead and his legs drawn up and driving him harder and harder into his refuge.

A remarkably similar attitude, on reflection, to that of another of the *Auriga*'s Damned; to that of little Donkeyman Trott, in fact; who had seemingly been destroyed by sheer fright only a little while before.

But Seaman Chikwanda wouldn't die in that manner. Seaman Chikwanda had too strong a heart to afford him the mercy enjoyed by Donkeyman Trott. All Chikwanda could do during his first touch of The Madness was to huddle there and mumble half-remembered prayers and watch for the sting of the arachnid hideosity.

He wasn't fooled by the General-spider's cunning. The fact that it had vanished from the space above his shattered bunk was only a ploy to lure him back into an invisible web. And, shocked as he was, there was no question in Chikwanda's mind that the horror *did* exist; that it hadn't been a vivid recollection from a nightmare suffered during an after-dinner doze.

He knew precisely where the thing was, you see.

Every time the *Auriga* rolled he could detect it, or part of it anyway. Every time the curtain lifted away from the porthole opposite he could see what lay behind, clinging to the side of the ship.

One spiky, hair-covered leg. Thicker than a man's finger now. And getting larger with each sluggish roll . . .

Chapter Nine

And so, with eleven hours of that North Sea night still to pass before they were scheduled to embark the Inchkeith pilot, the bizarre affliction of the *Auriga* had established a bridgehead.

Protected by ignorance it could infiltrate further now; activate the cancer of its main assault. It wasn't in a hurry; all it had to do was to spread the numbness of confusion. Many of its first victims were already too far gone to indicate their distress — men like Chikwanda grovelling before an ever-dilating awfulness; Seaman Grainger, who'd started it all and now lay unconscious in his cabin; poor little Monaghan still drooling in the galley; and Radio Operator MacNally, who had never moved from his disordered bunk and lay, staring up at a fiercely-clutched tube of indigestion tablets with liquid-eyed detachment.

There were others who recognised some perturbing condition had arisen within themselves — Second Officer Yancy and Second Engineer Beckman for instance, who realised they were doing odd things yet couldn't seem to help it; Ordinary Seaman Reid, who had scratched himself raw in places; Slimy Simmieson, who kept falling over for no apparent reason, and Greaser Behrens with his crawly skin and his phantom cat. They all suspected there was something not quite right but wouldn't say anything about it because . . . well . . . it was embarrassing. A bloke doesn't like to publicise his own infirmities. Not to those he lives with, who can't do much to help anyway.

Then there was a third group of victims aboard the *Auriga* by 2100 hours that night and they, perhaps, were the most unsettling of all — the men who were unaware. Chief Engineer Webster and

Fourth Bench, conspirators over the amazing pencil; Wimpy Jennings, who'd seen the incipient dementia in them but couldn't face it within himself; Third Officer Sandy Garvie, smiling secretively in anaesthetised menace, who would be in sole charge of *Auriga*'s safety until midnight; the self-destructive Derek Guy, who didn't need the added touch of an alien lunacy to be a lunatic; even Captain Charles Mowat himself, approaching a period in his life when he would be called upon to command a nightmare, fight an enemy a thousand times more horrifying than any storm or torpedo or beckoning lee shore — yet already finding it difficult to accept that there might be something odd about a young man who stuck pins through his neck.

Finally there was the fourth and still largest group — that of the unremarkable; the ordinary, the unsuspecting or the suddenly apprehensive remainder of *Auriga*'s complement, who revealed as yet no sign of having been visited by The Madness.

Chief Steward Sullivan was, if anything, stronger than ever in the face of young Monaghan's imbecilic torment. Chief Cook Holmquist might have displayed unexpected diffidence when faced with the same situation, but that didn't mean he was mad; merely that Sven Holmquist was revolted or scared or just plain bloody indifferent to the sufferings of others. A lot of ships' cooks have to be; they couldn't live with their jobs otherwise ... or that's what their captive messmates would claim, anyway.

Hughie Baird? Well, he was even more of an aggressive bloody nuisance than he usually managed to make himself; but the headache and indisposition he was feeling at that moment could at least have been accounted for by the unusual amount of work he had been asked to do. Cadet Kennedy's major concern was still his voyage study programme; Cadet Simpson had, admittedly, vomited during the Third Mate's afternoon teach-in but he'd quickly recovered and was now glumly becoming as involved in Kennedy's metacentric heights — *he'd* been told to redraw the rotten diagrams, having been sick across the originals. Bosun Peak still suffered a painful throat, but since Trotty's inexplicable death that discomfort had been overwhelmed by his sense of loss.

And Chief Officer David Temple? Well, he was still O.K. A bit confused certainly; and shaken not only by the frightening incidents he already knew about but also by his mounting suspicion that other things were happening that *none* of them were yet aware of. But otherwise the *Auriga*'s second-in-command was perfectly unaffected, and quite capable of taking over from the Captain if necessary.

Well he *was*, wasn't he? Surely the fact that, for the first time in his career he'd become involved in a fracas with a junior member of the crew didn't mean he was *ill*, did it?

That The Madness was secretly corroding David Temple's brain as well?

Captain Mowat's outward imperturbability was severely tested on his way down from the bridge as he absorbed Behrens' garbled account of attacks by cats and the sudden death of Donkeyman Trott all mixed up together. By the time he arrived in the galley to be confronted by Terry Monaghan's bizarre transition, he was visibly shaken. To those waiting, the Captain's reaction seemed natural; the sort of shocked disbelief to be anticipated from anyone plunged from routine into sudden awareness of the appalling. And Mowat's reaction *was* normal, come to that − as yet The Madness had only brushed him with a breath of ice, a hint of pallor. His mind, though sluggish and hesitant, was still that of a perfectly ordinary man.

Terry never moved or displayed any hint of intelligent awareness while they grimly examined him. All the time Chief Steward Sullivan cradled the boy's head in his arm with firm reassurance, and Chief Cook Holmquist watched impassively. From a distance.

'May God be with the lad,' the Captain said eventually, 'for there's nothing we can do to help him, Mister Temple.'

'Why the hell can't he unbend just once?' the Mate thought savagely. 'Call me David; ease off the formality . . .'

'We can get him to his bunk, dammit! And put out a Pan Medic call for advice,' he found himself retorting angrily. Then he became conscious of his own temerity; the way his nerves appeared to explode into violent over-reaction at the slightest provocation, and he shrugged weakly.

'We've got to do something, sir.'

'Then see he's left in the coma position,' Mowat said quietly. 'Lying over so he won't drown in his own vomit. And have someone with him all the time. Mister Sullivan.'

111

'Aye?'

'Could Monaghan have injured his head recently? Any accidental blow?'

'Now wait a minute, Captin. I don' hit Terry; I haven't no need to bash my assistant.' Holmquist broke in with considerable heat. 'You got a good boy there. I do all I can to help Terry, ya?'

'Just so long as 'e's healthy anyway,' the Chief Steward observed pointedly and to no one in particular, but the enigmatic comment was lost on all including the Chief Cook.

'I said "accidental", Holmquist,' the Captain countered tartly, much more his old self when stimulated by the adrenalin of crisis. 'So don't read more into what I say. My own feeling is that the only medical explanation for this boy's condition is some form of shock to his nervous system. Concussion? Possible damage to the brain?'

'Well I don' hit Terry,' the Swede persisted, but he didn't add anything more; not many people dared to once they saw Mowat really beginning to bristle.

'Hasn't banged his head as far as I know, sir,' Sullivan interjected hurriedly. 'Either way we'd better get 'im to his bunk. C'mon, Hughie. Fireman's lift, right? Get his arm round the back've your neck like that an' — HUP.'

Monaghan's head lolled against Baird's and Temple caught the flicker of revulsion on the young Steward's features as they turned towards the door. He couldn't help feeling relief that he wasn't forced to be that close to the sick boy, then was aware of a pang of shame.

'How long has he been like that?' the Old Man asked, as the shuffling trio disappeared into the alley. Holmquist shrugged.

'One hour? Maybe one and a half, Captin. Since he spilled the *Vitkalssoppa* while we was serving dinners.'

Mowat frowned at Temple. 'It hasn't been all that long . . .' Then he read the expression on his Chief Officer's face and snapped, 'Don't get disapproving before I've finished, Mister. We have two alternatives — either we keep the boy aboard and quiet for another twelve hours, then straight to an Edinburgh hospital with the minimum of stress; or we request a helicopter transfer to Aberdeen . . . and during the dark hours, remember. They won't be able

112

to reach us before then. Would you risk the added strain *that* particular operation would place on Monaghan?'

Auriga rolled a little further to starboard than usual and recovered. Temple noticed absently how the Captain seemed to stagger, bracing himself against the oven rail for support, but didn't think any more of it as he stretched a hand towards a carelessly stowed baking bowl. Holmquist took it from him and shoved it in the rack with a muttered, 'Blotty everyt'ing is blotty downsides up . . .'

'Then can we ask them to fly a doctor *out*?' he suggested doggedly.

The temporary vitality was draining from Mowat. His legs started to become cold again, while thinking presented an enormous effort. He was also sensing a growing uncertainty; a desire to postpone action, to avoid commitment.

'We could, Mister Temple, but on what grounds when you really analyse them? We have a seaman who appears vacant; staring; not in full possession of his senses . . . Dammit, the lad could be drunk to all intents and purposes!'

'Terry don' drink booze,' Holmquist interjected aggressively. 'I never seen Terry drinking, Captin.'

'Are you suggesting Monaghan *isn't* ill, sir? That he doesn't require medical aid any more than an ordinary drunk?'

The Captain passed a hand across his brow — dear God but he was weak now. Decisions . . . decisions couldn't, mustn't be made under pressure. Unnecessary alerting of the maritime emergency services; the risks attendant in any air-sea operation; the expense to the company and his being called upon to justify what could easily prove an over-hasty act . . .

'I'm suggesting nothing,' he countered sharply, a little desperately. 'I'm telling you, Mister! I do not intend to activate a major mercy mission to this ship until we have watched the progress of Monaghan's condition for considerably longer. Or until we have discovered the likely origin of it.'

Temple felt the rage detonate inside him again; frighteningly. 'And Trott?' he heard himself snarl. 'Are we going to watch an' see if *he* gets better as well, dammit?'

Then, just as suddenly, the fury had gone. Perhaps it was only a

113

reflection of Mowat's own vacillation but Temple, for the first time, began to wonder at himself too. To question whether the strange things happening about him were real; or whether his fears were from within, products of his overstressed imagination.

There was another factor which was affecting him. All his life at sea had been a process of conditioning to acknowledge the Divine superiority of the Master; bowing to the unquestioned omniscience of his various captains. Ships functioned that way, survived peril and hazard that way — because no responsible seaman ever disputed, certainly not openly, the decisions taken by the Master.

Like most systems there were flaws. Had David Temple at that time been more perceptive and a little more ready to question Mowat's fitness, then The Madness would have been denied one of its closest allies — that same virtue of uncritical obedience. But David Temple was, above all else, a traditionalist.

'I'm sorry, sir,' he muttered tightly, beginning to give way. 'It's just that Monaghan and Trott together, within an hour of each other . . .'

'Trott?' the Captain echoed in a rather querulous voice — or was it merely the detachment of a man engrossed in deep thought? The Mate forced himself to disguise his impatience; obviously he was reading Mowat wrongly again. He knew the Old Man had visited Trott's cabin on his way down from the bridge and there was no way anyone could overlook an experience like that.

'The Donkeyman. Dying the way he did, allied to Monaghan's condition?'

'Ya, a blotty queer thing I tell you,' the Chief Cook growled uneasily in the background. 'I be glad when this sheep's alongside an' no kidding.'

Temple directed a warning glance at Holmquist but, at the same time, couldn't help reflecting a fervent 'Amen to that . . .'. If he hadn't taken his eyes from the Captain during those few seconds, he couldn't have failed to miss the this-time-unmistakable expression of uncertain comprehension dawning through Mowat's frown.

'I see no connection between the two incidents,' Mowat snapped, unease at his own mental inertia sharpening his tone with defensive certainty. 'Trott obviously collapsed under a massive heart attack; Peak says there was a tragic family history. While the boy

Monaghan, whatever the cause of his problem, certainly isn't suffering a physical weakness of that nature.'

The *Auriga*'s Chief Officer drew a deep breath; there *was* something; there *had* to be some common link between the events. The time scale indicated that his earlier apprehensions had some basis for concern. And the other incidents, each significant in isolation: the blood at Garvie's throat; Reid's constant scratching; Derek Guy's outlandish reaction to Trott's death; the apparently pointless violation of Radio Operator MacNally's cabin; the paw marks on the deck — all reinforced by a sudden awareness that the ship itself had been too quiet, too inactive, without the routine mutter of friendly rivalry from mess-rooms, the odd lounger at the rails enjoying a post-dinner communion with the sea, even the occasional slam of a cabin door. It all added up to an ill-defined but certain conviction that something was terribly, unnervingly *wrong*.

He *had* to brace himself for a last-ditch stand against the disciplinary values he cherished to plead with the Captain to act immediately — to alert the maritime authorities at least to the possibility of a threat to *Auriga*; to have them institute some form of periodic radio check during the final stages of her passage . . .

'Sir, I must formally request that you . . .'

Abruptly, he became aware that nobody was listening any more. His voice trailed away as he swung round, following the querying glances now directed towards the galley doorway.

Fourth Engineer Bench stood there. He was still uniformed as he'd been for dinner earlier, only now the reefer jacket was rumpled; his hair awry; a shiny oil smear shaded one cheek and he seemed flushed, as though something portentous had occurred.

Yet when he did speak it was calmly, almost too calmly in a flat monotone.

'Captain, sir,' Bench began with impeccable correctness. 'The Chief Engineer sends his compliments, and asks if he may see you as soon as convenient.'

Temple knew then that his protest was over. One glimpse of the relief in Mowat's eyes as the pressure was eased, the need for immediate decision averted, was enough. It could be claimed, perhaps, that in that critical moment Chief Officer David Temple also became an accessory to the killing of *Auriga* when, no matter how reluctantly, he relinquished his moral duty; bowed to the already faltering judgement of Captain Charles Mowat, Master before God; and thereby acknowledged the proxy command of The Madness.

The Captain half-turned towards him, offering him one last chance by staring at him queryingly; but Temple also saw the glass-fragile promise of impending fury and dropped his eyes.

'It's not important,' he ground out savagely. 'Not immediately.'

There was snap to Mowat's tone as he swung back to face Bench. 'Is it really urgent for Mister Webster to see me, Fourth?' he asked, yet buried underneath the new-found briskness was an element of gratitude.

'Yessir!' the youngster answered in that same measured manner. But then Bench couldn't hold it in a moment longer and smiled; an exhilarated little-boy smile with the barest hint of triumph.

'It's Wimpy Jennings, sir,' he blurted out, '. . . something's happened to him.'

Chapter Ten

Ten p.m. — halfway through the evening watch — and still neither the Captain nor Chief Officer Temple had returned to the bridge.

Cadet Kennedy saw the trawler, well out to starboard and a good five miles off with its steaming lights already showing as red and white pinpricks against the darkening horizon. He saw it, noted it was under way heading south and duly wandered through the wheelhouse, past Quartermaster Mulholland tidying away the remnants of the signal locker, and out to the opposite wing where the Third Mate leaned idly against the bridge front.

'Ship, sir. Two points on the stab'd bow and crossing.'

'Yeah?' Garvie acknowledged but there was no sign that he'd actually hoisted the information in. Certainly he never lifted his head to indicate the precautionary interest expected of any officer of the watch. Kennedy wondered if he should report it again, emphasise that there *was* something over there which might demand avoiding action on the part of *Auriga*; but that would imply that Mister Garvie *needed* a reminder of his O.O.W. responsibilities, and Cadet Kennedy was already in enough trouble with his metacentric heights without committing suicide. Anyway, there were still fifteen, twenty minutes to run before their tracks crossed and no confirmation at that range that they were actually on collision courses.

He hovered a minute longer, hoping Garvie might remark on the curiously long absence of the Captain from the bridge, maybe even speculate on the reasons behind it, but there was no response as the Third Mate continued to gaze absently ahead. Kennedy eventually idled back into the wheelhouse and stared with ill-concealed boredom into the hood of the radar.

That trawler was there, of course; a bright orange blip constantly pulsing and fading with every scan. There were two targets high up in the top left quadrant of the P.P.I., just inside the thirty-six-mile range; while the random geometrics of the rigs they'd passed two hours before were still cutting the periphery at six o'clock. For a few seconds Kennedy toyed with the idea of practising his blind pilotage by plotting and extending the course and speed of the trawler image just like they'd be doing in poor visibility, but he couldn't find a Chinagraph pencil and wasn't that bored anyway — not bored enough actually to do something to pass the watch — so he decided he'd just keep an eye on it until it had crossed and was clear. Just in case the Third really was dozing with his eyes open.

Mulholland glanced up from the flag locker as he passed and Kennedy smiled shyly. He'd never quite figured where he stood with the crew; a youngster with many of an officer's privileges but lacking the weight of rank. Some of the seamen tended either to ignore him completely unless forced to acknowledge his presence; or to be too familiar, too patronising. But most of them were O.K.; not yet alienated by the prospect of the ever-widening disciplinary gulf between them. Mulholland was like that, and Able Seaman Reid; easily informal without seeming to take advantage of his naiveté.

'I'm nearly finished here,' Mulholland said. 'If you want to put the kettle on I'll make the tea. It's all in the chartroom, ready.'

Kennedy hesitated; usually he'd wait until the Third Mate told him to, but tonight Garvie gave the impression of being unapproachable, and Kennedy possessed more than his share of boyish reluctance to disturb authority unnecessarily. He looked at the clock, noted it was already well past smoko time, and nodded.

'I'll do it now. Will Reid want any or has he gone below for good?'

Mulholland stowed the last numeral pennant and stood erect, dusting his knees. 'He hung around for a while waitin' to find out what the flap was about but 'e's itchy — sweat rash or somethin' — and he don't feel so good. Gone for a shower and to turn in.'

'I wonder what it was about; Baird's panic?'

'Dunno. Sammy Behrens seemed in a right state an' all when he dragged the Old Man off as well. I . . . ah . . . thought you might have known why. You bein' an officer an' that?'

Kennedy didn't have a clue.

'No. It couldn't have been much. Though the greaser did seem terrifically worked up, and Baird, too.'

He wondered if he shouldn't add something else, something profound to support Mulholland's recognition of his bein' an officer an' that; but he couldn't think of anything significant and suddenly felt quite thirsty, unusually anxious to get that cup of tea. Maybe he should take a couple of aspirins too; the way his head was beginning to ache for no apparent reason.

The Quartermaster shrugged. 'Yeah, well . . . Mind you, knowing Sammy Behrens, he'd probably jus' met a new variety of pink elephant, him boozin' the amount he does. An' Hughie Baird — he'd get all panicky an' dramatic if a galley spoon was missing. D'you want *me* to put the kettle on, then?'

'Oh, sorry. No, I'll do it.'

Cadet Kennedy went into the chartroom and plugged in the watchkeepers' kettle. He switched it on, passed another two or three minutes in idle contemplation of the chart, which was as long as he dared be absent from the port wing without risking the Third Mate's displeasure, then wandered outside through the wheelhouse again. Lord, but he wished it was midnight an' time to get his head down. He was awfully tired and his eyes had started to ache now. He primly resolved, there and then, never to drink as much as some of the *Auriga*'s complement did. That greaser — Behrens, was it? He'd looked dreadful; a shambling example of what alcohol could do to a chap's brain.

The trawler was a lot closer when he finally arrived back on the port wing; making good speed and apparently intending to hold on to cross *Auriga*'s path. If she *was* fast enough to cross ahead ... otherwise Mister Garvie should be preparing to alter to starboard and go round the other vessel's stern.

Still secure in the knowledge that Third Officer Garvie carried the responsibility for dealing with what was, after all, a routine case of nautical right-of-way, Kennedy wasn't concerned. He'd reported as required; the O.O.W. would order any necessary action.

More out of habit than anything else he lined the trawler's silhouette against the forward corner of the wheelhouse, waiting to see if the bearing remained constant. If it did, if the wheelhouse corner and the approaching ship remained in line, then they would eventually meet; in ten minutes or so from now, unless *Auriga* gave way, there would be an unavoidable collision ... but Cadet Kennedy was only passing a few more dreary moments and trying to forget his headache. Fantasy disasters like that simply didn't happen.

Well, not to well-found ships manned by competent and certificated British officers they didn't, anyway.

Or not very often.

The bearing didn't change at all. It was then that Cadet Kennedy felt his first niggle of doubt. When he noticed that Third Officer Garvie hadn't yet entered the wheelhouse to stand by the autopilot over-ride.

Radio Operator MacNally's right foot suddenly jerked spasmodically. It was his first movement for nearly two hours, ever since he'd stretched out on his bunk and begun to stare so fixedly at the plastic tube of tablets suspended above him.

The hand gripping them was white, spectral and claw-like as if drained of all blood; but that couldn't simply have been caused by the strange attitude he'd adopted, for his other hand — still resting normally beside him and clutching nothing more outrageous than a rumpled ball of coverlet — was bleached and dead too, now, and terribly cold.

MacNally's foot stirred again, and gradually the plastic bottle wavered, lowered stiffly. A whimper escaped through cracked and dehydrated lips as the agony of returning circulation began to penetrate the vegetable consciousness of Radio Officer MacNally. It took several more minutes before his fleshy shell had eased, zombie-like, from the bunk to stand erect and expressionless before the mirror; but even had he been capable of taking in the apparition gazing back at him MacNally would never have recognised himself — only the hair line would have been familiar, and possibly the rugby-flattened nasal bridge; but otherwise, no. His cheeks were grey and cadaverous, his mouth slack; dried saliva meandered across the left side of his face and his eyes, uncomprehending, focused far beyond that inconsequential image in the looking glass.

Had The Madness, so elusive in its infinite variety, presented a typical form, then, most certainly, it existed now aboard *Auriga* in the cabin of Radio Officer MacNally.

The apparition opened the door and, falteringly, stepped into the alleyway leading to the electronic wonder box which contained the only loud voice *Auriga* possessed should she need to scream for help.

The radio room. As vulnerable as an exposed spinal cord.

On the bridge Cadet Kennedy was watching the converging trawler with growing apprehension. The bearing still remained steady as a rock, warning without the slightest doubt that — unless someone did something very soon — both ships were on course to occupy the same square metres of the sea's surface at precisely the same moment.

And the trawler wouldn't give way — the trawler *couldn't*! Not if she observed the demands of international procedure and held to her course and speed. *Auriga*, being the vessel approaching on her port side, had to be the one to take avoiding action. If the fisherman's nerve broke, if he suddenly panicked and swung away or reduced speed unexpectedly in the same late instant that *Auriga* made *her* correction, then the coincidental alterations could easily cancel each other out, and make a full speed collision inevit. . . .

'You see her, do you?'

Kennedy jumped; maybe it was the snap of anxiety in

Mulholland's voice but it confirmed his own uncertainty — they really were rapidly approaching an irretrievable disaster. Ten thousand tons of charging steel didn't magically dart off at a tangent just because you put the rudder over; ships carry considerable inertia, their centre lines respond quickly and their bows start to come round, but the actual bulk continues to crab slightly sideways along the original line of their passage.

He blurted, 'Yes! Oh *hell* . . .' and threw an appealing glance across to the other side, still loath to challenge what could — what surely *must* represent the Third Officer's more experienced assessment of the risk. But Garvie's silhouette still remained hunched in apparently placid reflection against the starboard bridge front.

'You'd better do something, kid,' Mulholland urged with growing urgency; a comment that, in itself, reflected yet again in the inflexible hierarchy of command — and it never occurred to Able Seaman Mulholland, though five years older and more sea-wise than the boy beside him — to *make* a move himself; not when there were two officers' uniforms on *Auriga*'s bridge. Not even when he himself could see the disastrous situation developing.

'F'r Christ's sake do something!' he repeated.

'Sir . . . Mister Garvie.'

Cadet Kennedy began to hurry through the wheelhouse in an agony of indecision. He heard his own voice rising to a squeal and felt embarrassed; childishly inadequate because of it.

'SIR!'

Only then did the man who carried the ultimate responsibility for *Auriga*'s safety stir, swivel to face him. Kennedy ground to a grateful halt and stammered, 'The trawler, sir. She's crossing pretty close ahead . . .' and felt enormously relieved.

Or at least he did until Mister Garvie fixed him with a stare of such malice that the boy jerked a full step backwards with the shock of it.

Then the Third Officer said, quite deliberately, 'About time, you apathetic little bastard! So we got twelve, fifteen wooden-topped fishermen dozing under the bows up there. Well, you have the watch, Mister Kennedy . . . and maybe thirty seconds left to decide what to do about them.'

Things were actually getting better below decks; certainly tidier anyway, during the period when Cadet Kennedy and an unspecified number of Grimsby trawlermen were about to become victims of a most malign practical joke; and while Radio Officer MacNally was embarking upon his ominous advance towards the *Auriga*'s communications centre.

Chief Steward Sullivan and Hughie Baird had eventually managed to slide Monaghan's inert frame into his own bunk and arrange him in the coma position, on his left side with his right knee drawn up and his head tilted slightly down so he wouldn't drown in the continually forming mucus. They were engaged in what was, for the catering department, a routine and comfortingly familiar difference of opinion.

'Oh f'r cryin' out loud, Hughie! Of course you can stay with him on your own. I mean it's not likely you could catch somethin', is it? It's not as if whatever 'e's got is infectious, is it?'

The Assistant Steward stared back at his senior officer in unconvinced resentment. 'How do you know? You havenae even seen the Donkeyman yet, have ye, and what it did tae him if it wis the same thing? The ... the Chef obviously thinks that it's the same thing. Or 'e would if he'd seen Trotty, anyroad.'

'The Chef?' Sullivan jeered, anger fuelled by steadily mounting frustration. 'It's the first time I've ever heard you agreein' with anythin' the *Chef* bloody well thinks, laddie!'

'And Mister Temple,' Hughie claimed desperately; prepared to change allegiance if needs must. '*He* thinks mebbe Terry's got the same thing, an' the Mate's no sae bluidy daft.'

Sullivan flinched as if struck across the face; a Caesar to Hughie Baird's Brutus − *Et tu ...?* That a once loyal servant in his catering staff should ever have a good word for a ... a *deck* officer. The shock of hurt in his eye faded under the threat of retribution, even observed through the self-righteous myopia of Assistant Steward Hughie Baird.

'Meaning I am?' Sullivan prompted, in a voice of pure silk.

Hughie shuffled awkwardly, realising he had gone far beyond the pale but still graceless in defeat. 'Well I'm no' touchin' him again. Ah'll stay a while seein' it's an order, but I'm no' goin' to touch Terry; no way.'

The Chief Steward opened the door, then turned back, carelessly unforgiving.

'I'm glad of that, Hughie Baird,' he announced stiffly, ' 'cause Terry Monaghan's already *had* all the unpleasant experiences he can do with f'r a long time to come.'

. . . and they'd tidied things up a lot in the deceased Donkeyman's cabin too.

Slimy Simmieson had stayed to help Peak with a previously unsuspected gentleness; straightening the already-stiffening match-stick limbs; arranging and cleaning the feather-light corpse; closing Trotty's eyes for the last time and, ultimately, drawing a clean white sheet over what had once been a man. Actually Slimy had left the Bosun to complete that somehow terribly final rite on his own, turning discreetly away to examine the darkening seascape through the scuttle with only the set of his shoulders to betray any embarrassment he felt. And the sympathy.

Oh, the Captain had called briefly while they were doing what had to be done, but the Old Man was on his way through to the galley where something bad had happened to the kid Monaghan apparently, and that may have accounted for his seeming preoccupation. Typical though, wasn't it? That no one had any more time for Trotty in death than they'd had for him in life.

Sammy Behrens eventually discovered his way back too, before they'd finished, but Sammy was just as distracted as the Captain, only he was gabbling on about bein' attacked by things an' that up on the boat deck, which disappointed Slimy a lot seein' Sammy hadn't met a proper hallucination monster since he'd kicked the booze back in Helsinki. It wasn't until they'd completed making Trotty shipshape that Peak suddenly remembered *he'd* seen some-thing cat-like slipping out of the dead man's cabin as he'd first entered. From then on they listened a lot more attentively to the awesome tale of Greaser Behrens . . .

. . . and Seaman Chikwanda? Well, things weren't exactly better for Seaman Chikwanda during that rapidly-shrinking time span while *Auriga* and the Grimsby fisherman headed towards high-speed unification; but on the other hand they hadn't got much worse.

The spider had grown a lot — its repulsively articulated leg was as thick as a man's thumb now — but it hadn't moved again since Chikwanda first compressed himself into the corner of his cabin.

Though his eyes still stared and his sweat-shiny torso trembled continuously, at least the Ugandan was trying to come to terms with his extraordinary situation.

If he could only escape now, before the creature sprang, it would give him time to plan. Oh, he realised the General-spider would never give up — would continue to stalk him relentlessly in eight-legged hideosity — but perhaps he would be able to prepare some defence. Maybe even devise a weapon.

You see, The Madness permitted a certain crazed logic to evolve in most of its victims. Even when confronted by the spectre of a monstrous arachnid like that.

The Captain never spoke to Temple or Fourth Engineer Bench during their hasty walk back to the Master's quarters. It was as if Mowat had conditioned himself to an acceptance of fact without feeling the necessity to probe the deeper cause. One man was dead, one gravely and inexplicably stricken — yet the Captain didn't want to talk about it.

'Christ, but he hasn't even questioned Bench about what's happened to Jennings,' the Mate brooded savagely, following in tight-lipped silence along the internal stairways. 'And the Fourth's gone bloody secretive about it too; as if the Chief's warned him to keep his mouth shut. But *why* f'r . . .?'

Webster was already waiting for them outside the Captain's cabin. Mowat pushed the door open and said, 'Come in, Eric, all of you.' There was a weary anticipation in his tone. Nobody sat down as he turned.

'Well?'

Temple couldn't help noticing the curious look which passed between the old and the young engineer, the almost conspiratorial nature of it; but then Chief Webster smiled diffidently and shrugged.

'It's the Third, Charlie — Jennings.'

'Yes?'

He's . . .'. The Chief traced a pattern across the carpet with his toe and scratched his head as though it were all too ridiculous. 'He's seeing things, Charlie. Imagining things, like he was drunk or someth . . .!'

'Oh for Christ's SAKE,' Temple exploded. 'Within the last couple of hours that makes thr . . .'

'Mister *Temple*!'

Mowat's reprimand slashed across the cabin. Twenty years of discipline silenced David Temple, as effectively as a gag. The Captain swung back to face Webster.

'What sort of things?'

'Eh? Oh, daft things, Charlie. Stupid things.'

'I didn't ask for an impression, Mister Webster. I asked you for specifics.'

The Chief stared at his friend in surprise; Charlie Mowat had never snapped at him like that in the five years they'd sailed together. He began to wish he'd never started on this elaborate ploy, but the illness in him compelled him to go on; to attempt to destroy Wimpy's credibility so as to protect the incredible.

'All right. Jennings believes there is a pencil on board with certain . . . ah . . . strange properties. He is under the impression that it can, well, float in the air . . .'

'Float? In the *air*?'

Webster managed to inject just the right amount of deprecatory embarrassment. 'He claims he saw me — I'm sorry, Charlie, I told you it was daft — he is adamant that he actually saw me trying to hold it down. Stop it from floating up to the deckhead.'

'It was too heavy with me, sir,' Bench blurted, then got uneasy and confused at having nearly given away the real truth, and added hastily, 'I mean Wimpy believed I couldn't even pick it up. That it weighed a ton.'

There was a long silence. Not even Temple could think of a way to follow a story like that. It was the Captain who marshalled his thoughts first.

'Where is Jennings now, Eric?'

'Sleeping. We took him to his bunk.'

The Chief Officer looked interrogatively. 'Sleeping, Chief? Or in a coma?'

Webster seemed uneasy for the first time; frowning. Again Temple caught a flicker of furtive understanding passing between the two engineers but it didn't suggest anything to him — *they* were obviously perfectly healthy; it was Jennings' behaviour which indicated derangement.

'I suppose you could say he sort of passed out,' the Chief ventured cautiously. 'Now he's asleep, David, and I'd like him left that way.'

'That's *it*. Now you've no alternative other than to radio for medical assistance, sir,' Temple urged, gazing hard at the Old Man. 'That's three men down already — and God knows how many others for that matter. We haven't checked; half of 'em are in their cabins either asleep or ...'

'*Three* men?' Webster demanded abruptly. 'Who the hell else is seeing things aboard the ship, Charlie?'

His concern was genuine. The Madness presented many different faces, and the fact that Chief Engineer Webster was convinced that he had to neutralise Wimpy Jennings so as to ensure no one searched for that wonderful pencil, didn't mean he was any less shocked by the prospect of mental imbalance within the rest of the crew.

It was Mowat's turn to look uneasy. 'I'm afraid it's more serious than mere delusions, Eric. Donkeyman Trott died a short time ago from a heart attack, while the Second Cook, Monaghan, has also suffered some form of stroke.'

'No!' Temple snarled. He shook his head violently. 'You don't know *what's* happened to them, Captain. What caused Trott's heart to stop; what caused Monaghan to collapse, and now Jennings. Christ Almighty, Mowat, how many coincidences do you need before you'll take some bloody action?'

Suddenly the fatigue and the worry dragged the Captain's features into those of a very old, sick man. He sagged into his chair and Temple, despite the raging frustration in him, couldn't help a surge of sympathy, almost pity, as he watched the curiously white right hand of his Captain absently reach out and caress the one secure thing he seemed to have left.

His Bible. Resting on the desk.

It had carried him through hazard and fear once before; many years ago on a liferaft crewed by dead men. It would sustain him again in this, perhaps his ultimate test.

'Charlie?' Chief Webster probed uncertainly. 'David's right, Charlie. You've got to notify them shoreside.'

The ship rolled to port as an extra-large swell nudged her but nobody paid any attention. Temple gave a mental shrug; after what he'd just yelled he was already committed. At least the Chief was behind him and could still think straight. No fancy delusions about Chief Engineer Webster.

'I'm going topside now to shake Sparks and get him to transmit a Pan Medic, sir. We'll inform them of our situation and ask for advice in the first instance!'

The ship was still falling to port; harder suddenly. A glass ashtray shot off the Captain's desk and tumbled across the carpet. Even Temple hesitated, waiting for the roll to complete itself and for *Auriga* to recover.

But she didn't. She just kept on lying over, harder and harder.

Bench suddenly lost his grip on the door frame and hop-skipped with flailing arms down the hillside towards the Old Man's sleeping quarters. 'Sorry! That wave . . .'

The Chief Engineer snapped anxiously, 'Wave be damned! We're in a turn. Some bloody fool up there's put the wheel hard over.'

And that was the moment when, from high above, *Auriga*'s siren began to blare. One long, nerve-freezing blast . . . *I am directing my course to starboard.*

At full speed in the middle of the North Sea it could only mean one thing.

. . . that they were in imminent danger of collision.

Chapter Eleven

Chief Officer Temple was right; the social whirl among the off-watch crewmen of *Auriga* really had been uncharacteristically subdued after dinner that night. Mind you, as social whirls go *Auriga* always did tend to have more in common with a monastic brotherhood than a party-orientated fellowship, but usually there was someone dropping into someone else's cabin for an evening beer; a few bored seekers after card-partners, or conversation or simple companionship idling in the recreation spaces.

Tonight there wasn't. As the darkness gradually obscured the surrounding sea even that desultory round of fraternisation was strangely lacking. And that, in the progress of the *Auriga* horror, had already been a major factor — because the early victims were as yet isolated and undiscovered, not included in any assessment of the true danger by the most perceptive, not even by David Temple who, at ten thirty p.m. on her last evening, still only knew that three men had been stricken by some unidentifiable cause.

He still wasn't aware of the plight of Radio Officer MacNally for instance; not then as the ship lurched and all thoughts were diverted to immediate threat rather than long-term unease. Nor did he or anyone else know about Chikwanda's fantasy of terror, nor of Grainger's collapse, nor of Second Officer Yancy and Second Engineer Beckman's anxiously concealed worries. The Madness, which fed on opportunity, would capitalise further on that weakness of liaison. Already a vital call for help had been delayed by underestimation of the magnitude of the crisis.

Now it was to be postponed again. When the whistle blew.

Cadet Kennedy had never been very quick to catch on. The difficulties he was having in absorbing the elementary laws of stability proved that; allied to the expression of puzzlement he seemed to wear whenever confronted by anything new or in the least bit complicated. He'd always been like that, ever since he went to sea — always giving the impression of being bemused by the most ordinary things. For instance, every time he looked outboard over the rails one was left with the feeling that the boy had never expected there could be that much water in an ocean and, furthermore, would never get used to the idea. His senior officers in preceding ships had often wondered why Cadet Kennedy hadn't decided to be something else; anything, come to that, in which split-second appreciation of a situation wasn't quite so vital. Like, say, a career as a test driver in a mattress factory. Or as understudy to a tortoise hunter.

Yet Cadet Kennedy's inadequacy was the element which neutralised the mind-freezing shock administered to him by Third Officer Garvie, under the guidance of The Madness. To anyone else in Kennedy's position the problem of what to do next would have been enough in itself to delay a quick response. Any switched-on youngsters would have been so taken aback by the outrageousness of Garvie's command — to say nothing of its likely consequence — that he would have hesitated too long while querying it; attempting to make sense out of the obviously grotesque . . .

. . . but Kennedy didn't. Kennedy wasn't bright enough to hoist it all in, not right away. Oh, Kennedy was terrified all right, mostly by the unexpected demand on him to redress an error of judgement already verging on cataclysmic — but the improbability of it didn't have time to sink in. Kennedy was programmed for hair-trigger if blind response; so aware of his failings and, because of them, so anxious to please, that he invariably tended to act first and ask why afterwards.

So, while Sandy Garvie's dementia would have rendered any other deputy impotent during the few remaining seconds left to do anything other than pray, Cadet Willie Kennedy merely jumped a foot in the air; squealed, 'Yessir! Ohhh Lord, sir . . .' and galloped for the wheelhouse, the whistle lanyard and the autopilot override.

He hit the green starboard dodge button; watched the rudder indicator start to clock right; lunged for the whistle because he vaguely remembered you blew one blast to let the other chap know you were turning to starboard; closed his eyes . . .

. . . and hoped to God he wasn't goin' to get into any more trouble!

MacNally never even heard the siren as he opened the radio room door, or if he did then certainly his lack-lustre eyes never indicated any awareness of it. He entered the compartment, deliberately locked it behind him and advanced towards the operator's chair like a man in a dream.

Then he sat down. It was an action he had performed before prior to an eternity of listening watches. He slipped the headset over his tousled hair with slightly stiffer formality than usual but then, instead of reaching for his seemingly inexhaustible store of reading matter, MacNally leaned back and fixed the brass clock before him with an unblinking stare. He never stirred again all that time in which *Auriga* was shying to starboard and bellowing her fear across the North Sea.

But MacNally was a very special person now; because MacNally had been favoured with a presentiment. It had come to him a little before, while lying in his bunk; a forewarning of a vital task he was about to be called upon to perform. Not that MacNally was totally convinced, of course. You'd have to be *mad* to believe a thing like that without any confirmation, and there was only one way to receive confirmation aboard a ship at sea — MacNally knew that because MacNally was a radio man, and accepted the evidence of his senses only when the radio told him it was so.

It would tell him at ten thirty precisely — if it really *was* true, and they *did* exist — and it would come during the next three-minute transmission-silence period when ships of all nations listened and were themselves quiet, keeping the distress frequencies clear in order that any of their sisters in hazard might cry SOS and be heard without interference.

MacNally's message would be sent then, even so. Because MacNally's instructions, if verified in the proper manner, could very well save the world . . .

At 2230 hours minus thirty seconds he leaned forward, stretching for the signal pad. At 2230 minus five seconds he steadied his headphones with an in-built thoroughness not even The Madness could annul, and gripped his pencil with resolute fingers.

At exactly 2230 hours British Summer Time he began to write. Occasionally he would key acknowledgement with deft precision . . . *Mike Lima Delta Tango Auriga* was reading an incoming transmission with the same calm precision it would afford any routine signal. Suddenly everything was normal, methodical, reassuring, after MacNally's earlier eccentricities.

In fact there was only one anomaly; one somewhat singular departure from standard communications practice.

In that Radio Officer MacNally had never made the main power circuit as he'd entered; he had never switched his equipment on. Which meant that every module in the electronic array before him — including the receiver he was reading so assiduously — was silent.

It wasn't that Able Seaman Reid hadn't tried to sleep since he went below. It wasn't that he was all that curious to discover the reason for the panic caused during the earlier change of watch by Hughie Baird either, because he, like his relief Mulholland, had eventually decided no news was good news an' that Baird was a bloody flapper anyway. Seeing his itching was getting worse and worse he would do as well to get his head down as hang around for confirmation of a non-event.

Only he hadn't been able to sleep. The irritation had driven him frantic, and the longer he had lain awake the more he'd begun to worry about the debts he had, and how many more he would have when he got home to discover what irresistible luxuries the furniture vans had delivered to Helen this trip out. Then he'd heard the mutter of voices and, eventually, the sound of a scuffle outside the Donkeyman's cabin a few doors down the alleyway; but he hadn't responded because he knew Bosun Peak would still be there an' Reid had enough troubles without openly inviting the bloody Bosun's as well. Apart from which personal conflicts in the crew-quarters of a ship were usually best kept out of.

So he had simply lain, and scratched, and worried, and wondered; and almost wished it were four o'clock in the morning so's he could at least go back on watch to occupy his mind — until the *Auriga* suddenly began to turn and the siren, muted as it was within the accommodation, started to blare ... whereupon Able Seaman Reid added apprehension to his other miseries, and raised himself to clamber out of his bunk.

The cramp, when it took him, was scalpel-honed. Reid sensed he was screaming but it was like listening to somebody else from a long way away; keening on a fortissimo of agony. With every abdominal muscle knotting and distorted he slammed into a foetal attitude, keeled helplessly sideways until the leeboard acted as a fulcrum, shrieked again with the pain and the shock and the knowledge that he was falling.

He hit the deck just as his cabin door burst open and a voice blurted out, 'Aw f'r Christ's sake what's ... Easy, son, EASYYYY!'

But he couldn't take it easy. He couldn't take it any way at all, the torment he was in. Yet even that wasn't the worst part of his misery; for despite his condition he knew that something horrifying was happening to him which far transcended any ordinary

131

illness. He sensed that as clearly, as certainly as he knew he was going to die.

Able Seaman Reid could actually feel the blood in his veins beginning to bubble. To boil, as in a superheated kettle.

The trawler had begun to turn even as Cadet Kennedy seized command of *Auriga*.

She shouldn't have done so according to *The International Regulations For Preventing Collisions At Sea*. Still being fine on the *Auriga*'s starboard bow and suddenly turning away herself, presenting her own stern to *Auriga*'s previously steady progress, the fishing vessel was aggravating the situation by reducing her relative crossing speed while still remaining stolidly within the arc of danger Kennedy had now selected.

But then ships aren't supposed to collide at all, not according to those same *International Regulations For The Prevention Of Collisions At Sea*; and everybody's nerves have a breaking point, even trawler skippers'. So when you are in a small craft and you watch a large one bearing unerringly down upon you, and see in intimate detail the white water exploding under her closing bows, and even hear the thunder of her displacement and the ever-nearing throb of her engines; and disbelief suddenly gives way to the conviction that she bloody well *isn't* going to go round you — then your mistrust screams *SOD the Regulations . . .!* and you do something; anything you can to present a narrower target and minimise the impact.

Quartermaster Mulholland wasn't even aware of Garvie's dementia and Cadet Kennedy's frantic doubts, being transfixed as he then was on the port wing of *Auriga*, with the expanse of the wheelhouse separating him from his officers — apart from which he was rather more preoccupied with the disaster now looming ahead. All *he* was conscious of was the tiny figure of a man staring tensely from the trawler's postage stamp bridge; then the man abruptly disappearing — he was a stout, balding man; Mulholland could make that out despite the falling dusk, they were so close by then; and suddenly the trawler was altering, swinging away with her length foreshortening and the red blob of her ensign arcing towards him on the taffrail of her shelter deck.

Then the bald man came out of her wheelhouse again and there was something in his hand. He pointed it skywards and there was a puff of white smoke while a white flare rose warningly, almost pleadingly to explode with a *plop* and a splurge of incandescent despair.

Mulholland started to will aloud, 'Over! Oh, get . . .'

Only then, slowly, did *Auriga*'s bow begin to swing; hesitantly at first, but then faster and faster as thirty degrees of rudder shied from the pressure of the sea. While her whistle began to clamour from the unbeautiful rectangular funnel surmounting the bridge . . .

The spider had heard the whistle; Chikwanda could tell by the way its leg jerked spasmodically and only slowly relaxed again as it digested and analysed this new stimulus. He could see the curtains move too and, while many would have been fooled into imagining they were only stirring under the lateral pull of the ship's turn, Chikwanda knew it was the reawakening of the bulbous abdomen concealed beneath.

He also realised that his fear-sweat and his cringing couldn't protect him for much longer, because the Amin-creature thrived on the impotence of the meek and spat poison in contempt for the defenceless. With this recognition in mind Chikwanda became a man again — terrified, stare-eyed, but a thinking man nevertheless, and with all a man's instinct for survival.

He had to gain time; to slip away before the obscenity came scuttling towards him on these claw-hair legs and with that piercing sting, but before then he must learn to think as the spider did, with a rigid determination to kill; to come to an unflinching acceptance of the fact that he only had one choice now — either he must be the hunted, or the hunter. His Ugandan forefathers had lived under that primeval law; kill or be killed; and they had survived, hadn't they? Chikwanda's existence was the living proof of that.

Therefore he would become like them; a predator-cunning savage in every respect. Such was the logic struggling in the pitifully ravaged mind of Seaman Chikwanda. Carefully, ever so cautiously, he began to slip out of his bloodied shirt, watching, all the time, for the assault of a monstrous fantasy.

In the Captain's quarters the initial reaction to *Auriga*'s massive

133

course alteration was remarkably restrained. It wasn't because The Madness slowed the mental processes, certainly not in Temple's case, while Mowat himself had already demonstrated that he was quite capable of normal behaviour under the snap of crisis. Partly it was because the Captain was of the old school, where dignity demanded calmness and a British master would rather have died than be seen to panic. There was also a somewhat more mundane reason. Every one of them realised that if, in these days of high-speed catastrophe, the ship was already committed to such a drastic emergency evolution, then by the time they reached the bridge the outcome would be long past human resolution anyway.

So when the Chief Engineer pronounced, '. . . some bloody fool up there's put the wheel hard over!', just before the reinforcement of the whistle confirmed it hadn't been an act of folly after all but one of deliberate intent, all Captain Mowat actually said was, 'I'm sorry, Eric. We may have to continue this discussion later.'

And walked purposefully towards the door. Not hurriedly even then, but with a grim urgency which boded ill for anyone foolish enough to delay his passage.

Temple followed in similar impassivity even though his mind was seething with apprehension, torn between his conviction that there *was* some menace in their midst, and the even more imminent danger now apparently threatening them from without.

He didn't run either, though. It wasn't British. A chap simply didn't overtake his Captain and show panic. But by *God* it took every ounce of his crumbling self-control not to.

Eventually, a million years later it seemed, the senior deck officers of *Auriga* arrived on her bridge.

The first thing they saw was a navigation light — a masthead navigation light — sliding down the port wing of their own bridge so close you felt you could've leaned out and touched up the chipped black casing with a long-handled paint brush . . .

. . . and then something white and incandescent rocketed inboard; struck the wheelhouse in an explosion of sparks; ricocheted crazily aft in Catherine wheel hysteria, and disappeared again below the level of *Auriga*'s rail before you could blink a disbelieving eye.

'It's mad,' reflected Chief Officer Temple with by now detached resignation. 'I know it's quite mad, but I could swear someone's just fired at us. From the sea. With a bloody flare pistol!'

Mulholland had showed remarkable restraint too, in the few seconds preceding that frantic not-quite-collision, but in his case it had been more through paralysis than British phlegm.

For all the Quartermaster had been able to do was to grip the rail before him with knuckle-straining hands; and stare ahead as *Auriga's* jackstaff swung ponderously towards the trawler's stern, bisecting her wake, married exactly in line with her fluttering ensign and swallowed up the gap between the closing vessels like the maw of an overtaking juggernaut. Then he winced as the smaller ship disappeared completely, masked by the overhanging flare of *Auriga's* bows.

All he could think of doing even then was to rush to the outboard end of the wing, already reflecting the red warmth of *Auriga's* port steaming light against the falling dusk, and frantically jerk at the release toggle of the lifebuoy stowage. The buoy tumbled away, a bright orange ring hitting the sea far below, even as Mulholland realised distractedly that it had been a bloody inadequate thing to do as restitution when you'd just killed ten or fifteen men.

Until, miraculously, the trawler's stern reappeared round *Auriga's* port bow, and then the rest of her; still steaming the same way but steadily being overhauled by the length of the bigger ship. The bald-headed man was still staring upwards from her minuscule bridge, only now he was exploding with fury and outrage at them irresponsible, toffee-nosed bastards on that great super-bastard above 'im; and more sleepy-eyed men were tumbling out of the trawler's deckhousing, wearing vests and underpants an' not hellish much else other than expressions of shocked indignation that they could've fished f'r twenty-odd days through the dangers of the Bering Sea only to get this near home an' suddenly meet a homicidal bloody maniac what shouldn't even be in fuckin' charge o' a fuckin' rubber fuckin' DUCK.

Then, even while they were still rolling aft along *Auriga's* towering steel side, the bald man lifted his Verey pistol once again in an excess of rage and pointed it, quite deliberately, straight at

135

Mulholland — whereupon Mulholland's jelly legs dissolved and he fell flat behind the protection of the wing just before the phosphorescent resentment whooshed above his head to erupt in fiery contempt . . .

. . . which was the moment when Temple an' the Old Man clattered up the internal stairway to hear Third Officer Garvie's voice, charged with all the concern and perplexity and barely controlled anger that you'd expect, ring out accusingly, 'Kennedy! By God but what've you done, laddie? What the hell possessed you to alter when she would've passed well clear?'

That was one of the greatest weapons of The Madness during what was still the opening phase of its assault on *Auriga* — its very elusiveness, the manner in which it appeared, struck, then retreated, leaving not only the onlooker but also the victim himself uncertain whether anything strange had taken place. It was still, in the majority of cases, a will-o'-the-wisp affliction; just as the real truth behind the near-collision remained uncertain even after Mowat's interrogation.

'It was Mister Garvie, sir,' stammered a white-faced Kennedy on the verge of tears while torn between loyalty and self-preservation. 'He did tell me to take action, honestly, sir! An' . . . he was sort of laughing when he said it. As if it was funny.'

'Yeah, well *I* couldn't be sure, sir,' Mulholland had emphasised with cautious neutrality. 'Not *sure*, you understand? I mean the fisherman did look like he was steaming a bit too fast for us to pass ahead and clear, yeah; but then again Mister Garvie's an experienced officer, isn't he? It was definitely the apprentice what altered . . . No, sir, I couldn't *say* whether he got a direct order or not. Certainly I wasn't even put on stand-by at the wheel an' I am the Quartermaster, all said an' done! Christ, imagine him firin' that Verey at me. Me, mind you! Jus' the bloody Quartermaster an' nothing to do with makin' decisions.'

Finally Sandy Garvie himself; disillusioned naturally, yet obviously anxious to be fair. As concerned for young Kennedy's future as for his own.

'My fault quite frankly, sir. Pushed the lad too far on what was intended to be a hypothetical collision situation — what he would have done if he'd believed I'd underestimated the risk; if we hadn't been heading to pass well clear. Then he panicked, hit the button before I could stop him. Nevertheless my responsibility, sir. Entirely mine.'

Chief Officer Temple didn't believe one word he'd said apart from, possibly, the last part. He liked Garvie; he considered him a good officer and had always trusted his judgement implicitly until now. Only he couldn't help noticing the blood still marking the Third Mate's collar and remembering that earlier expression of devilment. The one Sandy hadn't quite concealed during the changing of the watch.

So when he and the Captain finally walked together out to the wing, staring grimly astern along *Auriga*'s wake to where an angry trawler wallowed in fading isolation, David Temple shook his head defiantly, this time without the slightest compromise.

'Garvie's lying,' he stated flatly. 'I can't understand why, or what the hell's got into him, but I do know he's covering for something a bloody sight more serious than his own simple negligence.'

When Mowat's answer came it was completely unexpected. 'I agree, Mister Temple. I am also forced to accept your other observations. Too many riddles; too many damnable co-incidences.'

Temple said, 'Oh!' and felt ridiculously deflated; he'd never really expected the Captain to concede even then. It made him feel relieved yet, in a perverse sort of way, more nervous as well. As if his own fears, having finally been confirmed by higher authority, had suddenly adopted the status of fact.

'Then you will radio for help, sir?' he added hurriedly, anxious to retain his advantage. 'Or for medical advice, at least?'

Mowat turned, apathy overcome for the moment by the realisation that his command — his very own *Auriga* — had nearly pulverised a dozen men through criminal irresponsibility. Only action could help neutralise the horror he'd felt.

'More than that. I want Mister Garvie relieved by the Second Officer immediately, Mister Temple; we'll reschedule the night's watches later. Then I want you personally to check every man in every compartment through the ship for indications of illness or mental disturbance. I also want another meeting with the Chief

137

Engineer and Mister Sullivan in my cabin as soon as possible after that ... but before everything, get MacNally up here now while I draft a precautionary alert to the shore authorities.'

Temple nodded, aware of a heady gratitude. For a time he'd begun to imagine that even the Captain had been affected by ... well ... whatever it was. Now he felt everything would be O.K. The Master was in charge again and already the night promised less strain. Oh sure, he was concerned for Sandy Garvie — it was a hell of a thing to suspend any officer from duty, but the Third Mate wasn't himself; Temple was certain of that now. You can't risk leaving a sick man in charge of a ten-thousand-ton meat axe ...

'I'll get Sparks, then shake Bill Yancy. Do you want me to explain ... ?'

He broke off abruptly, looking over the Old Man's shoulder. Radio Officer MacNally was already on the bridge, standing in the wheelhouse door with a signal pad in his hand and gazing at them, yet Temple got the weird impression that he wasn't really seeing them, somehow. It made him curiously uncomfortable.

He forced himself to grin, aware how weak it must look. 'Talk of the devil. Is it me you want, Sparks, or the Captain?'

MacNally didn't answer immediately, and Temple only needed to note the stiffly articulated manner in which he tendered the signal pad to feel the first prickle of renewed apprehension.

'Immediate action,' MacNally intoned eventually. 'They told me I had to take immediate action.'

The Captain gazed uncertainly between the two men before his eyes dropped to the message written on the pad. Then he appeared to read for a long time, as if having difficulty in deciphering the text — or in accepting the evidence of his senses.

When he did finally lift his head to meet his Chief Officer's anxious query it was a look of such disbelief, such frowning incomprehension that David Temple feared for one chilling moment that he was alone again, and that whatever had previously stiffened Mowat's resolve had just as suddenly evaporated.

Until the *Auriga*'s Master silently presented him with MacNally's signal pad, and he also digested its content. And felt exactly the same incredulity.

The crisply printed characters at the start were as familiar to

Temple as a thousand weather forecasts and navwarns and company telegrams before them. It was only as the text continued, and MacNally's dementia had impaired his physical co-ordination, that the writing began to falter, and then straggle, and then become spidery and illegible until, finally, it trailed in mad slashes clear off the bottom of the pad.

'Immediate action,' the Operator repeated woodenly, as Temple stared. 'They told me to take immediate action.'

But Temple didn't raise his eyes. Not for a long, long time . . .

> TO MLDT AURIGA – PRIORITY FLASH:
> ROYAL OBSERVATORY CONFIRMS EXTRA TERRESTRIAL SPACE VEHICLES ANTICIPATED NORTH EUROPEAN THEATRE WITHIN NEXT TWELVE HOURS STOP ALIENS CONSIDERED HOSTILE STOP MONITORING DEFENCE TEAMS INDICATE AGGRESSOR GUIDANCE SYSTEMS CALIBRATED TO COMMUNICATIONS INSTALLA-TION MIKE LIMA DELTA TANGO AURIGA STOP IMPERATIVE ... ESTROY ALL RADIO EQUIP ... EDIATELY STO ... ITAL REPEAT VITAL THIS TASK COMPLET ...

'Ohhhh Jesus,' Temple muttered. 'Oh Jesus Christ Almighty!'

'Immediate action, they said,' MacNally explained laboriously for the third time, and then he sighed. Neither Mowat nor Temple were quick enough to catch him before he slumped to the deck.

Perhaps the Captain had been given a little longer than Temple to adjust mentally; whatever the reason he reacted quicker than the younger man as he knelt beside the moaning victim.

'I'll stay here with him,' he snapped, almost as briskly as if Mac-Nally had tripped and wasn't a lunatic at all. When he did look up there was a reassuring urgency in his gaze, even though they both already knew, deep down, that the time for urgency was past.

'You'd better get down to the radio room, Mister Temple.'

Chief Officer Temple began running. *An' this time,* the little voice in his head was screeching, *the hell with staying calm an' bloody British . . .*

He was so preoccupied with his panic that it never occurred to him to wonder why the Old Man suddenly became so competent after his earlier uncertainty. As if some powerful outside force had begun to sustain him.

Chapter Twelve

There is a rift in the bed of the North Sea, lying well off the east coast of Scotland, which leaves a sharp one hundred and thirty fathom trace on the sounder and provides a splendid check for mariners against their course made good and their distance run. It isn't so necessary now, of course, when ships tend to follow the electronic guidance of Decca chains and D.F. beams and the precise digital fixing of satellite navigational aids; but the chasm still appears on the charts, and still bears the name it always did.

They call it *The Devil's Hole*.

Quite apt, really, considering the thoughts that were infiltrating her Captain's mind at the moment when *Auriga* passed over it.

Oh, not that Charles Mowat himself was remotely aware of anything interfering with his thought processes. In fact, Mowat was pleasantly satisfied with his adjustment to what he had at last accepted *was* some form of threat — Garvie's apparently deliberate folly coupled now with MacNally's crazed offering had exploded any doubts he'd felt earlier. It had also made him acutely conscious of the need for authoritarian control to be exerted.

A crew in jeopardy demanded an undisputed Master to ensure their collective survival and Captain Mowat, who loved his complement with fiercely autocratic devotion, was not prepared to abrogate that ultimate responsibility simply because his limbs were chilled and his brain a cobweb snare for doubt. God would strengthen him; God would guide him. The Lord had always guided and delivered him out of hazard.

. . . and that was where the irony lay and his consequent vulnerability to the seductions of The Madness. For the regenerated Charles Mowat was now possessed of an inflexible determination to impose his will — which was merely a reflection of God's will —

on those in his care, with the firm conviction that divine providence would sustain his faltering intellect.

Yet it was that same great force which would eventually turn against them. With such strength of purpose vitalising the Captain as *Auriga* passed over The Devil's Hole and stood firmly for the Isle of May at the entrance to the Firth of Forth, what man would question his orders? Certainly none of his subordinates could ever have suspected that God and The Madness were increasingly becoming as one in the deteriorating mind of Captain Charles Mowat.

So that from henceforth, when God spoke, it might possibly be with the true and reasoning voice of a saviour. Or possibly with the malevolent exhortations of The Madness.

Third Officer Garvie's whimsical experiment with terror affected a larger part of *Auriga*'s crew than simply her Captain; especially those others already subjected to the vagaries of The Madness.

For most of them it acted as a sharp arousal; a temporary stimulant to counter their steady regression into unreality. Suddenly those who might have been identified as afflicted — men such as Second Officer Yancy and Second Engineer Beckman, who had slipped into a half-sleeping, half-waking limbo by that time — were snapped into shocked wakefulness by the blare of the whistle and, like Mowat, were able to camouflage their inadequacies.

It had overshadowed the symptoms of the lesser sufferers as well. The Bosun's painful throat condition; Slimy Simmieson, with his still manfully controlled lack of stability; Greaser Behrens' itchy crabs and his confused recollection of a homicidal cat; Fourth Engineer Bench who preserved the most exciting secret ever kept, and Chief Engineer Webster who believed in it too: all were abruptly dragged back into the real world of seamen as their own special brands of The Madness submerged under the demands of professional concern.

Of course some of them weren't. The ones who were irretrievably affected by the time *Auriga* steamed across The Devil's Hole in the North Sea.

There were seven of them altogether — apart from Donkeyman Trott, who was already dead and totally unperturbed by the fears of mortal men: Terry Monaghan, who only clung to life as a slobbering shell; Chikwanda, engrossed with a survival game in which the penalty for failure far exceeded any conventional dismemberment by imploding steel or wood; Wimpy Jennings and Seaman Grainger, both in coma; and the most recent victim, Able Seaman Reid, who now felt his whole body engulfed in flame. Oh, and young Derek Guy of course, who'd heard the siren but had refused to have anything to do with the bloody thing because he was still upset at bein' upstaged by that ol' bastard Trott and who — without being remotely affected by The Proper Madness — was nevertheless so suicidally determined now that if *Auriga* had gone down he'd have considered tying himself to the rail just for bloody spite. In full view, naturally. Smiling contemptuously at whatever audience managed to make it to the liferafts.

None of those advanced sufferers recovered even slightly; but the majority did. This might have seemed a setback to the progress of The Madness, yet it wasn't for it masked the true extent to which the *Auriga*'s complement had been affected while it hadn't made her any less at risk. It meant that her final capitulation had been postponed until she had time to sail into even greater hazard; to run out of sea room and be overwhelmed in a restricted channel where others, too, might become involved.

Until, in fact, *Auriga*'s death might escalate beyond disaster, and assume the scale of cataclysm.

It was well after one a.m. before the senior officers again assembled in the Captain's cabin. Temple and Chief Steward Sullivan had only just completed their check of the crew's health and done what they could for those discovered to be seriously ill — snugged them down into their berths, ensured they were constantly attended by a reliable shipmate. They had become more and more disquieted themselves as they tallied the full, or the apparently full, extent of whatever contagion had stricken the ship.

Less than five hours now remained before *Auriga* entered the Firth of Forth; less than seven before she was due to board the Inchkeith pilot. No warning had yet been passed to any shore authority and, after one appalled glance into what had been the radio room, Temple now assumed there never could be.

Chief Webster confirmed his opinion. 'Buggered!' was his technical and succinct opinion.

142

The Captain eyed him, grimly reflective; very much in command, though his fingers constantly toyed with the Bible beside him. Very white fingers.

'No prospect of even temporary repair, Eric?'

'What? With every chassis withdrawn on its maintenance slides so's he could do a thorough job? There's valves and condensers smashed; wires ripped out; main and emergency aerial connecfions severed.' Webster shook his head positively. 'Beckman's still down there fiddling with it but he's not looking so bloody bright himself an' there's no chance, Charlie. No way!'

Mowat turned to his Chief Officer. 'And Chikwanda. What about him?'

Temple shrugged tiredly. 'As I said, he's missing. Bunk board splintered, clothes torn and lying in a corner . . . they're looking for him now — and for that cat we apparently have aboard at the same time.'

'Christ but it's weird,' Sullivan muttered uneasily. 'Cats and staring eyes and disappearing men. Christ, but it's unsettling.'

It may have been imagination but Temple thought he caught the Old Man glancing sharply, almost disapprovingly at the Chief Steward as he spoke. There was no reason, surely? After all, Sullivan was dead right — it *was* weird!

'But what made MacNally *do* it?' the Chief growled, still thinking about the radio. It underlined the perversity of The Madness — Eric Webster calmly accepting his own delusion, yet unable to understand a similar condition in others. 'Why all that rambling nonsense about aliens and space ships an' stuff? What put all that into the poor sod's head?'

'Auto-suggestion?' Temple hazarded. 'This thing . . . this illness we're hit by; it seems as much a mental as a physical condition. And Sparks is a sci-fi buff, remember. Spends half his watch reading about U.F.O.'s and green men. Now it seems they've taken over. It's crazy.'

'Aye,' Sullivan blurted out, for Chief Steward Sullivan was still severely shaken after having been the first to answer Able Seaman Reid's scream for help. 'Crazy's the word, Mate. That young kid . . . Christ but he was shrieking before he passed out, d'you know that? Shriekin' and screeching his blood was boiling — that his whole body was on fire, dammit . . .'

'Mister Sullivan!'

This time there was no mistaking the displeasure in the Captain's tone. 'I'll thank you not to blaspheme quite so liberally, Mister Sullivan. I realise that you have undergone a most unpleasant experience, but . . .'

Mowat hesitated when he caught the disconcerted frowns around him. He smiled quickly, trying to take the sting out of what he already realised had been a stupid mistake. 'I suggest we should reserve the Lord's name for a more considered appeal, gentlemen. Considering our situation.'

Temple began to grow angry again: there was a lack of urgency even now; Mowat seemingly more preoccupied with what had been a hitherto well-concealed religious conviction than with assessing the situation. Yet he did appear to be firmly in command. Just got his priorities a bit odd, that was all.

Sullivan obviously wasn't mollified either. He'd had one hell of a night already an' now he was being told off like some precocious little kid. For *swearing*. Aboard a bloody ship! Suddenly he didn't give a damn any more; not for Master's personnel reports or Company Catering Superintendents or . . .

'Ohhhh f'r Chr . . .' he started to protest before Chief Webster leaned forward hurriedly, grabbing the stage. But Eric Webster wasn't *that* mad. Disturbed and vague, yes, but not crazy enough to let Arthur Sullivan commit professional suicide.

'How many seamen sick so far, Dave?'

'Four,' Temple was as quick to answer. 'Reid, Monaghan . . .'

'Monaghan's not a seaman; Monaghan's a caterer,' Sullivan niggled peevishly, still resentful of the Captain. Who was a seaman.

'Monaghan,' Temple persevered with tight self-control, sick of the bickering and the worry and the awful helplessness now the radio was gone. 'Grainger and, presumably, Chikwanda. Oh, and you can add that odd-ball Guy to the list; he's not comatose like the others but he's gone peculiar. Always was, actually, but now he's even more bloody objectionable and introverted.'

'Do we count him as sick then, Mister Temple?'

'Good as, though possibly not with the same thing, sir,' the Chief Officer retorted impatiently. 'Either way we can discount him as a useful hand.'

144

The Captain frowned, attempting to evaluate the limited options open to him. Silently, he was praying for guidance. God required him to do that much; to make that effort. God, in His wisdom and when He was ready, would propose their course of action but until He did, Mowat would continue to delay.

'Then would anyone care to suggest the possible cause? We know the symptoms: mental derangement, loss of consciousness, severe pain in the case of Reid, yet apparently, in the Third Officer's case at least, a diametrically-opposed form of anaesthesia. I don't believe Garvie was even aware of that pin through the flesh of his neck. And, of course, this inexplicable coldness in the limbs . . .'

Temple looked up curiously. 'Coldness? I don't remember anyone complaining about that?'

Mowat covered himself well; only his fingers, chilled and practically numb now, pressed the Bible a little harder. 'MacNally mentioned it. During dinner if my memory serves me. Before it held any significance, of course.'

'All right. Then what about the cat?' Sullivan exclaimed.

Webster was the first to catch on. 'Rabies, you mean?'

God help them if it is, the Mate reflected sickly.

'Trott had scratches on his forearms,' the Chief Steward pursued grimly.

'None of the others did,' Temple countered.

The Old Man shook his head. 'The incubation period must be too long. The cat, if there is a cat, can't have been aboard before Helsinki. Two days ago.'

''Course there's a cat, Charlie,' the Chief put in with a touch of asperity. 'I told you I'd seen it myself, remember?'

But Chief Engineer Webster had seen a pencil lighter than air for that matter. He pulled a face and added, 'Anyway, you could say that about any epidemic — not enough time to incubate or whatever, an' too bloody coincidental it's hit them all within a matter of hours.'

It was noticeable that nobody queried the 'All', as though each of them still clung doggedly to the assumption that *Auriga's* tribulation had reached its peak.

Temple started, galvanised by a sudden thought. 'Food poisoning. That can affect people very quickly.'

The Chief Steward rounded on him furiously. 'There's bugger-all wrong wi' my food, Mate! I run a hygienic ship; the Chef keeps that galley spotless, not like some've *your* crowd on deck.'

'All *right*, Sullivan!'

This time there was no hint of apology in the Old Man's growl. 'Cut out this inter-departmental wrangling! Something of a particularly virulent nature has struck this ship and it could very well be of a toxic origin. Temple is not reflecting on your efficiency — tinned and packaged foods; fish; meats; any of them could be contaminated without your being aware or responsible.'

'But you only get sick with food poisoning, sir,' Sullivan appealed, drawing back a little from the brink. 'It'll make 'em spew their rings; stomach pains, maybe headaches an' even coma . . . but some of those blokes are hallucinating. It's their brains that are affected, not just their body functions.'

Mowat felt utterly weary. Imploringly he pressed his deadened fingertips hard against the worn red binding of the Good Book and almost immediately sensed the spiritual strength bolstering his faltering intellect.

'I would to God we did have more medical knowledge, Mister Sullivan. But for the moment we can only take every sensible precaution . . .'

The bridge telephone rang. It seemed very loud. Mowat reached to answer it but completed his instructions before he spoke to Yancy; a man totally in control.

'. . . therefore you will ensure that any unused food from yesterday's meals is retained for analysis, and you will break out fresh stores for breakfast. Yes, Mister Yancy?'

All eyes watched as he listened sombrely. After he'd finished he hung the phone back on its bulkhead mounting and turned. 'They have found no trace of Seaman Chikwanda. It's dark but they claim to have searched pretty thoroughly. The Bosun is of the opinion that he is either hiding or has gone overboard.'

Temple shrugged wearily. 'Then I suppose we turn back. He's a fit bloke; probably swims like a fish . . .'

His voice trailed off as he caught the Captain's expression. Deliberating, yes, but also placid. Too placid.

'Last seen during dinner; which could place him up to five hours and seventy-five miles astern, Mister Temple. And we are into the dark hours as Peak has already emphasised.'

'You mean you're not even going to try and search for him?' the Mate echoed disbelievingly. Mowat looked unhappy but inflexible.

'We already have several sick men aboard who require urgent hospital treatment . . .'

'One sick man should've been enough, dammit! You should have shown that much concern and taken action on Monaghan's behalf alone . . . before we lost our bloody radio.'

Suddenly the tension had reached hysteria pitch. Mowat's features flushed, perhaps understandably outraged at such a blatant attack by a subordinate. 'Are you daring to question my decisions, Mister? Or implying I had prior knowledge that MacNally would become deranged and destroy all means of communication?'

'I'm saying there's been too much procrastination. Too much bloody complacency on your part.' He swung round, glaring at them all. 'What the hell's wrong with us? That we never do anything? That we reduce every bloody emergency on board to the level of a discussion . . .'

'Belay that, laddie!'

Temple's jaw shut with a snap. When Eric Webster bellowed on the few occasions he needed to, it was loud enough to freeze a piston in mid-cycle. Yet when the Chief spoke again it was mild as mother's milk, and without the slightest trace of censure.

'What's all this about communications, Charlie? We've still got a radio — the V.H.F. on the bridge.' He smiled uncertainly, trying to lighten the strain with a joke. 'You'll tell me next you'd forgotten it. Both of you.'

The Captain's expression was a mixture of comical disbelief and . . . could it have been anger? At himself? As if another crack had suddenly been revealed in his veneer of infallibility. Not that Temple noticed, or even gave a damn right then — *he'd* forgotten it; he bloody well had forgotten it! But his pride wasn't important, not right now.

Optimism began to lift him again, dampening the fear and frustration. So they did still have a link, albeit a tenuous one, with the world beyond *Auriga*'s bulwarks. The drawback was that V.H.F.

147

had a maximum range of, say, thirty miles under normal conditions. Line of sight transmission. But this was the North Sea, and you were very seldom alone in the North Sea; not nowadays with oil service vessels trundling back and forward to the rigs like heavy lorries down a motorway. Switch any radar to thirty-six miles and there was almost invariably an echo to keep you company somewhere on the P.P.I.

'So we could have a Pan urgency call relayed back along our track at least,' he urged, willing Mowat to respond. 'Alert all east-lying vessels to keep look-out for a man overboard between here and, say, our nineteen hundred position last night.'

'If we can relay back, then why can't we relay ahead?' Sullivan probed forcibly, probably the most unlikely ally Temple would ever have. 'You say we can't risk a Medevac by helicopter at night, sir, but we can warn 'em shoreside to have ambulances and medical help waiting in Leith; maybe even have a doctor board with the pilot.'

The Captain stirred unhappily. Dear God, but he was as anxious to get help for his crew as anyone — to get help for himself, for that matter, for Mowat was only too aware that, while the Lord would undoubtedly make his physical as well as his mental suffering bearable, a little assistance from the medical profession wouldn't go amiss.

'Of course we will put out an all-ships Pan regarding Chikwanda,' he said carefully, 'and assuming we *can* raise a relay station close-to, then I shall alert the shore authorities. It will have to be a limited description of symptoms at this stage but by daylight we will be within direct V.H.F. range of Forth Radio anyway and we can reassess our situation then.'

'Thank God,' the Mate exclaimed without thinking.

The Captain of *Auriga* stared at him dryly yet, for the first time, there was a faint trace of humour. 'Not yet, Mister Temple,' he retorted, 'but if prayer does have any power at all, then I pray to Him to give us reason for thanks by this time tomorrow.'

None of those present could have guessed how deeply Charles Mowat meant it. Not right then.

Temple glanced anxiously at his watch as they moved towards the door. It was 0200; four bells in the graveyard watch ... they had six hours to go before they picked up the Inchkeith pilot.

'It's going to be a long night,' Sullivan said, back to preparing the ground for efficiency reports. 'I'll be pushed for staff to do a proper breakfast but I'll get the Chef to knock up some sandwiches for the lads a bit later.'

He couldn't conceal a mischievous grin at David Temple as he watched the prospect of a sanny-in-the-hand replacing the Mate's previous anticipation of eggs, bacon, toast an' succulent, thick-cut marmalade. The Captain hesitated too, though.

'Then tinned fillings only, Mister Sullivan. From different batches to any previously used, if you please.'

'Aye, aye, sir,' the Chief Steward acknowledged without the slightest resentment. Already he'd recovered his spirits at the evidence of action being taken — apart from having delivered the *coup de grâce* to his adversary's most cherished joy.

Of course they'd have to use Holmquist's ship-baked rye bread again — none of them fancy Scandinavian fillings, obviously — but thanks to Hughie Baird an' Grainger's vandalism they didn't have much choice about the casings.

Still, for hungry men working short-handed watches they'd be more than acceptable.

And it was hardly likely that anyone was going to go stark, raving mad over a thing like *that*. Not just from eating a slice of bread.

Chapter Thirteen

They weren't quite alone at 0210 in the North Sea. They weren't exactly in imminent danger of another collision, either. There were three targets creeping like glow-worms across the periphery of the Decca P.P.I., but all were more than thirty-five miles away and southbound, running parallel to the Scottish coast. None of those anonymous blobs would pass any closer to *Auriga* and, until a new echo appeared on the screen, no one else would be able to hear.

Mowat passed a general call on Channel 16, though. And

someone did hear — the answering break in the static hiss showed that some unidentifiable second officer on at least one ship's bridge was trying to acknowledge their transmission; must therefore have been able to read some of its content ... but how much was uncertain. Whether he was aware of their request to relay it shoreside was even more in doubt. V.H.F. radio at extreme range is a fickle servant; men talk to astronauts on the bright side of the moon through it, yet can be deaf and dumb to a colleague dipping just below the curvature of their immediate horizon.

PAN, PAN, PAN RELAY! ALL SHIPS, ALL SHIPS, THIS IS MIKE LIMA DELTA TANGO AURIGA ... WE HAVE SEVERAL SEAMEN SERIOUSLY ILL SUSPECTED FOOD POISONING. REQUEST MEDICAL ASSISTANCE AVAILABLE ON ARRIVAL FORTH. OUR E.T.A. INCHKEITH 0700 G.M.T. WILL TRANSMIT AGAIN IF FURTHER MERCY ACTION REQUIRED.

PAN, PAN, RELAY! BELIEVED MAN OVERBOARD EAST OF POSITION ...

'We'll try again in an hour, Mister. Someone should be well within range in another hour,' the Captain finished confidently, passing the handset back to the man who'd been in charge of *Auriga* ever since Sandy Garvie had been relieved because he was mad.

'Yessir,' said Second Officer Yancy. And smiled. Just as Third Officer Garvie had done a few hours before.

Chikwanda stirred warily in his hiding place. He had watched them searching without concern because it was a good hiding place, worthy of a crocodile or a hunting lizard; one as secure as the river bank where the saurian waits openly yet is not seen because it has become a log. A log is unremarkable among other logs ... animal guile was rapidly replacing human logic — he was naked now and as different from his companions as a savage from a scientist. He had no hate for them, not as he did for the spider-thing, but his mistrust was a relic from the heritage left to him by his forebears.

So was his cunning. As the crocodile capitalised on its ugliness, so Chikwanda employed his own natural advantage. They had briefly switched on the *Auriga*'s cargo lamps during their search, flooding the forward deck with stark brilliance, but glaring light creates equally dense shadow, and Chikwanda had chosen one of the most obvious hiding places of all, yet one where his physical appearance rendered him unnoticeable to all but the most perceptive eye.

He decided to remain there a little longer, even though the search was abandoned and darkness had settled over the decks of the ship. Oh, he knew they would see him as soon as dawn exposed his deceit, and that he would have to find a most powerful weapon before the crawling monstrosity came upon him . . . but there was still time. And the primitive that was Chikwanda had a new-found patience.

All creatures which hunted required patience. Until the moment when they were ready to kill.

Derek Guy blinked at his watch, the one Mum had given him before he sailed on his first trip, then turned over in his bunk staring bleakly towards the washbasin and mirror. Unconsciously his thumb found its way between his teeth and he lay there sucking absently. Like a baby.

It was two thirty, the darkest part of the short summer night. If he was going to do it — accomplish the two things he wanted so badly; to be reunited with his mother and go out've this life wi' such a blaze of derisive glory that every single one o' these bastards aboard'd wish they'd been a lot more appreciative of Derek Guy — then the time had come. Now was his ultimate hour. Or moment, anyway. Well, surely to Christ it wouldn't take an *hour*? He didn't think he'd like it to last as long as an hour. Still, better get on with it. Now.

He didn't actually move, though. Just lay there brooding darkly. And sucking his thumb, of course.

The trouble was that his enthusiasm had been . . . well . . . dampened. Or if the truth were told, criminally undermined. The way they'd all acted; dead nasty an' brutal an' that, just because he'd got a bit upset over the self-indulgent way that the Donkeyman had selected to pre-empt his own intention — dying like that, an' in a manner that reeked of crude melodrama, what with the starin' eyes an' the pathetic attempt at mystery. But still, the old soak had done it. Spoiled a lot of the impact . . .

Mind you, there was still Mum; his original motive for suicide. She'd be disappointed or then again, maybe not; maybe when you got wherever it was you went you couldn't even get disappointed. Sure as hell ... oh, sorry! Sure as *Heaven* you didn't get none of the real miseries any more, like grief and people being aggressive to you, an' Liverpool losin' at home by a last-minute penalty.

Right. So he'd compromise; not actually make up his mind finally until he got up there. He swung his legs off the bunk and brought out the special suitcase with slightly less enthusiasm than before. But he still intended to do it, remember. Derek Guy wasn't a bloke to back down once he'd made up his mind an' that was f'r sure. But you didn't rush self-destruction. It wasn't something you could exactly postpone once you were halfway down.

Christ, but that razor was sharp, man! He looked at it apprehensively, thinking how much it might hurt, with or without five hundred aspirins inside him. Even the suggestion of pain made Derek feel squeamish. An' the blood. All over everythin'.

He put the razor back in the case with relief at having come to a decision. No mess.

So what was next? Yeah, the roll of Elastoplast. He'd bought that because it had occurred to him that if he did cut his wrists he'd maybe yell a little despite his resolution ... but he'd decided against the wrist thing now — purely because of the mess an' that, of course — so there wasn't a lot of point in abandoning dignity by slapping an uncomfortable sticky plaster across his mouth.

He put that back in the case too.

The plastic bag? Derek frowned uncertainly. It had only been a last-minute inspiration during the planning stage; some idea of a fail-safe back-up. He'd reckoned if he put that over his head an' tied the neck, then even if the rope didn't work he would still suffocate. But his original resolve was wavering and prolonged dying held less and less attraction. Goin' purple-faced inside a stupid plastic bag was about as laborious as you could get. Anyway, there wasn't no point in over-kill. They'd just think he'd gone a bit unbalanced if they found 'im dead stuck in a plastic bloody bag!

He put the bag back in the case. The little shudder of revulsion he betrayed might have led an astute student of human behaviour to wonder if Seaman Derek Guy was *quite* as daft as was originally assumed. But there were still the aspirins, and the bottle of hydrochloric acid. And the rope.

Derek weighed the little bottle thoughtfully in his hand. Very carefully indeed. Well, his plan had been to show everybody how thorough he'd been. All the times they'd bawled at him for doin' jobs half-hearted; Temple an' the Bosun an' the rest've them — so he knew if he killed himself with one hundred an' fifty per cent super efficiency, then that'd really be twisting the knife in 'em; make 'em really sick about losing him.

He'd worked out the most fantastic *hara-kiri* routine, belt an' braces certain. He was going to hang himself, of course; that was the keystone of the whole thing. From some part of the ship nice an' high up. But first he planned to take five hundred aspirins, which was clever because not only would they poison him but they'd make the rest of it pretty damn painless. Anyway, then he was going to put the rope around his neck and get ready for the big drop, but not right away. No! Nothing so unsubtle for Derek Guy, wishful-thinking nutter supreme . . . because he'd have the plastic bag over his head as well, in case the jerk didn't work. An' before even that, he would have slashed his wrists so's he could bleed to death on the way down. And then finally — ultimate stroke of genius — he was intending to soak the hanging rope with acid, which would take a minute or two to burn through probably; so if all else failed — the poisoning and the suffocating an' the slashing and the hanging — then the rope would eventually part and Derek Guy — the *late* Derek Guy — would smash hisself to bits on the deck.

Bloody fantastic!

He put the bottle cautiously in his pocket. He didn't actually have to use it but it was as well to be prepared. Of course he didn't have to do it at all tonight. Not if he really didn't want to. Now, where were those aspirins? He could risk a few of them an' see how he felt. He didn't have to swallow all of them if he didn't want to, either. But a few wouldn't harm. Maybe a coupl've hundred . . .

He managed four, and even the last two took a bit of getting down with his throat so dry. First night nerves, probably . . . he looked anxiously at his watch again and guessed he'd taken about four minutes to swallow four aspirins. That would mean five hundred minutes for five hund ... Christ, it would take him over eight hours just to get *started* on his suicide.

He knew he shouldn't have left it so late. He should just have missed out on eatin' Scandinavian tonight and got on with it.

Derek put four hundred and ninety-six aspirins back in the bottle, put the bottle back in the case along with most of his other death support systems, and headed not too enthusiastically for the door.

He still had the rope, and the acid. He'd still go up there an' see how he felt.

It would be chilly though, even on a midsummer night in the North Sea. So if he got up there and did find it too uncomfortable he'd maybe put it off f'r this trip.

Not for long, mind you. No one could say Derek Guy was all mouth an' no action.

Second Cook Monaghan died at three in the morning.

Noisily.

Hughie Baird was there. He'd been dozing actually, slouched with his chair tipped back and his feet up on Terry's bunk board, dreaming resentful dreams which covered a vast spectrum from the iniquities of Chief Stewards an' bluidy wee hard men sailors that used fire hoses instead o' their ain two fists, to a Finnish tart called Olga who couldnae appreciate the difference between a suave, accomplished man of the world — like hisself, who was an officer too — well, sort of — an' a bluidy wee hard man sailor!

The sounds filtered slowly through his subconscious and in a somewhat confusing manner — according to his dream Arthur Sullivan had just been told by the Company Catering Superintendent precisely what the Company Catering Superintendent thought about Arthur Sullivan's competence as a Chief Steward; whereupon Arthur was kneeling over the Company Catering Superintendent and choking the Company Catering Superintendent to death, while Hughie stood watching with a great big smile on his face an' the anticipation of quick promotion ... until the gagging, rattling noises the Company Catering Superintendent was emitting became so real compared with the ethereal quality of the rest of the dream — meaning that, after reading the

Old Man's report on this particular voyage, it was more likely it would be the Superintendent tryin' to throttle *Arthur* — that Hughie Baird eventually opened one uneasy eye, and saw Terry and what Terry was doing . . . and fell backwards off the chair with a shriek of wide-awake panic.

The Second Cook was sitting bolt upright with his eyes protruding and the saliva flooding down his chin. His hands were plucking — *clawing* for God's sake — at his arms and his chest and his face and anywhere else they could snatch about his body, while all the time the youth jerked and arched convulsively, scrabbling with his legs to jam himself against the back of the berth as if recoiling from something coming through the door.

The door?

But there *wasnae* anything comin' through the door!

And then Terry shrieked, 'Help me, Hughie! Oh, Mother, please help me! I'm burning . . . Ohhhh please I'm burning; I'm on fire! Hughie please put out the fiiiiire . . .'

Baird made it out of the alleyway while still on his hands and knees, yelling for Sullivan, Holmquist . . . anyone. By the time *Auriga*'s Mate and the Chief Steward had forced their way through the white-faced knot of crewmen jamming the door to Terry Monaghan's cabin the Second Cook was dead.

No cat, of course. No scratches. No signs of charring, scalding, not even the slightest reddening of Terry's skin.

Only the fear remained. But that was the most contagious element of all by three o'clock that morning; it was rapidly becoming the single common link between them all, certainly between those who outwardly retained an appearance of normality. It was kept well concealed by most, though; battened down under expressions that were only a little grimmer than usual.

Men in danger fight hard to look impassive. It can become important not to be seen to be more vulnerable than those around you — apart from which there were only five hours to go now before they embarked the Inchkeith pilot, and were safe.

Second Engineer Beckman was feeling sick and dizzy by the time he'd given up trying to make anything of the wrecked radio equipment. He knew he wouldn't be able to stay on his feet much longer,

155

yet he was still scared Webster would change his mind and not let him go home tomorrow − or today, was it? − if he thought he wasn't up to travelling.

There couldn't be all that much wrong with him, surely? Not coming on as quickly as it had? There was an old sailorman's adage about heavy weather which kept running through his mind − *long foretold, long last; short notice, soon past* . . . Yeah, O.K., so maybe this wasn't quite the same thing, being ill, but the rhyme couldn't be entirely unconnected; they even talked about *being under the weather* when you thought about it.

All he needed was a few hours of decent sleep; not the kind he'd had with those frightening dreams before they'd called him to say MacNally had flipped his lid, poor bastard − though he always had figured Sparks was a potential nutter with his sardonic disregard for authority . . . funny, the way the ship was rolling an' pitching yet there wasn't even a slight swell outside. So who was on watch up top, then? Bloody inadequate bloody seaman officers; can't even keep the ship right way bloody up . . . Christ but he could feel it coming on again − the remoteness; the same weird sensation he'd felt earlier when he knew he was squeezing the toothpaste tube but couldn't bring himself to stop, like he'd been outside his body an' gazing down in critical detachment.

Beckman staggered from the radio office and leaned uncertainly against the rail at the head of the internal stairway. He knew he should go looking for the Chief − report his big zero on the radio repairs − but he was loath to in case Webster noticed how ill he was . . . an' that was another thing; the way they couldn't mind their own bloody business. If a bloke wanted to feel sick, then who the hell had the right to stop him going home because've it? But Webster would. Oh, Chief Engineer Eric bloody Webster would; like a shot. All hypocritical concern . . .

Beckman became aware of a savage anger rising within him; he knew it was silly, but he still couldn't stop it. In fact he didn't want to suppress it; it was such a good anger, such a satisfying rage. Maybe MacNally hadn't been so crazy after all, with his protest against the System. Oh boy, were their faces white when they found what Sparks had done to his equipment − stuck two fingers up at the whole bloody lot of 'em by putting a hammer through every radio set in his shack.

The ship rolled without reason again and Second Engineer Beckman almost fell. Bastards! Criticising and superior an' stopping blokes going home to see their families f'r spite, yet they couldn't even steer the ship properly themselves. All that guff about calling the shore, the need to warn the authorities that the *crew* was sick ... except it wasn't the crew, it was the bloody senior officers couldn't do their jobs; couldn't make the ship run straight so's blokes like him wouldn't keep fallin' down an' ...

... a cover up; that's all it was. All the supposed concern for the crew's health. Just so's they could say *We told you so* when things really went wrong and the boat rolled clean over on a flat calm sea jus' because nobody was steering it right. MacNally had the right idea. Good old Radio Officer MacNally. Screw the bastards; pull the plug on 'em. Stop 'em settin' up alibis f'r their own rotten inadequacy.

Beckman suddenly knew what he had to do. Well, somebody had to do it. Somebody had to take a stand for the little men against the System, and they'd stopped Sparks before he'd had time to finish. Boy, when they discovered jus' what Second Engineer Beckman intended to do would their expressions be sick? Not the crew's — they were O.K. No! Jus' the bosses — Mowat. Webster. Prissy bloody Chief Officer bloody Temple!

The Second wandered unsteadily through the light trap curtain and into the darkened wheelhouse. It was very quiet, just the occasional click of the gyro and the low hum of the radar. Just like any ordinary night watch up top ... the dimmed glow of equipment monitors, the orange flare reflecting from the P.P.I.; the wash of red to port and green out to starboard where the nav lights overspilled their warning. Two figures leaning over the bridge front — Yancy probably, an' the other duty quartermaster; name of Grimm, was it? Ignoring everything an' not giving a damn even though *Auriga*'s deck was rolling and pitching like crazy. Inadequate. Bloody useless inadequate. But he'd show 'em. He'd give 'em all something to explain away to the Owners.

Calmly Second Engineer Beckman disconnected the V.H.F. radio power connection and aerial plug. Then he depressed the clips retaining its smooth, nylon-coated casing to the after bulkhead. There were two chromed handles, one on either side, which made it easy to carry even though the deck kept lifting and falling ... carry it carefully. Through the port door; out on to the wing, an' keep going.

Someone behind him was yelling suddenly; Bill Yancy? From the other side? Beckman couldn't help grinning to himself. They'd all have to shout after this; shout at the tops of their voices; shriek their bloody futile excuses to the wind.

Second Mate Yancy wasn't able to run because he was too ill; almost as ill as Beckman. All he could do, along with Quartermaster Grimm who was every bit as shattered as anyone, was to watch in disbelief while Beckman heaved *Auriga*'s last link with the outside world clear overboard.

It was 0320 British Summer Time. Now they could never be certain of how much − if any − of their earlier appeal had been passed to their only source of aid.

Derek Guy got as far as the operator's cab platform of the crane and hesitated, panting for breath. Lord but it was dark up here above *Auriga*'s foredeck. Certainly there were a few floods illuminating the superstructure aft, and the red and green steaming lights positively sparkled in the clear night air, but down here − right forr'ad on the port crane where he'd selected what promised to be the stage for his ultimate performance − it was ... well, dark. And kind've creepy.

It was deathly quiet, too, with just the swish of the sea under the bow and the putter of the funnel throwing an almost incandescent trail of exhaust into the black sky. Quite exciting, standing up here with his back against the guard rail and virtually on a level with the bridge. Secretive too, knowing the Second Mate was probably out there on the wing somewhere gazing right towards him yet not having the first inkling that Derek Guy was as high up as he was and totally invisible.

High? Derek glanced down involuntarily and swallowed. Jeeze but it really *was* high up here at that. Well over forty feet an' a sheer drop to the base. It wasn't even like there was a clear space if you did fall; nothing but a forest of protrusions what with number one hatch coaming and the ventilators an' ring bolts an' ... He closed his eyes for a moment and forced himself to reason. Now look, pal; you're gonna hang yourself − or you're *thinking* about hanging yourself, anyway. So what does it matter what there is below you? I mean, you aren't goin' to fall far enough to hit it, are you? Not *hit* it? Or not till the acid burns through and the rope parts, but by that time you'll be a long way away, with Mum. Laughing at 'em all.

He actually found himself smiling at the prospect, but it was a pretty weak smile and without a lot of enthusiasm. Without a helluva lot of conviction either, suddenly.

It would probably have been fair to say that, had Derek Guy been aware of Terry Monaghan's death half an hour before, he'd never have made even this rapidly faltering gesture towards his own masochistic daydreams. Only he hadn't heard the rumpus caused by the Second Chef's terminal agony — or by Beckman's inexplicable disposal of *Auriga*'s last radio transmitter either, for that matter — because ever since he'd left his cabin he'd dawdled and dithered half-heartedly in the general direction of the foredeck cranes, and fiddled with the rope in his hand, and hoped desperately that someone would meet him on the way so's his plan would be compromised and he would be forced to call the whole thing off.

But only temporarily, mind you. Until, maybe, the next trip out. Or certainly the one after that, anyway.

Derek frowned petulantly. Well, it was fact, dammit! He bloody DID intend to do it some time soon, whatever you think. D'you really imagine he'd've come all this way up here in the middle've the night just because he was some kind of self-absorbed fruit cake, huh? Some psychological nutter who needed to make up for his inadequacy in life by fantasising over his power to end it any time he wanted to?

Well look, pal! It's all planned, see? Right down to the last detail. He was gonna secure the rope there, up on that ring bolt above the platform, like that. An' then the noose — a proper noose, mind; tied in a genuine hangman's knot — well that got placed around his neck, like *that*. An' pulled tight. Right? And then he was goin' to climb up on the middle rail of the safety barrier like . . . Jeeze but it was more awkward than he'd figured, with a rope already round your neck . . . but like so. And then he would smile. A really contemptuous smile at the whole inferior bloody world. And then he would jum . . .

Christ!

For a long time Derek didn't dare move one muscle. Because he suddenly realised how far he'd gone; and then he'd stared down to see the steel deck all black and horrifying and dizzy-making a long way below ... whereupon the last cherished fantasy of Derek Guy disintegrated in a spinning nausea of vertigo and explosive reality. Yet ironically there was also the glimmering of a hitherto unsuspected peace of mind for the lonely boy. In that split-second of his charade of self-destruction he discovered he really wanted to live very much, and that Mum was a memory and that you couldn't *join* a memory; you could only continue in gratitude for the warmth of it.

Ever so slowly, carefully, Derek began to feel with his foot for the lowest rail beneath him. It was nerve-racking, stuck up there feeling a bit silly and still dangerously off balance; but at least he was better now. Much better.

He was so relieved he never even sensed the crouching figure inching along the *Liebherr* platform behind him. Or the outstretched hand reaching towards the small of his back.

In the Cadets' half deck sleep had long been abandoned; excitement barely suppressed. Two lads, the oldest only nineteen, were participants in a full-scale mystery of the sea. An' not only that — one of 'em had already saved his ship from certain disaster when the Third Mate had gone ga-ga, while the other ...

Yeah, well, Cadet Simpson hadn't actually *done* anything heroic yet; all he'd done was to spend yesterday afternoon being sick and yesterday evening re-doing Willie Kennedy's metacentric heights *because* he'd been sick in the afternoon. Still, it was a tremendous adventure now, with everything happening, and he didn't feel ill any more, and he didn't really mind helping Willie out because, hero or not, Willie Kennedy needed all the help he could get. Mister Garvie had emphasised that regularly. Three times a day. Before he went loopy, of course.

'I wonder if it'll be in the papers,' Kennedy speculated hopefully. 'About us, when we get in.'

Simpson looked gravely considerate. He was a full nine months older than Willie, and that made him the Senior. After he'd evaluated the prospect and arrived at a decision, he gave his verdict.

'Mmmm ... maybe.'

'You . . . ah . . . you think they'll mention names, do you? Like the ones who played a sort of leading role.'

Simpson's response this time was a little more direct. Brutally so.

'Like yours, you mean?'

Willie blushed modestly. 'Er, no. Good Lord, no!'

'No,' Senior Cadet Simpson agreed with the callousness of youth; but even a nice lad has a trace of jealousy in him somewhere. 'No, I shouldn't think so. Not yours, anyway.'

There was a long silence pregnant with Kennedy's disappointment. Eventually he shuffled his feet, a bit niggled, and blinked around the four bulkheads of the half deck. 'I still don't see why Temple ordered us to stay in here an' not go on deck. None of the others has been told that; except the ones that are sick and don't want to go out anyway.'

Simpson frowned. He agreed with Willie, in fact he had even more reason to want to help run the ship than Kennedy did — who'd already had his moment of glory up on the bridge — but nevertheless there was a leadership problem here. Simpson, as senior man, was bound to maintain unquestioning obedience to authority.

'Because they don't know what's causing it,' he explained with just the right amount of censure — not too much so's to cause a row, but enough to remind Willie of who was in charge. 'And if they let us catch whatever it is, an' we die, then there'll be hell to pay.'

'I know,' Kennedy endorsed feelingly. 'My Dad'll be bloody furious.'

'I meant the Company,' Simpson retorted, loyal servant to the core. 'From the Department of Trade an' that.'

'Well, I still think the Mate's treating us like kids,' muttered the youngest kid of all. But no wonder he was feeling bolshie; saving the ship an' then being sent off to bed. Next time he wouldn't *bother* to save the ship, he'd just let it steam strai . . .

'What time is it now?' Simpson asked, bored with being responsible and fed up with being treated like, well, like a kid.

'Nearly four o'clock. In the morning.'

Simpson wandered over to the door and opened it with defiant trepidation. Nothing came in; no ghosts or mythical cats or germs;

certainly none large enough to see with the naked eye. He stuck his head into the alleyway and gazed wistfully aft, out through the open exit to the officers' deck. It was still dark and quiet, just the steady throb of the engine below and the stark white geometry of rails illuminated against the last of the night.

'Careful,' Kennedy warned waspishly. 'Temple might see you an' log you for mutiny, Senior Cadet!'

Simpson shut the door hurriedly. Not that he was worried, of course, but a chap had to set an example. He turned back into the cabin just in time to see Willie Kennedy diving forward, scrabbling to hide himself under the table, with a look of horror on his usually bovine features.

It all happened so quickly. Talking to Willie one second, yet the next . . .

'Get them out!' Kennedy shrieked. '*PLEASE,* Simpson — the birds! Those *BIRDS*. Get them *OOOOOUT!*'

'Wi . . . Willie?'

'Oh, Mummy . . . the birds. Those black decomposing birds, Mummy! All flying and screeching an' rotting away. Oh, God, it's all *over* me! The filth, the putrefaction! Get it *OFF MEEEEE . . .!*'

But Senior Cadet Simpson wasn't there any more. He was already out on deck and running without the slightest regard for orders to stay put. It wasn't a mutiny, though. Just the terror of a nineteen-year-old boy.

And Willie Kennedy? Well, it looked as though he'd suddenly got an awful lot closer to getting his name in tomorrow's papers.

Chikwanda had been watching the spider-thing ever since it first began to climb towards his secret hiding place. He hadn't dared move at first while it hesitated on the platform of the crane, presumably sensing the nearness of him, its potential victim. Even with sunrise imminent it was still too dark to make out detail and Chikwanda's fear was further stimulated by his dismay that it had out-guessed him so quickly. Obviously its arachnid intellect was nearly a match for his own, which meant he would have to take the initiative yet again; surprise it before it had time to locate him precisely.

He took one tremulous step and then hesitated, uneasy. It was a curious silhouette for a spider, and so big now; it seemed to be levering itself upward, mounting the rail encompassing the platform. He could only detect four of its eight legs, and a hideously elongated abdomen as the Thing poised, stretched. That was when Chikwanda shuddered uncontrollably, for it suddenly dawned on him that the spider was preparing its trap. For him. A web! The first glimmer of light from the horizon was more than enough to reveal the pale silken cord now linking the creature to the structure of the crane itself.

He was running out of time. He had to force himself to approach the spider once again. He knew his hand was shaking, deathly cold as he reached out towards the obscenity; only a shimmering image now seen dimly through his sweat of revulsion.

Close now. And closer . . . and then it had sensed his presence. It was swinging back . . . reaching. Clutching for him!

He pushed . . .

And Chikwanda's spider — which was, of course, only young Seaman Guy caught off-balance and in the middle of changing his mind about his suicide project — went cartwheeling outwards and downwards from the platform of *Auriga*'s port forward cargo crane. He was so disenchanted that he never even got around to screaming that he'd just decided not to do it tonight. Not to bloody do it at *all* f'r . . .

It wasn't the fall that killed him; it was hitting the deck at the end of it which did that. And that, perhaps, was the saddest thing of all about the dying of Seaman Derek Guy — that he didn't manage to prove to those who mattered that he really was capable of fulfilling the simplest task correctly; not even after all that planning.

Well, you could hardly claim to be a practical genius, could you? Not if you attempt to hang yourself with a forty-five-foot length of rope; but only step off a forty-foot-high scaffold.

Captain Mowat received the news of Terry Monaghan's tragic end at the same time as he learned that Second Engineer Beckman had finally isolated them from the world over the horizon. He wasn't, however, aware of the fact that Derek Guy had also, in that short span of time, transferred his death wish into high impact reality.

Even if he had been conscious of a third member of *Auriga*'s crew succumbing to the horror of the night, it was unlikely that his attitude would have changed. For now there was something more than sadness over lost shipmates in the Captain's eyes; there was also an aura of quiet determination which should have bolstered the flagging optimism of every man aboard. As he sat alone with his thoughts, and the ship raced nearer and nearer to the approaches to the Firth of Forth, he was no longer downcast as he had been by adversity — only the ignorant had need of solace, and Captain Charles Mowat was ignorant no longer.

He knew, now, the true nature of the threat which hung over *Auriga*; and with that knowledge came the power to use it; to overcome the awful hazard they faced.

So it wasn't significant that his legs had become so cold they transmitted the pains of amputation. Nor did it matter about the constriction gripping his chest, nor the waves of nausea attacking his concentration; for he had discovered that they were merely physical manifestations of the True Evil and would ultimately be destroyed by his, Charles Mowat's, Faith. His bodily suffering was simply a distraction sent by the supreme enemy, as was the derangement of Beckman and MacNally, Jennings and Third Officer Garvie — all plainly revealed now as a diabolical contrivance to shake his allegiance to God's Blessed Guidance.

For the Word lay before him at last; the Lord's identification of the malevolence which moved among them. Denounced through Peter in the New Testament:

. . . Be sober, be vigilant; because your adversary the Devil, as a roaring lion, walketh about, seeking whom he may devour . . .

His hands rested lovingly on the Bible across his knee.

While they still betrayed the white transluscence of death, there was a further subtle deterioration noticeable; the rims of the Captain's fingernails and the tips of his fingers themselves were darkening; gradually betraying the first indications of cyanosis.

It all suggested that the Faith of *Auriga*'s Master would indeed require divine patronage in order to survive.

For by 0400 hours British Summer Time on that final morning, Captain Charles Mowat's hands were becoming gangrenous. Slowly but relentlessly they were beginning to decay.

Chapter Fourteen

Fatigue was becoming an ally to The Madness. Not one man, either normal or apparently normal, had slept since the collision alarm the previous evening. Compound that lack of rest with the strain of fear and the debilitating and still unsuspected affliction they all suffered to some degree or other, and you produced a crew of stumbling, red-eyed shadows.

By five o'clock in the morning, even with the Scottish coast now an incandescent barrier across the top of the radar screen and the Bell Rock racon flashing a regular electronic sector bearing only a few miles off the starboard bow, there was no euphoria; no sense of deliverance from the Captain's Valley of the Shadow. There was only their dull concern for an ever-lengthening list of moribund shipmates and an increasing dread that — within maybe the next sixty seconds even — it might be you, yourself, lying there in torment ... and the next death-watcher would be watching over you.

They were falling fast, now; two more seamen had buckled and whimpered that their blood was boiling and their guts had split; Beckman, Garvie, Jennings, Radio Officer MacNally had all lapsed into comatose raving. Cadet Kennedy, who'd felt himself interred under the still fluttering corpses of putrefying birds, was now mercifully unconscious. Too many victims to nurse together; there was no compartment large enough on a ship such as *Auriga* to accommodate an epidemic on the scale they now faced. Only individual cabins; individual bunks — which meant the diminishing number of able crewmen were fragmented in their efforts to tend the casualties, spread throughout the accommodation and isolated from each other.

That enforced separation allowed The Madness great latitude, because it permitted only fleeting observation of other men who should easily have been recognised as first-stage sufferers — such

165

as Second Officer Yancy, still doggedly manning the bridge, and skin-crawling Greaser Behrens; topsy-turvy Slimy Simmieson; Chief Webster and Fourth Engineer Bench; Bosun Peak: all flawed, all dangerously irrational and all men who should, in the interests of safety, have been relieved of their responsibilities. Along with Captain Charles Mowat. In fact especially Captain Charles Mowat.

For he still maintained his traditionally undisputed place in command of *Auriga*. Under God, of course. Or so he devoutly believed.

They discovered the late Derek Guy just after the wheelhouse clock struck two bells in the morning watch — the golden sun was well above the horizon by 0500 and Yancy, up on the bridge, had been the first to notice the unseamanlike strand of rope dangling unsecured from the port forr'ad crane. Then he'd stared a little harder, struggling against the nausea now flaring as regularly as the radar image of the Bell Rock racon, and detected an equally untidy blue-denimed leg protruding from the mess of crushed ventilators and piping around the *Liebherr*'s base.

Yancy hadn't dared believe it at first — he was still plagued by the worrying memory of his earlier experience when he'd suddenly snapped out of that trance to find his mouth kiln-dry with aspirin crumbs. He'd rubbed his hollowed eyes and blinked down at the foredeck again, then staggered for the wheelhouse telephone.

There hadn't even been any nervous chatter to camouflage revulsion; they simply took Derek away in silence and put him in Terry Monaghan's cabin to await collection on docking. Trotty wouldn't have been offended at being denied the privilege of Derek's company. He'd been a solitary man while he lived; there wasn't a lot of point in starting to be gregarious now.

They never even connected Chikwanda with the kid's death. Obviously a suicide — bumbling and unnecessarily overdone, jus' like you'd have expected from Derek Whatsisname, but gorily effective in the end. Success despite Stupidity; the epitaph for a born loser.

And Chikwanda? He was hiding again, this time in the steering gear compartment aft. He hadn't been distressed when he'd realised his mistake, for Chikwanda was long past feeling anything but a savage hatred negating even his fear. The Amin-spider had made a fool of him, but it wouldn't again. Not ever again.

Now he intended to go hunting for it when the moment was right. Because insane Chikwanda had finally found a weapon every bit as lethal as any mutant arachnid's sting.

When Arthur Sullivan had observed his assistant's condition immediately following Monaghan's death he was shocked. Oh, sure, anyone being left alone with a thing like that happening before their eyes would've been shattered by the experience, but Hughie had appeared to be even more deeply affected, grey-faced with a wild haunted expression. Though on reflection the lad had been steadily getting more and more depressed since the previous evening — since he'd first run up to the bridge for help a million years ago. At eight bells following dinner, when it seemed to have all started.

Yet now, over two hours after the Second Chef's passing, Baird still looked as shaken as ever; standing and watching while they eased Derek Guy into the darkened cabin and laid him gently down. They all looked pretty rough, come to that — Temple, Peak and the three seamen volunteers — but Hughie seemed worse; a helluva lot more worrying.

Of course the young Scot had suffered the traumatic experience of finding Donkeyman Trott as well. He'd claimed then that he'd read a lot more from the old man's dead eyes than anyone should have seen in the stare of a corpse. Chief Steward Sullivan felt the pangs of guilt. He understood now that he should never have pushed Hughie into nursing Monaghan. Not all on his own like that.

Firmly he guided the Assistant Steward from the knot of grim watchers crowding the alleyway. Hughie didn't budge at first but Sullivan just kept shoving; sometimes you had to be cruel to be kind.

'Sandwiches,' he said matter-of-factly. 'You, me an' the Chef, Hughie. We're going to make up sandwiches for the lads.'

Baird frowned at him dully and Arthur felt overwhelming compassion. All he actually did was to jerk his head towards the galley.

'C'mon,' he ordered. 'We're nearly up to May Island an' the

whole bloody ship's out've bed. They'll be screaming for vittles before long.'

'Terry screamed,' Hughie muttered. 'Terry screamed a lot with the pain.'

'It happened and it's over,' Sullivan snapped. 'We're looking after the rest as best we can, so forget it, Hughie. At least for now.'

He watched the youngster with covert apprehension, waiting for the hysteria to detonate. But after a long silence Hughie Baird's tense expression relaxed and he looked much more his usual pugnacious self. Strangely, that was the moment when Chief Steward Sullivan became even more disturbed about Baird. There wasn't any reason for it. Just a premonition.

'Whit time is it?' Hughie asked.

Sullivan looked at his watch and then cautiously at Baird. 'Twenty past five. In the morning.'

Hughie turned towards the galley. Far too placidly. 'Sandwiches it is, then.'

It was only when he glanced back almost as an afterthought that Sullivan knew there was something terribly wrong with Hughie.

When he added, in a tone casual enough to be enquiring about the weather forecast, 'Whit about yon bastard Grainger, by the way? He'll no' be such a hard man now, eh? Or is the wee lecher dead already?'

Slimy Simmieson lay stretched out on the crew's mess settee and tried to sleep; anythin' to overcome his horrible sense of disorientation. Hell, but it was getting so bad there were times when he could sense himself rolling off've the bloody couch yet the ship wasn't moving at all ... He sat up suddenly, staring around — there had been an odd noise, a scraping unlike any shipboard sound he'd ever heard before. Like ... like something heavy. Bein' dragged along the alleyway outside the door.

He began to wish Sammy Behrens was there to keep him company. An' that wus a laugh — most times it was the other way round, with Sammy needin' to lean on him for support against the drink. Now he suddenly needed a familiar presence; even a bit o' good-natured argymint. Only Sammy was up top somewhere, doin' his spell of looking after the sick lads. Heh! Talk about the blind leadin' the blind ...

Slimy tried to swallow and found it wasn't easy. Lor' but his throat was parched; dry as the cynicism in the Second's eye when he'd tried to explain how he'd fell off've the engine casing yesterday wi'out no apparent reason. He wished he hadn't thought about a drink, now. What wouldn't 'e give for a nice long can o' lager?

Sssssssh! Weren't that the noise again? The odd noise.

He forced himself to think about Majorca next week, and how Jessie would enjoy it — but he couldn't. Concentration was becoming bloody impossible what wi' the dizzy spells an' the thirst. He was feeling really cold too, now. Chilled to the bone like it was winter.

There was something. Tapping, suddenly. Tapping and dragging and easy to hear above the throb of the engine and the whirr of the blowers.

Slimy eased his legs off the settee and stood shakily erect. There it was again. Just outside the door. A heavy, kind've a sluggish movement. He moved apprehensively to the door, holding on to the mess table for support. Peculiar things had been happenin' on *Auriga* — maybe someone was trying to attract attention. Maybe some poor bastard needed help.

He jerked the door open abruptly. He had the feeling that if he didn't do it right away he never would. Because he was dead nervous now; proper uneasy about what was out . . . but there wasn't nothin' out there. Both ways up and down the alleyway — clear!

Slimy Simmieson wandered aft, towards the exit to the open deck.

It was only when he'd actually stepped out over the coaming and stared warily around the deserted poop, seeing nothing but the flap of the Red Ensign bright against a blue Scottish sky, that he heard the noise again. The dragging, tapping noise.

But *behind* him, this time.

Slowly, Greaser Simmieson began to swivel round.

Fifteen miles from the entrance to the Firth. One hour's steaming.

Fourth Engineer Bench sat in the engine control room thinking about the pencil. It was becoming an awful worry, much greater even than trying to work out how he was going to fashion the rivets for his 1866 tandem compound steam engine model . . . nobody would try and steal *that* when they got in, but he knew they'd be desperate to get their hands on anything as special as the pencil.

He was glad Chief Webster had put it in his safe, just as he was grateful that the Chief was on his side and understood how fantastically important the pencil was — the impact it would make on the scientific world once they examined it. The upheaval to all the laws of physics governing mass and gravity and molecular structure an' . . . but that was where the danger lay, too. The risk they would face as soon as they got in. There would be a lot of unbelievers — accredited scientists that was, not mere laymen cynics like ol' Wimpy Jennings — who would be determined to destroy the pencil to protect false values and theories because their minds were too closed to revolutionary discoveries.

Like the pencil.

He knew precisely *when* they would be most at risk, as well. In two an' a half hours when the pilot boarded. How could they be sure he *was* a pilot? How would they know he wasn't really a spy for the Other Side; the jealous, stop-at-nothing scientists' side?

He started to hum a tune. *Pom tiddley pom pom, tiddley om pom pom*. Then he stopped singing abruptly and began to worry about the anti-revolutionary scientific fraternity again, and how subtle they would be in their attempts to discredit his, Benchy's, evidence, and Chief Webster's of course. Then he thought of using ordinary dressmaking pins cut down as rivets for the tandem compound steam engine, and forgot all about his paranoia over protecting the pencil.

For a few minutes, anyway. For The Madness lurked very near the surface of Fourth Engineer Bench's mind by half past five that last morning. It would only need the slightest jolt to erupt in unpredictable frenzy.

Aft, up on the open deck where the Ensign flapped and the wake joined them to the past horizon straight as a hydraulic rule, Slimy Simmieson stood with hair prickling on the back of his neck and mystification screwing up his eyes.

There wasn't nothin' there behind him after all. Yet he could've sworn there was something . . . and then he heard it again. Clear as a bell or whatever. A tapping, tapping, tapping. But again *behind* him!

170

He whirled a second time, mouth opening to shriek for help, taut with the fear of it — and then stopped dead. Halted in mid-scream.

Tap, tap . . . tap, tap, tap . . .

Slimy felt so daft; so bloody foolish as he walked back a couple of paces to the Ensign staff and gazed at it with comical resentment.

Tap, tap . . . tap, tap, ta . . .

He placed an oily hand on the halyard, choking it to the staff itself and cutting short the intermittent vibration of metal against wood. 'Cause that was what was doin' it, ye skittery ould idjit! The brass Inglefield clips securing the Ensign hoist to the halyard itself; every time the Red Duster caught the wind the whole shebang tightened, pulled against the staff an' . . . *Tap, tap. Tap.*

Smiling self-consciously Slimy eased it from its cleat, frapped the halyard firmly around the staff and secured it with an admonishing tug. Funny, mind? That he'd heard a little thing like that all the way back there, inside the accommodation itse . . .

Tap, tap, tap . . . tap, tap, tap.

This time Greaser Simmieson didn't turn round — he spun forward to face *Auriga*'s superstructure.

And then he did see it.

'Awwww Mary Mother o' GOD!'

It came around the starboard side of the deckhousing. Enormous; waving jerkily, and the dragging, slithering, rattling sound again, like a bag o' bone-white skeletons being tumbled into an ivory grave. Only it wasn't white — it was black. Greenish black and the colour of a nightmare.

The claw. On the end of the leg.

Feelin' an' fumbling blindly towards him; reaching further and further round the corner of the deckhouse. A claw that made you shriek just with imaginin' what repulsive form of carapace might have the strength to wield it. Exac'ly like a lobster's claw; a sea tank's claw — except f'r one staring-eyed detail . . .

Tap, tap, tap, tap . . .

It was as big as a man's whole torso by itself. And waving a clear six feet off the *Auriga*'s suddenly reeling deck.

Second Officer Yancy had watched the target closing at a combined speed in excess of thirty knots ever since it had first appeared on radar — steaming a reciprocal course but a few miles to the north of them; probably outward bound from the River Tay. It was the only ship they'd raised that would pass close enough for visual communication.

He tried hard, sheer willpower forcing the sickness in him to the back of his mind. Quartermaster Mulholland stood beside him, signal pad ready to take down the other ship's reply as Yancy interpreted it. Mulholland had doggedly returned a little earlier, partly to relieve Grimm and partly to get away from the smell of suffering below. Mind you, nobody had relieved Yancy. Temple was up to his eyes in other people's troubles; 3/0 Garvie was . . . well, unfit for anything other than a padded cell right then, poor bastard; and the Old Man? They hadn't even seen the Captain; not since two thirty a.m. after he'd put out that one and only V.H.F. relay. But Second Officer Yancy wasn't too resentful. Mowat had a lot more to worry about than simply driving *Auriga* an' there was no way Bill Yancy intended to sleep again tonight; not to expose his imagination to those nightmares. No way!

The approaching vessel was coming up forward of their starboard beam now, the sun striking her superstructure with a brilliance of white and the bone in her teeth tumbling and rolling astern. Yancy placed his alarmingly clumsy fingers over the signal lamp key and muttered, 'Ready?'

'Aye,' Mulholland nodded, then he grinned unexpectedly. Reassuringly. 'Not too fast, mind. None of your ten words a minute, sir.'

Yancy had to smile back, even though he couldn't quite conceal the wry twist to it. 'Don't worry, I'll keep it slow. She's probably foreign anyway . . . most've 'em bloody are nowadays.'

It was all there before him; concisely drafted in hopeful anticipation of this event. The only way left to them to prepare the shore for their coming.

MLDT AURIGA: I HAVE A MEDICAL EMERGENCY ON BOARD: MY RADIO U/S: REQUEST YOU ALERT FORTH TO RECEIVE TWENTY PLUS CASES SUSPECTED FOOD POISONING . . .

. . . he began to key the masthead signal lamp. Slowly. With all the care of a prayer. AA . . . AA . . . Dot dash dot dash . . . *Calling unknown station . . .*

Nothing. No response.

AA ... AA ... AA ...

'Dozy bastard!' Mulholland snarled with feeling. Yancy fought the rage in him and kept keying. K ... K ... K ... *I wish to COMMUNICATE with you.*

In fact Second Officer Yancy kept on flashing until the other vessel was well astern. With her national ensign now plainly displayed over her counter but not the slightest sign that she'd either seen, or had wanted to see, *Auriga*'s plea.

They would never know whether her mute passing had merely been the fault of some criminally somnolent watchkeeper, or symptomatic of a disease increasingly more dangerous and certainly every bit as senseless as The Madness itself.

If it had been the latter, then while it hardly presented as imminent a threat to *Auriga* it did starkly underline the ever-widening gulf separating those British seamen and at least one Russian.

'Well?' Hughie Baird demanded with disrespect as near suicidal as possible without actually committing it. 'Is he dead or isn't he — yon Grainger lad?'

The Chief Steward took a long, deep breath. 'Still in coma. Very ill,' he retorted stiffly. There was still a chance that the Assistant Steward was only baiting him. Hughie could be an infuriating little sod, especially when he was covering for his own shortcomings by acting the wee hard man.

'Oh aye?' said Hughie, revealing total indifference. Then he frowned erratically. 'He had it off wi' mah Olga, ye ken? That's why ah sorted him oot in the provisions store ... bang, bang! One two!'

Arthur shuffled uncomfortably. He didn't quite know how to handle this situation, while the reference to the store room fiasco disturbed him out of all proportion to its importance. It raised the spectre he'd previously tried to avoid — for it had only been after that incident that things had begun to go wrong. And the provisions store was his responsibility. If he'd allowed food to be served from there while failing to appreciate that it might have been contaminated, then he would carry a lot on his conscience as well as losing his job and pension.

But *what* food? Everything they'd salvaged had either been

tinned or above suspicion — eggs; foil-sealed mixes; all meats and fish taken straight from the freezer compartment; certainly nothing even touched by Grainger's sea water hose. That flour, the rye flour had been dry as a bone an' definitely . . .

'Yon Grainger,' the Assistant Steward mused. 'Now there's one randy bastard ah do hope dies screaming, an' that's a fact.'

This time the callousness was unmistakable — as was the obvious conclusion that Hughie Baird, too, was steadily succumbing to the *Auriga* nightmare. But Sullivan had a breaking point as well. Christ he was human, wasn't he? All the time it was strain, aggravation, strain . . . Nobody else in the lousy ship seemed even to *care* about what was happening to 'em any more. Sickness; madness; death . . . Yet none of 'em gave a damn except maybe David Temple — while some of them like Garvie and Sparks and Second Beckman, an' now Hughie here, actually seemed to be wanting the misery to be compounded.

'Right, that's IT!' he snarled, unable to keep his fury in check any longer. 'You jus' got yourself paid off, Hughie Baird. The minute this hulk docks you're goin' straight down the gangway with your sea bag, laddie. Fired. Like a bullet from a bloody gun.'

'Oh, aye,' said Hughie. 'Then I'd better get on wi' the sandwiches, hadn't I?'

There it was again. Total bloody indifference.

'Ahhhhhh shit!' snarled *Auriga*'s Chief Steward, and swung furiously away.

They trailed the distance to the galley in stony silence. When they got there the door was firmly closed with its dogs in place. Sullivan knocked them off and tried it savagely. It was locked.

'Chef,' he called, frustration tinged once again with alarm. 'You in there, Chef?'

There was no answer. Behind him the Assistant Steward began to giggle. 'Ye canny make a sanny if ye're . . .'

'Shut up!' Sullivan bellowed, panic welling inside him. He banged on the door with the flat of his hand. 'Holmquist. Are you in there, f'r Christ's sake?'

The voice, when it came, was muffled. 'Go away, Chief Stewart. I don't open this door for no one. Not till this sheep goes alongside.'

Chief Steward Sullivan blinked. He didn't say anything for a full

174

minute; simply blinked owlishly at the door and wondered if he'd heard right. That he was being locked out. Of his own department!

'Smash it down, Chief,' Hughie suggested. Sullivan closed his eyes, praying for sanity to return to his world. He began to bang on the closed door again desperately.

'What's wrong, Sven? Let us in f'r . . .'

'Go *away*! I got a wife; three childs. I ain't getting near to no disease like Terry got . . .'

'O.K. Then ah'll smash it down,' Hughie offered cheerfully.

'Come out o' there, you great Scowegian bas . . . It's mutiny, Holmquist; d'you realise that? Onna British ship it's blatant bloody mutiny.'

The routine black comedy relationship of the *Auriga*'s catering department had reached a new high. Prompted by The Madness it was soaring to the peaks of farce, only it had ceased to be funny. From the second that Terry Monaghan left the cast all the humour had died with him.

'See me?' Hughie Baird cackled. 'Ah can smash through doors. Ah can smash through onything, Mister Sullivan. Ah'm Hughie Baird; ah'm the Bionic Man.'

'Go 'vay. Everybotty go avay!'

'I'll kill you, Holmquist! Oh, I'll bloody kill you . . .' The craziness behind Sullivan finally burst in a paroxysm of hilarity. 'Ah'll smash it, Mister Sullivan . . . watch me smash clean through it.'

The *Auriga*'s Chief Steward blanched, whirled, understood too late.

'No, Hughieeeee!'

The clenched fist of Bionic Hughie Baird impacted against the galley door with every bit of strength the lad could muster, a roundhouse swing which started from way behind him and was further accelerated by The Madness. The crunch of fragmenting bone was heard even above Sullivan's horrified cry.

Shock delayed the Assistant Steward's immediate reaction, but when it finally did come it was shrill enough and distraught enough to bring even Chef Holmquist out of hiding at a white-faced run.

They had to pin Hughie to the deck while they rough-splinted his shattered right hand and the compound fracture of his wrist. He didn't seem to know where he was or what had happened to him.

175

But that wasn't really surprising, under the circumstances.

Everyone with a pair of eyes could see it was a steel door, the galley door. A solid, white-painted, five-millimetre-thick steel door. And even a hard man like Hughie Baird just had to be insane to try and punch a hole through a door like that.

And Slimy Simmieson? Well, he wasn't much happier where he was, come to that. Out on the afterdeck.

He wasn't making a noise like Hughie, though. The loathsome grotesque his short-circuiting imagination had come up with was enough to paralyse the vocal chords of any human being, sane or mad.

It came around the corner of the deckhousing, that monstrous decapod, with a clanking and a rattling and a tap, tap, tapping that caused Simmieson's eyes to bug and the marrow to freeze in his bones. And it kept on coming slowly, waveringly; ballet-light on constantly twinkling points; approaching and feeling for him all the time with those gigantic scissor pincers that clicked an' clacked an' . . .

The taffrail came hard against Slimy's back. He hadn't even been aware of his own retreat.

It was actually taller than a man. He was gazing up at it now, while the stalk eyes swivelled and the articulated spiny-legs danced their grisly tattoo. And then it reared, with its black fan tail spreading a smear of foulness in an arc across the deck, until Slimy was goggling into the yawning, fronded gullet of the giant crustacean.

Steadily a creaking shadow encircled him. He shied away, squirming dementedly as the pendulous lobster claws, still trailing drabbles of putrefying sea-stink, skreaked jerkily downwards; inwards . . . An' he was trapped there; right in the middle. Where they'd meet!

No one would ever know whether Greaser Simmieson fell, or threw himself clear over the sternrails of *Auriga*; or, for that matter, actually was flung into the North Sea to drown fifteen miles off the Firth of Forth by some hideosity rather less spectral than the mind of any man untouched by The Madness would ever dare to contemplate.

Chapter Fifteen

The time-scale of catastrophe was critical now.

Had The Madness overwhelmed *Auriga*'s remaining crew before she entered the Firth of Forth, then she might well have driven harmlessly ashore at Gin Head or the Great Car, or eviscerated herself on Podlie Craig or Scoughall Rocks, or even telescoped her ten thousand tons into the towering east face of the Bass Rock; but she could never have penetrated the navigational hazards of the narrowing Firth without human guidance. Thus her self-destruction would have involved herself alone.

If, on the other hand, *Auriga* had betrayed her faltering command too soon; given some warning of the threat to the waterway by its erratic behaviour as she proceeded towards its most vulnerable point; then perhaps some desperate precaution could have been devised. The Firth of Forth, even in time of peace, is still a naval base where lean grey warships lie on constant alert. And the Royal Navy can be swift and resourceful in the art of stopping ships when ordered to.

So timing was vitally important for the ultimate triumph of The Madness.

But time had already declared itself liege to The Madness as also had the dulling edge of complacency; and complacency confounds man's instinct for survival. Not one officer or rating aboard raised doubts about the risks of proceeding further, despite their awareness that the mystery epidemic was still escalating with terrifying speed. They could have heaved-to off the mouth of the Firth; they could even have anchored safely in the lee of May Island and flashed for help; hoisted the international flag V — *I require assistance* or W — *I require medical assistance*; simply the red diamond on white F — *I am disabled. Communicate with me.*

But they didn't. Because The Madness had taken charge.

So, at 0630 British Summer Time, *Auriga* passed inside the line of May Island.

Chief Officer Temple and Second Officer Yancy leaned over the after end of the bridge together and watched as the May, hazy grey in the early morning sunlight, fell slowly astern.

To look at them they were as mirror images; red-eyed, unshaven and with the pallor of nervous exhaustion etched deep into unhealthy skin. Yet neither remarked upon his companion's condition — not Yancy because he was afraid to draw attention to his own illness and thereby forfeit any prospect of flying out to that desperately-wanted *Aries* promotion; and not David Temple, because he could sense the tight-wound spring that kept Bill Yancy going and was loath to disturb it, and also because he was, perhaps, afraid to admit even to himself that his fatigue might be aggravated by some force more dreadful than a night of sleepless worry.

Stretching fretfully he turned forward and forced his attention to port. The unmistakable silhouette of the Bass Rock stood clear and broad on the bow with the smaller hump of Craigleith three miles to the west. The Firth was welcoming them now; or swallowing them. Like a great, gaping maw.

'Well, we're nearly in,' he said, conscious of the need for encouragement but aware, at the same time, of his own growing torpor.

'Ninety minutes,' the Second Officer muttered. 'Ninety minutes to the pilot.'

There were ships around them too, now. A Danish short sea trader coming down outward bound; a bulker north of May and running parallel to their own course; a handful of distant fishing boats farming the Rath Grounds. Temple knew they should be making contact, calling through the signalling lamp at least, but it didn't seem so vital suddenly — that solitary V.H.F. warning must have been relayed shorewards over four hours ago; somebody had acknowledged it — therefore there was little to be gained at this late stage.

Complacency again. A blind man who still believes he can see, following a guide who continued to lead even though *his* eyes were already picked clean from his skull.

'Good morning, gentlemen. Once again!' their guide said. And it sounded just like the Captain's voice.

They swung, blinking at his quiet approach. Mowat smiled as if amused. He looked fresh, invigorated, and both officers drew strength from his normality even though Temple might have been excused a cynical reflection — it was the first time since it had all started that Mowat had done anything but depress him further. Still . . .

'Morning, sir.'

Just like any other day for entering port, before the stand-by whistle blows and sea-weary mariners stare with hopeful anticipation at the nearing skyline.

The Captain himself gazed critically ahead, scanned north to the May, south towards the Bass, and then gestured satisfaction. 'Still on time I see, Mister Yancy.'

'Keeping to our E.T.A.; yessir.'

'Then God is still with us,' the Captain said, and again his Chief Officer felt a sardonic niggle; God might have placed a little less strain on Bill Yancy had the Old Man spent more time on the bridge during the past few hours. But he didn't say anything; it would only have led to another bloody argument and that could wait until later, until the ambulances had left and the need for sleep was satisfied.

They talked in low tones as the Bass Rock came broad on the beam, while Temple learned with a slight surge of shame that the Captain had been to visit every sick man below and already knew of Baird's crazy assault on the steel galley door, and about the two ratings who'd added themselves to *Auriga's* casualty list in the past hour by vomiting without the slightest warning.

They never contemplated turning back to investigate the strange disappearance of Slimy Simmieson, because nobody knew that he had been flung over the side by a lobster as big as a steamroller; there simply weren't enough fit men now to keep track of each other's movements. Mind you, there were a few sad souls by then who would have been prepared to believe it. That bit about Slimy's homicidal decapod . . .

Until, at ten minutes to seven, Captain Mowat stirred and said in a quietly competent manner, 'Stand-by for the pilot from half

179

seven, gentlemen. Mister Yancy, I shall take the ship from now, if you please. Perhaps you will attend the telegraphs while we're manoeuvring; Bosun Peak can take charge aft for going alongside. Mister Temple.'

'Sir.'

'Have both anchors ready to let go if required. Do you have enough hands to cope?'

'I'll have enough if you keep Mulholland on the wheel,' Temple replied. 'Peak and young Simpson can help break out the mooring lines. Grimm should be down there now with the two remaining O.Ds.'

It was all so normal. And reassuring.

Particularly because neither Yancy nor Chief Officer Temple thought to wonder why the Captain had brought his Bible to the bridge.

Nor why Captain Mowat was wearing black leather gloves on such a lovely summer's day.

With the majority of her fit complement engaged in preparing *Auriga* for going alongside it was hardly surprising that, when Ordinary Seaman Grainger regained consciousness just before seven thirty, he found himself alone in his cabin with the door hooked open but not a sight or sound of anyone.

He was shivering uncontrollably, his throat was painful and his breathing seemed tight, yet all Grainger could think of was his still-vivid resentment at the way he'd been elected to carry the can for the provisions store affair of . . . when was it — yesterday? While *now,* even though he was obviously crook, they weren't even botherin' to keep an eye on him. Ohhhh boy, but was he goin' to make an issue out've this. Was he not goin' straight ashore to the Union office to get this lousy, irresponsible shipping company sorted out proper?

Of course Grainger wasn't aware of what had occurred since his collapse; about the manner in which the sequel to his fight with Hughie Baird had escalated; but it wouldn't have made any difference to him if he had — nothin' was mere chance, and nothing was the fault of the working class; it was always the responsibility of the bosses. The officers! Like high an' mighty bloody Temple . . .

Christ but he had to get to the heads. His guts were beginning to rumble again but the crew toilets were further aft, down the alleyway. He struggled from his bunk, getting more and more outraged all the time that there wasn't anyone detailed to him — the Union would've made damn certain he was nursed O.K. . . . There were agreements; conditions of service . . . It was only when he noticed the shoreline sliding past outside the port that he felt any satisfaction at all. That looked like Fidra out there; the trip was nearly over an' then there'd be a reckoning; a settling of old scores.

One thing about Ordinary Seaman Grainger — he was certainly in a class of his own. Apart from the fact that he personally had been the prime cause of *Auriga*'s agony — aided by Olga the athletic Finn and Bionic Hughie Baird, of course — he was also the only critically sick man aboard who was more anxious to get to the offices of the Seamen's Union than to the bloody hospital. But there's always one; on every ship at sea there's always an Ordinary Seaman Grainger. Except on Russian ships, admittedly. They don't have the same democratic problems on Russian ships.

It was only after he'd staggered the short distance to the heads, and had managed to make it into one of the cubicles and squatted without even having time to shut the door, that he noticed it.

The cat.

It was half-crouched, half-lying under the line of washbasins opposite, and Grainger could tell at a glance that there was something terribly wrong with it.

Suddenly it began to crawl, claw itself forward in a slithering, dragging motion as though its hind legs weren't synchronised with its forr'ad end. Grainger became aware that he was trapped inside the cubicle without any escape other than past the awful cat, and too weak to move anyway, so he could only stare in horrified revulsion as the creature skittered closer and closer across the wet-tiled deck.

Then the abominable feline fixed Grainger with a glare of green-eyed venom, and began to hiss and, incredibly, to gather its crippled form in preparation for a spring. Grainger cringed further and further back against the bulkhead with his hands reaching for the top of the cubicle partition, and started to whimper and forget all about his bodily weakness, overwhelmed by a hysterical disbelief which not even a Union statement could have assuaged.

That was the moment when Ordinary Seaman Grainger again became unique in the social structure inhabiting *Auriga*.

When he became the first member of her crew to discover precisely what *had* killed Donkeyman Trott.

Despite his own growing discomfort Chief Engineer Webster had done as much as anyone to aid the stricken. Most of his night had been spent prowling anxiously through the accommodation, calming the delirium of Radio Officer MacNally who had never recaptured reality since his collapse on the bridge the previous evening, and of Third Mate Garvie, of course, who'd spent all his short periods of wakefulness after the near-collision in staring up at the deckhead and ignoring anyone beside him — simply giggling and smirking through dry bloodless lips at some very private joke. And Second Beckman, whose trance-like quietude concerned Chief Webster more than the symptoms of any other man aboard, because he was fond of his assistant and frightened he might die. Then there was the unconscious Cadet Kennedy, transferred now to the Mate's cabin and possibly the greatest responsibility as well as the most pitiful of all those afflicted because he was the youngest of them . . . and poor Wimpy Jennings.

Eric Webster had felt an uneasy pang of guilt every time he'd looked in on Third Engineer Jennings because he had been subjected to ever-increasing doubts about the magic pencil as the time for docking drew closer. Oh, he hadn't lost his wonder over it, or even his conviction that it really did hold physical properties which could place it at risk in sceptical hands; but Chief Engineer Webster of the *Auriga* was also a very nice man and maybe The Madness, in his case, hadn't yet secured total victory — he could not bear to maintain the lie about Wimpy Jennings for much longer. Maybe they shouldn't be so protective of their discovery; the world would learn of it soon enough anyway, so why treat Wimpy's honest doubts as so fearful a danger?

He glanced into Jennings' cabin again, to find Greaser Behrens already sitting there. Behrens was the most unlikely nurse you ever saw, what with his two-day growth and his neanderthal frown of concentration on whatever it was he was concentrating on, and his eternal bloody scratching and wriggling and sniffling. Then David Temple came past, on his way down from the bridge, and said quietly, 'Fidra's coming abeam now, Chief. Stand-by for the pilot in ten minutes.'

'Thank God!' exclaimed Chief Engineer Webster. But he didn't say it as reverently as the Captain would have done. Nor as obsessively.

He decided to have a chat with young Bench while they were waiting for engine movement orders in the control room; trim the boy's sense of proportion a little better. No leaning on rank or anything; just a firm word pointing out that they couldn't keep the pencil a secret for ever.

Reasoning, that was what was needed. A presentation of the realities of life in a way that any sane young chap would understand.

At seven twenty-five Chief Officer Temple gave a last look around the foc'slehead and nodded curtly. Everything was ready for going alongside. He noticed Bosun Peak, breathing heavily, standing alone in the eyes of the ship, gazing down towards Inchkeith now showing as a dark shadow against the upper reaches of the Firth. It was a beautiful morning with little breeze and the sun already warm on their faces; only the fifteen-knot wind of their passage riffled the sparse hairs plastered across Peak's crown. Temple wondered precisely what thoughts were concealed within that doleful skull. The Bosun had never once referred to Trott's death since last night. He hadn't said very much about anything, come to that. But then again, he seldom did.

Temple motioned to Cadet Simpson. He felt sorry for Simpson; it had been a hell of an experience, even without the shock of Kennedy's harrowing fantasies, but action would occupy his mind. Anyway, they only had three seamen left apart from Mulholland already at the wheel; they needed all the hands they could muster.

'D'you think you could manage the pilot ladder seeing Mister Garvie's ill?' he said gently. 'I want the Bosun down aft to take charge going in. You can have two of the three seamen, then when you've taken the pilot to the bridge leave them to recover the ladder and you nip forward here again to help me. O.K.?'

'Yessir,' Simpson said, eyes growing wide as saucers at the responsibility of command. 'Pilot to the bridge, then back here to you, sir.'

'*Forward* here to me,' Temple corrected with a grin. 'We're in the bows now, right?'

He turned away and picked up the telephone, gazing aft and up at the bridge wing as he did so. He could make out Mowat's head above the dodger and for no reason his grin faded. Something still unsettled him about the Captain's bearing. What the hell *was* it?

Yancy's voice sounded tinny and weak at the other end of the phone.

'Bridge.'

'Foc'sle. Tell the Old Man we're ready forr'ad. And confirm we're preparing the pilot ladder port side midships.'

'Roger.'

Temple hung the phone back in its waterproof housing and faced ahead. They should be raising the white bow wave of the fast pilot cutter heading towards them any time now.

It was seven thirty in the morning. A long whistle blast shrilled from the bridge.

Auriga was on stand-by for her final berthing.

Chikwanda heard the whistle only faintly above the intermittent rumble of the steering gear but it struck a faint chord in his fast-fading brain. He was still vaguely aware of being on a ship — which to Chikwanda now merely seemed a steel jungle populated by alien and strangely pallid tribesmen — and some lingering memory also registered the urgency of what he had to do; recognition that his allotted killing time was nearing its end, as the first gleam of a rising sun blinks warning to any nocturnal predator.

The light struck on the long-handled fire axe he clutched with grisly intent. Uncoiling from his primitive crouch he opened the door and peered warily out towards the open afterdeck. The spider wasn't there. But it would be — somewhere. Waiting to scuttle from cover and overwhelm him.

Unless he surprised it first. Now he had a weapon.

Ever since Hughie Baird's bionic self-mutilation earlier, Chef Holmquist had remained alone and simmering in the deserted galley.

He'd kept the door wide open, though; hooked back to prove to Chief Steward Sullivan that it had all been a blotty bad misunderstanding an' that there wasn't nothing on no sheep what could scare him — Sven Holmquist — into hiding from his responsibilities . . .

. . . only there was, of course. Because Holmquist had been forced into betraying his one major weakness; his phobia over proximity to illness. Unsuspected by anyone aboard, his cabin drawers were stuffed with patent medicines and cures while his Scandinavian preoccupation with hygiene, as the washday hands of poor Terry Monaghan had so often revealed in the happier past, had gradually developed into more of a pre-emptive strike against germ warfare than a simple virtue.

And that was where the simmering bit came in. Previously the *Auriga*'s Chief Cook had maintained psychological superiority over Arthur Sullivan in their continually-running professional conflict.

Until now. Now his revulsion from the sickness around him had shown him to be every bit as vulnerable to doubt and fear as the next man. Furthermore Sullivan had immediately recognised it — the Chief Steward's contempt when Holmquist finally did bring himself to open the galley door had established that beyond doubt. So while Arthur Sullivan's confidence had been enhanced under crisis, the Swede's had been disastrously eroded.

Nevertheless even that defeat hadn't spurred Chief Cook Holmquist to resolute action. It wasn't his fault; his deep-rooted phobia was far too dominant . . . and so, as the stand-by whistle blew from the bridge, Holmquist realised he faced the final, yet probably the most difficult test of all if he was to remain in his self-imposed quarantine.

They would be alongside soon, and safe, but unless large scale medical aid joined with the pilot — which was unlikely as *Auriga* had been prevented from communicating the full distress of her situation — no nursing assistance would be available until they actually docked. For the next hour or so, all remaining deck and engineer personnel would be fully required for the task of berthing; and that was where Holmquist's problem lay. Only a few such as himself would be free to tend the sick, and Sullivan would be back to look for him . . .

He would have to hide. But where? His cabin was too obvious and the galley was out — and that was when the Chief Cook had his inspiration! There was one compartment of a ship that was always actively engaged prior to lengthy stand-by, yet rarely visited during one, as seamen, restrained by the jaundiced eye of the Mate, were forced to remain at their duty stations unable to still any growing discomfort.

The crew heads. The toilets at the after end of the ratings' accommodation.

Chief Cook Holmquist made it all the way without being observed. Better than that — by the time he got there he'd lost any sense of shame he might have felt; he'd actually managed to convince himself he was taking the only responsible course. He was a chef; he handled food; he was, accordingly, a natural transmitter of disease. He did, in fact, have a downright duty to avoid contact with those who were ill.

There were three cubicles, each separated by a partition which left space below to facilitate swabbing the tiled deck and a ventilation gap above between the partition top and the deckhead. They were all vacant but there was a slight chance that some last-minute call of nature might encourage a hurried visitor. Hastily Holmquist slipped into the middle one, locked the door firmly, dropped the seat over the pan of the w.c. and gratefully eased himself down.

He was safe. For the first time since it had all begun he was free of the demands of conscience and that blotty Chief Stewart. No possibility now of being discovered and forced into exposing himself to contact with what presented, to his distracted mind, the ultimate horror. Even the overpowering smell of fresh disinfectant was reassuring.

. . . the hand had a tattoo on it. Four tattoos. One on the back of each limp finger. The letters L . . . O . . . V . . . E.

. . . the nerveless hand which suddenly flopped downwards from above. And actually brushed against Chief Cook Holmquist's face!

Out on the port wing the Captain was as he had always been. Crisply competent.

He gave one critical glance down to the foredeck where Simpson and his seamen held the rolled pilot ladder balanced on the bulwark ready to be heaved outboard when required. He lifted his head, shading his eyes. The launch itself was beginning a wide turn astern in preparation for its boarding run alongside. Time to slow the ship a little more.

He turned towards the wheelhouse. Yancy and Mulholland both had their eyes fixed on him in anticipation.

'Half speed, Mister Yancy . . . Midships the wheel.'

'Half ahead, sir.'

'Midships . . . wheel's amidships, sir.'

The cutter was coming in fast now; handled with an expertise born of countless similar boardings. One man stood with hand already outstretched — the pilot; preparing to grip the ladder as it was lowered to deck level — while a second stood nervously waiting. Mowat wondered who the second man was. A doctor, perhaps? God willing!

'Stop engine.'

'Stop engine, sir . . .'

The telegraph jangled. '. . . engine stopped, sir.'

'Thank you.'

The pilot cutter brushed gently against *Auriga*'s towering side. Mowat was looking almost straight down now; there was no water between the two vessels.

The pilot, a white hat seen from above with a little bit of shoulder at each side, extended one foot and placed it neatly on the bottom rung.

Auriga was nearly home.

Chief Cook Holmquist was nearly having a heart attack. A real one. He was a fat man and his cardiac system was already under substantial strain — now it was fighting the shock of meeting a nightmare.

As he'd shrieked and jerked his head away from that limp hand from the sky, he found himself staring up towards the deckhead . . . and towards the apparition which owned the hand; lodged precariously along the top edge of the partition and directly above him. Even while the dangling appendage fumbled to maintain clammy contact with Chief Cook Holmquist, his shrinking gaze took in the apparition's awful appearance — the lolling, barely-recognisable idiot mask; the sweat of fear and the tremors of raging fever; the smeared black blood. And the mass of scalpel-fine lacerations striping the naked chest and shoulders.

Scratches? A berserk mutilation of scratches! As might have been inflicted by an animal such as a cat. But surely to *God*, only by a totally mad cat?

Ordinary Seaman Grainger's eyes snapped open and stared down at the corpulent, jellifying figure below. He didn't know where he was for he, too, had succumbed to The *Auriga* Madness in that appalling moment when he became the first man to understand why Donkeyman Trott had died simply through looking at a cat. Since then he'd exhausted his last reserves of ebbing strength in his demented scramble for refuge.

Slowly, pleadingly, his slack reach followed Holmquist as the Chef shrank further and further away. There was no sound now other than the stertorous rattle of Grainger's failing lungs and the gagging of the man who had tried so hard to insulate himself from just such contamination.

Consequently, when Ordinary Seaman Grainger did finally overbalance so as to smother Chief Cook Holmquist under the deadweight pressure of The Madness, it was an act which completed one of the most exquisite ironies of *Auriga*'s dying.

His last awareness as he clung to his saviour was one of enormous gratitude; that somebody, without a thought for themselves or urging from the Seamen's Union, had come searching for him even in this unlikely place!

Wimpy Jennings' eyelids flickered. It took him a long time to realise where he was — in his own bunk with the pillow soaked in sweat and his whole body seemingly burning up with fever. Yet that wasn't right either, because he could sense that his skin was icy cold, an' you can't be overheating from the inside while running a subnormal temperature from without . . .

Memory came flooding back, hazy but as terrifying as ever. The Chief an' the Fourth. The way they'd looked, an' his hysteria at what he thought they were going to do to him. Wimpy's eyes dilated and he turned his head pleadingly. Oh dear God but he was weak. Feeble and floating an' so very thirsty.

A figure was sitting in the chair beside his berth and it moved as he stirred, rising and practically gliding towards the door. It was unreal; like the continuation of a horrendous dream.

A distant voice called, 'Chief Steward — the Third. 'E's comin' round . . .' and suddenly there was another shape, another ghost looking down at him. He tried to move but a hand gently pressed his shoulder into the damp pillow and a second voice — Sullivan's this time — said, 'Easy, Wimpy. Take it easy, son . . .'

He struggled to move his lips but they were stuck together, fixed by a dried-up grue of thirst. Then a wet cloth was placed against them as wonderful as any nectar, and he could whisper again. Or whimper. It was terribly important that he should warn them.

'Chief Webster an' Benchy . . . they've got a pencil, Arthur. But they believe it's . . . it's . . .'

Chief Steward Sullivan patted Wimpy's arm with enormous understanding. 'I know, son. The Chief told us. You think you saw it float, right? Or was it too heavy or someth . . .'

'No!' Jennings cried. 'They saw it, Arthur. They believe it . . .'

The nausea hit him, arching him against the berth. Sullivan and Greaser Behrens — for it was still Sammy who had been watching over Jennings — grabbed him with the sweat equally evident on their own grim features.

'Steady as she goes, sir,' Sammy pleaded, all the time feeling his own skin creeping and crawling with them crabs or rabbits or whatever. 'We're gonna be in very soon now, an' then there's the 'ospital an' doctors an' that.'

'They're the ones that's crazy,' Wimpy Jennings shouted, as the black blood oozed from the corner of his mouth. 'The Chief an' the Fourth . . .'

'Sure, Wimpy; sure they are,' Sullivan panted. Even though he knew the need for compassion and understanding, he couldn't quite disguise the disbelief in his tone. Thank God it didn't matter now; thank God the pilot was boarding and it wasn't so imperative to distinguish who was sane and who was mad . . .

In that fleeting moment Chief Steward Sullivan actually held the power still to save *Auriga*. If he *had* believed the appeal of a distraught young man, acted instantly, then the full impact of the impending cataclysm might have been lessened at the least.

But he didn't. And so their last chance of survival died, simply because Wimpy Jennings' fantasy about the pencil proved he was the one who was deranged. And who had helped to prove it? Chief Engineer Webster and Fourth Bench, of course. Between them they had quite logically and sensibly established *that*.

But then the vitriol doused Jennings, flooded abruptly through his system to detonate in excruciating suffering. Yet he didn't immediately scream. Not right then. Because a curious recollection blocked the feeling parts of Wimpy's brain — a memory of a young Paisley lad of many years ago, and of the things he'd read, and of his childish fascination for the sea and for the bizarre. And of a story about lost sailormen and of ships which sailed unmanned; of names like *Mary Celeste* and of speculation and muttered rumour.

Whereupon Jennings suddenly tore himself free; sitting erect in his bunk while his shipmates stood aghast. And shrieked with bloodied incoherence before he finally fell back.

'Saint Anthony's fire . . .' they thought he raved. 'Saint Anthony's FIIIIRE is killing us all . . .'

And that produced yet another irony in a time when irony held supreme. For Fourth Engineer Wimpy Jennings — the one man whom nobody could believe — had become the one and only soul aboard *Auriga* to identify the true nature of The Madness.

Not that it mattered a damn any more. Certainly not to Wimpy.

Chapter Sixteen

Tradition; discipline; training . . . these were the strengths which had carried *Auriga* even this far.

Tradition was the factor which had compelled Captain Charles Mowat to maintain that outward resolution so desperately looked for by any crew under stress. If the Captain's inward determination was bolstered by his Faith, and even though that Faith had been perverted by The Madness, it had still proved him to be a courageous man loyal to the tradition of Master despite pain and mental suffering and the awful strains of doubt.

Tradition and discipline — they had been behind the superhuman efforts of Chief Officer Temple, and his loyalty to the

Captain irrespective of disagreement and constantly eroded confidence. David Temple's duty had been clear — to obey all lawful commands and do his utmost to ensure all others did so too, unless he had firm reason to believe that Captain Mowat was incapable of rational thought. And Temple had never been given cause finally to convince himself of that.

Tradition; discipline; training . . . all had combined to make Chief Steward Sullivan a tower of strength in adversity. All had combined to keep the sick and the faltering dedicated to the running of *Auriga*, even though they were unwitting allies of The Madness. Men like Chief Engineer Webster and Second Officer Yancy, both constantly battling against physical and mental distress yet carrying on with their responsibilities as they saw them in order to save the ship. And Greaser Behrens too; itchy, miserable through his need for drink, but still helping; still doggedly loyal to his calling . . .

Tradition; discipline; training . . . it was the saddest irony of all that those three strengths which had brought *Auriga* safely through her night of agony were also to prove the specific causes of her death.

As The Madness began its final assault.

Temple had heard the distant jangle of the bridge telegraph, then felt the foc's'le beneath him cease its vibration; stilled for the first time since *Auriga* had left Helsinki. He'd never been conscious of it before but it was an eerie sensation, slipping through the quiet water without propulsion with only the muted rumble of the slowly turning main engine and the whisper of exhaust to indicate there was still life within the hull.

Neither he nor A.B. Grimm, the only seaman left with him, spoke as they watched the launch with the large black and white letters PILOT blazoned across its streamlined wheelhouse make a wide flaring turn down-Firth before overtaking and closing *Auriga*'s port side; two figures clinging to her rails. Like the Captain, Temple breathed a silent prayer that the second one would be a doctor.

It was a good feeling, suddenly. Not euphoric — he was too tired to squander his last reserves in a selfish excess like that. No, it was more a warm peace within himself; the sort you get when you've come through appalling weather and still made your landfall on the nose despite wind, sea and lousy visibility.

Or at least you did in the old days. Before electronic wonder boxes took the need for a seaman's sixth sense out of the game.

But still, for David Temple it was a gentle triumph.

One last quick glance around the foc'slehead to ensure everything was prepared. Headrope ready to pass down to the Leith tug as soon as the pilot demanded; wires, heaving lines, power already to the windlass, anchors readied in case of emergency. Bosun Peak would have things just as efficiently organised down aft; Peaky was a good man even though he did tend to wallow in gloom. Sad about Trott, it had hit the Bosun harder than most of them realised; the old fellow had been pretty odd ever since that hellish scene of last night. Who the hell *hadn't* been odd during this Godforsaken voyage?

The pilot cutter was lost from sight now, already masked by the height of *Auriga*'s side. Young Cadet Simpson hopping with anxiety amidships while his lads unrolled the ladder outboard. Another figure leaning out and gazing keenly down from the lofty vantage of the port bridge wing — the Old Man. Everything back to normal ... except for an aptly-named skeleton crew on deck and a cargo of dead or maybe soon-to-be-dead sailormen ...

Temple gathered himself with an effort. Watch it, chum! Nearly over and time for reaction later; perhaps too much bloody time ... He stepped aft to the rail and looked along the deck. Simpson was stepping forward to the ladder now, hand outstretched to assist the pilot as he reached the top. Then the first indication of salvation actually arriving aboard as a white cap cover appeared, followed by a blue-uniformed arm.

... the new sound seemed to come from a long way away at first. A keening, barely audible stridency but rising steadily, like a train whistle shrieking in the distance and coming closer all the time. Shrieking? Now what made him think of a parallel like that ...? Animals in pain shrieked. Frightened men shrieked. Berserk men shrieked! There was nothing in the middle of the Firth of Forth that would shriek like that yet the sound was still getting louder. And nearer ...

The Old Man's silhouette turned to face the wheelhouse. The telegraph jangled once more and almost immediately Temple became aware of the deck beginning to bounce beneath him; *Full Ahead* had been called, which meant that the second visitor was also on the ladder . . . and the pilot launch coming into sight again as she cleared *Auriga*'s side, flared bow already lifting over the white surge as she circled protectively before heading back to Granton station. *Auriga* would be swinging to port as well, shortly; heading sou' west for the Leith Approach channel.

The pilot's head clear of the capping now and his right arm feeling for purchase on the safety stanchions, ready to climb over . . . but what the hell was that sound? That chilling, constantly rising shriek?

. . . and then Temple lunged forward as awareness jolted him, while the group at the ladder whirled, shying like terrified horses; a thunderstruck tableau with the two seamen and Cadet Simpson rooted where they stood and the Forth pilot a head and shoulders of frozen disbelief . . .

'No!' Chief Officer Temple bellowed through his horrified dawning that it wasn't over yet — it wasn't even over yet!

'Stop him for *Christ's* sake! STOP him!'

It was precisely eight o'clock in the morning.

Below in the engine controlroom Chief Webster was getting more and more frustrated. Young Bench had gone bloody peculiar since he'd suggested they might be a bit more open regarding the secret of the pencil. Nearly home or not, it was time he bucked his ideas up. There were only the two of them down there, and Bench was needed to log and note the time of each engine movement as the bridge called down for them. It was only when the final *Full Ahead* had rung, presumably as the pilot boarded, that the Chief became aware of the lack of associated activity from his junior.

Half turning from his place at the controls he glowered with ever-increasing irritation. His legs felt like lead, his stomach was one long burn of indigestion, his head was bloody splitting, while that floaty detachment he'd had last night was back with a vengeance. Chief Engineer Eric Webster was definitely not in a tolerant mood any longer.

Certainly not when he observed Bench. The Fourth was simply staring at him and doing nothing. Oh, the movement log was open before him but there wasn't one damn entry in it since the initial *Stand By; 0733*. Only Bench gripping his pencil and staring at him. With an expression of . . . well . . . 'childish petulance' was the nearest the Chief could get to it.

'The movements. Why aren't you logging them, Bench?'

Bench didn't say anything. Just kept on staring.

'Now listen, son,' Webster growled with ominous deliberation. 'I know you're tired; we're all bloody tired. But you get those move . . .'

'The Captain understands,' Bench muttered almost inaudibly. 'The Captain understands about Them. And our secret.'

The Chief blinked. He wasn't used to junior engineers ignoring his danger signals, apart from which he didn't quite grasp what Bench was driving at. It was obviously connected with the pencil, but they already talked that out; or *he* had, anyway — the lad hadn't actually *said* anything when he came to think about it.

'Secret?' he said emphatically. 'The Captain doesn't even know about it, laddie. An' even if he did, it wouldn't matter. I've told you; we don't need to hide it because nobody's goin' to steal it. We can't keep a secret like that, dammit, so get those engine movements entered up. Now!'

And that was that. Positively! Except that Bench still didn't move, and just kept on staring.

'The Captain understands, sir,' the Fourth intoned, and the inflexible determination in his flat voice should have made Chief Engineer Webster very cautious indeed — would have done so if Eric Webster's perception hadn't been so deadened by The Madness, 'That's why we're back to Full Ahead, don't you see? Because the Captain knows They're only trying to trick us into letting Them aboard so as to destroy the pencil, but he's too clever . . . now he's escaping from Them.'

That was when Chief Engineer Eric Webster made his worst mistake of all. Driven to distraction by his illness and his anticipation of the action shortly to be demanded, he lost his temper.

'We're going Full Ahead because we got a crew of urgent hospital cases an' a fair bit to bloody run to Leith Approaches,

194

laddie. And we'll be stopping engine again when we get there; not because They're tryin' to trick us but because we haven't got bloody wheels, Bench. The Captain'll stop us ... I'll stop us — so you get those bloody movements logged before I put your name innit!'

He swung back to the panel, eyes returning anxiously to the telegraph repeater and hands reaching again for the throttle and gear controls. God, this bloody voyage! *God* but he'd be glad when they handed that pencil over an' Bench could be a bit more reasonable.

Webster wasn't conscious of the young man behind him rising from his chair; he was too engrossed in checking the instruments, ensuring *Auriga* was prepared to respond to the first flurry of telegraphed engine orders as they came up to the lockway, to register Bench's disappointed, almost sad acceptance of necessity.

'I *do* wish you'd understand, sir. How important it is for us to escape. From Them.'

Chief Engineer Eric Webster certainly didn't observe the heavy Stilson wrench as it described an arc at the radius of Bench's arm. Or even realise he was dead as the base of his skull imploded.

Fourth Engineer Bench didn't log that particular movement either.

He was far too absorbed in easing the engine throttle forward to its maximum extent, you see. Because they *had* to get away before the pencil was stolen, and at least he'd given them a fighting chance now.

Wimpy Jennings had once told him that *Auriga* exceeded seventeen knots on her full speed trials.

Chikwanda had required the stealth of a leopard and the gliding silence of a snake to reach the forward end of the main deck alleyway. Almost as soon as he'd left the steering gear compartment he'd been forced to seek refuge again as those pink-skinned foreigners had moved industriously around their metallic jungle, doing meaningless things with coils of rope and wire; preparing, he assumed, for some obscure ceremony to take place shortly.

'Stop him, for *Christ's* sake! Stop himmmmmm . . .'

But he was berserk now; a hurtling fury with the rabid foam a mask and his eyes burning crazed malignance. Pilot William

Dornoch, who had visited many ships yet never before found himself aboard a nightmare, could only stare and whimper as the great flashing axe swung in ever-nearing circles around his executioner's head. And the *whup . . . whup* of displacing air a rhythm to the ascending shriek.

Pilot Dornoch tumbled from *Auriga* with the sound of splitting wood, and carried his medical aide-who-never-was below him into the Firth of Forth. They couldn't have guessed it then, but it hadn't made the slightest difference to those still left aboard, because *Auriga*'s destruction had been predetermined ever since the moment when two immature young seafarers had confused the professional expertise of a long-haired girl with an abstract thing called love.

Only the manner of *Auriga*'s dying had now to be decided. Chief Officer Temple, as had happened once before, was the first man to conceive of that awful prospect.

For as a seaman is part of a ship, so that ship is a part of the seaman. It is as impossible to be unaware of what is happening to the ship as not to notice that your lungs have stopped pumping, or your heart pulsating. When the ship behaves in an unexpected manner, then you notice. Even if you're fast asleep in your bunk and something not quite right occurs, then by God your eyes snap open and immediately you're alert.

Despite his shock David Temple was still alive. And because he was still alive he sensed what was happening to *Auriga*, just as he sensed his pulse racing in hysteria and the bile curdling in his mouth.

Which meant that he realised immediately that *Auriga* was still driving ahead, still increasing her propeller revolutions, even though two men had just gone over the side and the Captain knew it. And, furthermore, that she was beginning to swing to starboard instead of to port and towards her original destination.

To starboard?

But that could only mean she was heading for the *North* Channel. Up past Inchkeith Island and further up-Firth towards the Oxcars and Meadulse Rocks; Inchcolm; the Haystack.

'*Oh dear Jesus . . .*'

. . . and the fifty thousand ton triple cantilevers of the greatest railway bridge in the world.

196

Chapter Seventeen

Discipline; training . . . and The Madness.

They are already linked closely in any ordered service. No matter how sane a man is, once he has been thoroughly disciplined he becomes part-automaton; he is programmed to react to the word of command without questioning why. If he is a military man, then he will enter battle as his father, and *his* father before him did as soon as that command was given; even though he might consider — he might even know — it is a madness devised by politicians because of which he is virtually bound to perish, he will still obey. Still die with mechanical precision in the certainty of his own regimented insanity.

At one minute past eight on that last morning there were three disciplined men on *Auriga*'s navigating bridge — Captain Mowat, Second Officer Yancy and Quartermaster Mulholland at the wheel. Mowat and Yancy had evinced positive proof of their affliction; Mulholland had not. Other than revealing an inability to act on his own initiative during the near-collision of the previous evening — which was a weakness present in many men — Able Seaman Mulholland had never up to that moment felt particularly ill or displayed any signs of irrationality. But the sequence of disaster was gaining momentum now; no individual aboard *Auriga* could be guaranteed immunity for much longer.

Neither the Second Mate nor Mulholland actually saw Chikwanda's ultimate brain-storm, enclosed within the wheelhouse as they were when the order to recommence full speed was given. But the Captain did and, like every other observer, Mowat stumbled back a pace with ashen grey cheeks in the realisation that the danger thought to be past had suddenly become greater than ever before.

At one minute past eight there might even have existed a fleeting glimmer of hope. No one witnessing Charles Mowat's immediate reflex would have considered it unreasonable in any normal man catapulted into the midst of outrageous violence. He stood trans-fixed with his black-gloved hands clutching the weathered Bible and the shudders which ran through his body not entirely attributable to the ever-building vibration now stirring *Auriga* under the thrust of her propeller.

But the chain-reaction of The Madness had started many hours before. Its ultimate detonation had been as inevitable as the onset of a tide, and Pilot Dornoch's murder was enough to act as a trigger.

It was the moment when *Auriga* herself began to go mad . . .

Yancy left the telegraph and an open-mouthed Mulholland at the wheel, and ran out to the port wing as soon as he heard Chikwanda's berserk war-cry. Now his eyes were scanning uncom-prehendingly astern to where a dissolving pink stain swirled on the surface, through which the pilot cutter was drifting while her numbed crew tried to confirm if what they *thought* they had seen — but knew they could not possibly have done — really was true after all.

Abruptly he whirled round as the significance of what must have occurred filtered through the cotton-wool fatigue clogging his brain. The Captain was standing there; Bible hugged to his breast and gaze locked unblinkingly ahead; far out past the bows and the fast-closing hazard of Inchkeith Island dead ahead.

'Sir . . .' the Second Officer appealed while, from inside the wheelhouse, Mulholland's apprehension squealed a frightened, 'Course, sir . . .? I need orders f'r the wheel.'

Mowat still didn't move. More shouting drifted up from the foredeck, a hysteria of confused warnings and the clatter of run-ning feet, yet from the Master — nothing. No word; no order; no sign of awareness of what lay astern or what loomed directly ahead.

Yancy's mind was frozen; unable to think. 'Captain,' he whispered again. 'You *have* to stop the ship, sir . . .'

At last Charles Mowat's lips parted; but only his lips moved. His eyes remained steadily on that distant and unfolding vision. When he spoke it was as a riddle, and meaningless to Yancy.

'Satan's temple,' he intoned. 'Do you see it, Mister Yancy? Can you not sense its evil?'

'Please, sir,' the Second blurted out once more. All his senses were signalling an overwhelming plea for direction — he was just too tired now, too tired and too ill to decide what to do. Even the frenetic turmoil echoing from below the bridge aroused no more than a detached curiosity.

'We hear Your Command, Lord. You are our Power and we are merely Your Instruments . . .'

'SIRRRR!'

'We have now seen his violence. We accept in Your Name his Diabolical challenge.'

'Awwww f'r fuck's sake,' Mulholland bawled, as he focused on the solid reality of Inchkeith Island now rushing towards him at eleven . . . twelve . . . thirteen knots an' accelerating faster an' bloody faster.

'Hard to port,' Yancy finally screamed in despair. 'Hard to port the whee . . .'

'Belay that order!'

There was a very long silence. Slowly, tremulously the Second Mate turned. Captain Mowat's voice was crisp and firm as he gestured to Mulholland.

'Starboard twenty, Quartermaster. Quickly now.'

'Stab'd twenty, sir.' The wheel was spinning even before Mulholland had completed his startled reply. Discipline; training; instant obedience . . . Able Seaman Mulholland would not have dreamed of questioning supreme authority in his instant of relief, but Yancy attempted to. It was a last reasoning appeal before The Madness overcame him too.

'Starboard, sir? But that's heading for the North Channel. Leith lies south, Captain. Please . . . we have to alter to port in the name of God!'

'Wheel's twenty to starboard, sir.'

'Thank you.'

Polite. Normal. So horribly normal.

Auriga's head was swinging, now; reaching up towards the north with her bridge deck angling gently under the pull of the turn. Mowat said nothing more until Inchkeith slid safely away to port and the red can number two buoy marking the entrance to the deep draught passage up-Firth came ahead and then clear.

Then, and only then did he place his hands on the Second Officer's shoulders.

'In the name of God, Mister Yancy?' the Captain pronounced

sombrely, but with an inner strength enough to calm even the storms of Yancy's mounting hysteria. 'Aye, but it is in God's name that we are steering for the North Channel, Mister. For we have been chosen to carry out His Work, do you not see? Look, Mister Yancy! Look up ahead and you will understand.'

Whereupon the confused invalid that was Second Officer William Yancy did turn and gaze ahead of *Auriga*; up past Inchkeith and Inchcolm and Inverkeithing Bay, and past the bulk of the squat supertanker lying to the oil terminal off Hound Point.

And suddenly he, too, distinguished with ever-widening stare the towering obscenity crouching against the sky; corrupting the horizon with its dreadful, radiating evil.

That was the moment when he did understand. Precisely what they had to do.

Had the foredeck crew rushed Chikwanda in the first hush of disbelief following the pilot's disappearance over the side, then even at that late stage *Auriga* might have been brought to a halt on the edge of the grave. But initial reaction was numbed, shocked into staring ineffectiveness, and any prospect of overpowering the spectre during that glazed aftermath lost for all time.

When they eventually did dare to approach, it could only be in wary apprehension, for Able Seaman Chikwanda was now a cornered, red-splashed gibber of terror with haunted eyes locked on the encircling men; the gruesomely baptised fire axe scything erratically above his head ... and you'd have to be more than ordinary mad to tackle a raving nutter like that, f'r Chrissake.

While David Temple — appreciating that something was terribly wrong on the bridge, and sick with the realisation that he was probably the only officer left who could halt this ominous diversion through the North Channel — was stranded and a prisoner on that open forward deck with his only route to the superstructure blocked by a homicidal maniac.

There was a shriek ... he whirled round in desperation; little Simpson was sobbing convulsively with a great gash splitting his shoulder and one of the seamen dragging him clear. Damn the kid! Damn him for being so bloody stupid an' heroic ...

Able Seaman Grimm bellowed with rage at what Chikwanda had done to the Cadet; no fright there any more, just a fury of almost animal intensity. He and the other deckie — Drever, was it? — advanced, crowding the slowly retreating Ugandan with menacing crouch and vicious chain stoppers dangling from poised fists. *Auriga* was careering into bedlam, crewed by hatred and violence.

Temple blinked ... that was a white tower lighthouse sliding past to port; a white tower with a red band ... the Oxcars! And not sliding — bloody well *racing* down their length. Hell, but they must be steaming at sixteen, seventeen knots on full power.

Madness; terror; suffering ... and the navigating bridge high above them, an unattainable island where the solution to everything lay. Yet not one head showed over the front; not one sign from those controlling *Auriga*'s passage that they were even aware ...

Heedlessly Temple cupped his hands around his mouth, threw his head back with the anger bringing a flush to his cheeks. '*Briiiiidge!* Stop her f'r ... Ohhh stop her you *Bastaaaards!*'

His rising panic was perfectly understandable. Quite excusable, in fact.

Because the Oxcars Light in the Firth of Forth lies slightly less than four nautical miles down-river from the largest railway bridge in the world.

At seventeen knots, and even without the added impetus of a flooding tidal stream, Chief Officer David Temple knew they now had precisely thirteen minutes left before the run-away *Auriga* reached it.

Greaser Behrens had stayed with Wimpy Jennings ever since the Fourth had howled that plea to be believed just before they'd entered the Firth. He didn't quite know why — for one thing he was a bit disenchanted with Slimy Simmieson; he'd've thought that old woman would have been up looking for him by now. He was a bit disappointed too; Sammy was kind of dependent on his mate's bossiness, it gave him a feeling of being loved an' it helped keep him off the booze. Maybe *that* was what gave him his affinity towards Wimpy Jennings — Sammy saw things too, when he was smashed out've his mind with the drink. Not floating pencils, mind you. No, them kind of things was a bit too intellectual for Sammy Behrens' drunken forays into fantasy. Sammy tended to meet the more conventional screamers, like hairy monsters an' little green

201

men an' monkeys wearin' funny hats and wellington boots when he was befuddled with the grog.

Talking of grog it was odd, really — he hadn't touched a drop since they'd cleared Helsinki, thanks to Slimy's tightly disapproving support, yet now he felt like he'd been drinking steady the whole trip. Floaty, giggly, eyes all screwed up jus' to concentrate on little details like doors an' which end up the deck lay.

. . . in fact, apart from the rabbits itching him all over, and the occasional attack from yowling pussy cats, The Madness, for Sammy Behrens, was developing into a beautiful experience. The cheapest, most euphoric and glassy-eyed Bacchanalian hang-over he'd ever had in his whole intemperate life.

Then, just as Sammy was about to start singing, Chief Steward Sullivan hurried into the cabin looking pale and concerned. But the Chief Steward *always* managed to look pale an' concerned. Mind you, 'e'd done 'em proud this trip, Sully had. Change o' vittles — Scandinavian no less, on a bit o' proper ship-baked bread. Jus' the job.

''Allo, Chief Steward,' Sammy welcomed him gaily, but Sullivan only looked more worried and asked, 'D'you hear shouting, Sammy? From up forr'ad.'

Sammy scratched thoughtfully and frowned until his eyebrows collided in the middle. Sullivan interpreted this as an unfamiliar attempt on Greaser Behrens' part to think, but it wasn't — all Sammy was doing was trying to decide whether there were two Chief Stewards standin' in the doorway, or four.

The strain became too much for Sullivan. Nobody had bothered to tell *him* they were being diverted up-river, presumably to Grangemouth or a quarantine anchorage or something — not that anyone ever bothered to tell him sod all! He was only the Chief Steward an' head bloody nursemaid on this bloody madhouse . . . but then the screaming had started, and the shouting from forr'ad, and the fear had come back to Arthur Sullivan.

And that was the moment when he heard Temple's sudden roar — it *had* to be the Mate with a voice like that . . . '*Briiiiidge!* Stop her f'r . . . Ohh stop her you *bastaaaards!*'

'*Jesus!*' Sullivan bawled in matching panic. 'Somethin's wrong; we got to get down there, Sammy . . . C'mon.'

And then he'd gone. Disappeared. Which wasn't unusual, for

most of Sammy's fantasies tended to vaporise like that — like when the cat attacked him, then vanished. He sighed a tolerantly inebriated sigh and, rising unsteadily to his feet, shambled after the Chief Steward's running footsteps on a cloud of good cheer.

Actually, even if Greaser Behrens had anticipated meeting a homicidal black maniac swinging an axe he'd still have gone. It would make a nice change from beaming owlishly when you come face to face with one of them perfec'ly ordinary *hairy* monsters . . .

Eight minutes left to run. Seven. Six.

Viewed from the shores of the Firth of Forth the Railway Bridge is breathtaking — the mightiest cantilevered structure ever created out of human endeavour. Six million rivets holding fifty thousand tons of steel; one hundred and forty-five acres of surface exposed for more than three-quarters of a century to the shrieking ice gales of the Scottish winters. The misery, the agony, the triumph of five thousand craftsmen over seven years of fortitude; the blood and the sacrifice of the fifty-seven who died violently in the Goliath's making . . . you feel humility when you gaze upon its silent vastness. It is a place of wonder; an awesome monument.

To Quartermaster Mulholland, gazing towards it from *Auriga's* steering position, it was utterly terrifying!

Discipline; training . . . ever since they'd diverted from Leith. Mulholland's creed, as had already been proved, was not to reason why so long as an officer took the responsibility — but even his in-built inclination to avoid involvement in critical decisions had become less and less resolute. They were peculiar, bloody peculiar, both Mowat and the Second Mate. Both miles away out on the wing, like the engine telegraph wasn't ever likely to be needed to stop her in an emergency; an' the only wheel orders called by the Old Man in a flat, creepy sort of voice. And never a reference to a chart or the radar — mind you Mulholland had seen the Captain take *Auriga* right up to Grangemouth often enough to realise he knew the route like the back of his hand; but that wasn't the way they normally did it. Not without crisp orders and continual confirmation of each buoy as it came abeam.

And they didn't even have a pilot aboard. Mulholland had never quite discovered why, other than that something weird had occurred down on the foredeck. But the Captain didn't seem to be concerned, nor did Mister Yancy . . . and anyway, everything was gradually becoming hazy in the mind of Quartermaster Mulholland as well. Already concentration had faded; simply keeping the ship's head steering 248° and straight for the centre of the inward-bound north span of the Bridge was an effort in itself, yet there was still a sense of unease struggling for release under the awful lassitude. What *was* causing it? No need f'r getting uptight, the Old Man's in charge an' God's in His Heaven so why the sick apprehension?

Maybe five minutes between them and the Bridge. Two four eight degrees true on the steerin' compass an' concentrate. Foremast, jackstaff, windlass — all centred dead on the gap ahead. Easy, boy, ease the wheel; stop her falling off.

'Starboard ten.'

Discipline; training. His response was immediate. 'Starboard ten the wheel, sir,' with the spokes passing through his hands even as he answered.

Auriga's bows stirred. Slowly at first, then gathering speed as seventeen knots of rushing water forced her stern to port. But by then Mulholland was frowning, even at the start of the swing . . . he'd had her precisely lined to pass clear under the north span without any correction, so why . . .?

A frantic glance out to the wing. Mowat and Yancy still both standing like they were hypnotised or somethin'. Standing tensely with their heads angled slightly back, almost as though they were looking at the top of the looming cantilevers now?

Swinging too fast suddenly. Right off course to starboard with the whole Bridge skating crazily across his horizon; charging down towards its landfall end with the wheel still ten to starboard!

'The wheel's *still* ten to starboard!' Mulholland screamed warningly, yet his hands, even then, seemed unable to haul it — *Auriga* herself — back to port and towards safety. Discipline; training . . . they had turned into a vice; paralysing him; binding him on that course for disaster even when his every shrieking nerve told him to act on his own for the very first time in his life.

'Orders, Captain?' Mulholland bellowed again because he couldn't act, even then. *'Orders, or we're gonna hit the Bridge!'*

Then his Captain was beside him. Strong, resolute, commanding.

'Keep her ten to starboard, Mulholland. Keep her ten to starboard and the swing on her.'

'But we're gonna hit the Briddddge.' Mulholland repeated in terror-filled supplication.

'Look, son,' Captain Mowat said ever so gently. 'Look! Up there — above the Bridge. Do you see it? Do you understand *now*, Mulholland . . .?'

And the young man did look up. And did see it.

And that was the moment when Able Seaman Mulholland — the only sane man left with the opportunity to divert *Auriga*'s final berserk passage — also succumbed to The Madness.

Down on the foredeck the situation was still in agonising stalemate. There was only one ladder to the upper deck, and that only reached by running the gauntlet of Chikwanda's flailing axe . . . yet every man trapped there also knew the ship was swinging, angling obliquely across the west-bound channel and into the loom of the Bridge. Steaming pell-mell for certain impact.

And what would happen to them, to the ship, to the Bridge f'r pity's sake, when ten thousand tons of careering energy converged upon fifty thousand tons of unyielding behemoth? Would it still remain inflexible as *Auriga* crumbled and compacted while they, exposed right forward on the open deck, were smeared under rearing, saw-edged steel plates and tumbling cranes . . . or might the Bridge itself submit, obliterating every last one of them in its destruction?

Chief Officer Temple was as savagely uncaring as any now; crowding the berserk man back against the ladder in a final hysteria of panic. Grimm had already gone down shock-eyed with a slab carved from his thigh, but it didn't matter to his fellows; as their terror of certain extinction increased, so it balanced their fear of the bloodied lunacy beside them. They had to get past; one of them had to reach *Auriga*'s wheelhouse — swing the helm hard over; ring *Full Astern* down to Webster and Bench sitting isolated from the world in the engine control room, blissfully unaware that within seconds their steel cocoon was about to implode on them; cave astern to allow the ice cold waters of the Forth to come roaring and rampaging and . . .

. . . the engine *control* room!

Temple whirled, clutched at a last straw of hope. Maybe there was a slim chance of short-circuiting Chikwanda's crazed blockade; even to lessen the impact now virtually inevitable — the second telephone on the foc'slehead. Rarely used, it had originally been installed as a direct link to the engineer of the watch in case of emergency. Emergency! He heard himself cackling aloud as he raced forr'ad, ignoring the resentment of his suddenly deserted companions.

The yammer of the *Pielstick* muted the reply of Fourth Engineer Bench as the handset was lifted down below. His voice seemed almost as mechanical as that pounding machinery. Distorted and flat . . . an' why was the main engine racing like that? What the hell had possessed them to open up the thrott . . . concentrate, Temple. Keep yourself calm. Precise. You got a one-chance-or-bust opportunity of persuading them to act on your orders an' not on the bridge telegraph's.

'Temple here, Bench . . . Temple. The bloody Mate!'

He screwed his eyes shut, fighting hysteria. Get a grip on yourself, laddie.

'Tell the Chief there's no time . . . this is an emergency. He is to Stop Engine, Bench; d'you read me? And then come Full Astern immediately. I say again, Fourth . . . come Full Astern immediately!'

Bench's remote voice sounded quite jocular; not at all resentful.

'You're one of Them, aren't you, Mister Temple? Or have They forced you to try an' deceive me, eh? Only you can't, you see; because I know They won't catch us now . . .'

David Temple blinked dully at the telephone in his hand. Suddenly his head was bursting in great flowers of colour and his legs . . . his legs felt very cold. 'Bench,' he called pleadingly. 'Please, Bench, tell the Chief he — must — come — Astern. Now! Or we'll all bloody *die*.'

Bench began to giggle, a ghastly mutilation of humour over the telephone line. 'Mister Webster's asleep, Mister Temple. I had to put him to sleep to save the pencil, don't you see? Because he tried to trick me too, you know. Tried to get me to stop the ship, just like you're doing. But I won't. I won't, d'you hear? You tell Them that; tell Them They'll never get the pencil now . . .'

Chief Officer Temple replaced the handset carefully and stared through black-rimmed eyes at the frantic siege of the foredeck ladder. Dear God but his skull was exploding; the deck was vibrating; the northern buttress of the Bridge was rearing dead ahead now.

He began to run again, skidding uncaringly down the ladder from the foc'sle, stumbling and reeling with the certainty of imminent death acid in his throat. He knew he was going to climb that route to *Auriga*'s bridge deck even though the dementia of Chikwanda would most likely split him asunder as it had the pilot. They were all lost anyway . . . all drowning under the tidal waves of this monstrous *insanity*.

'. . . Wotcher, Chicky boy. So how's it goin' then?'

The raving stopped. The shouting stopped. Chief Officer Temple stopped.

Suddenly there was no violence; no movement; no moaning from the injured; no flashing axe chunking great gashes in the ladder handrails . . . only incredulous silence. Even Chikwanda, glistening with the blood and the spittle-flecked varnish of his rabid possession, stared in incomprehension at the unsteadily happy figure who blinked back at him from three feet away.

'Wotcher, Chicky boy,' Greaser Sammy Behrens said with enormous good will. 'Havin' a fire drill are we, then?'

Quartermaster Mulholland was staring as well. Up ahead. Up past the great stone supporting piers; past the soaring massiveness of the tubular arms; up and up high above his craning, angling head to the looming crown of the northern cantilever of the giant Bridge spanning the Firth of Forth.

. . . and that was when he, too, had *seen* it. The Awfulness which God had sent the Captain to destroy; and which Second Officer Yancy had first observed as the ship altered round Inchkeith Island — for Yancy was the first to experience that ultimate delusion which The Madness could inflict . . . its power to work on the brain so that the imaginings of one victim are duplicated by the insanity of his fellows.

Satan towered above them in the sky, squatting in gargantuan obscenity on the northmost cantilever; His goatish visage a diabolical contempt and His red eyes like monstrous suns flashing a terror no man had ever exceeded. His horns simmered with the crawling of putrefaction, and the aura of His malevolence reached down towards them in a putrescent fog . . .

'Our Father which art in Heaven . . .' Mulholland whispered, secure in the knowledge of his own selfless martyrdom.

. . . the talons of the Anti-Christ dripped spears of dead men's gore; Its tail entwined the Bridge like a red-slime serpent . . .

'Give us Your protection, oh Lord,' Yancy was crying, 'for we are Your soldiers . . .'

. . . His cloven hooves pawed an anvil of white-hot sparks from the fabric of His megalithic throne. And Asmodeus began to roar a hissing tumult in sudden fear at Auriga's *Divine assault . . .*

'. . . Hallowed be Thy Name . . .'

'We shall breach the walls of his temple, Dear Lord. We shall smite and destroy the foundations of Lucifer's Cathedral.'

Seventeen knots. Two minutes to Armageddon . . .

'Midships. Steady as she goes for God, Quartermaster.'

'AYE, sir. Steady as she goes.'

Chapter Eighteen

Two minutes to Armageddon . . .

Chief Steward Arthur Sullivan had arrived at the forward end of the main deck first, well ahead of the tolerantly trailing Sammy Behrens. When he'd finally burst out of the internal alleyway he'd stopped dead. Just like everybody else had done at that first moment when they'd looked up and realised *Auriga* wasn't heading through the Forth Railway Bridge; she was heading for it.

Arthur Sullivan had been given an additional cause for temporary paralysis — because it was also his first meeting with The Madness in its most violent form; represented by the gibbering mutation that was Able Seaman Chikwanda.

So the Chief Steward hadn't hurried any more; all he'd been able to do was draw back in fright and flatten himself around the corner of the deckhousing, and wonder hysterically what in hell's name he was goin' to do next.

That was when Sammy had turned up; having got lost a couple of times and eventually finding his way down through the opposite alleyway. Which meant he was out and creeping up to surprise his ol' pal Chikwanda before Sullivan even had a chance of stopping him.

But, you see, to Sammy it wasn't a frightening experience at all, this chance meeting with a shipmate familiar. Oh yeah, sure, Chicky did look a bit niggly an' bad tempered, in fact to anyone else he'd have seemed downright spooky — the kind've weird apparition they'd cross to the other side of the ship to avoid. But not in Sammy's eyes; bumbling, matey little Greaser Behrens had met an awful lot of screaming freaks during his alcoholic course through life and had discovered there wasn't nothin' scary about them. They never ackshully *touched* you, or did more than snarl at you — jus' like ol' black Chikwanda there who might or might not be f'r real.

To Sammy the apparition before him could just as easily have been another phantom of the bottle. For by then Greaser Behrens was enjoying the most satisfying delirium he'd ever experienced. And he would never know it was all a last gigantic drunk by courtesy of The Madness . . .

So . . . 'Havin' a fire drill are we, Chicky boy?' Sammy had enquired with sympathy, blearily focusing on the red-handled axe poised over him. 'You give it ter me, then. I'll be the fireman f'r a bit while you have a nice lie down, you lookin' a bit peaky an' that.'

Chief Steward Sullivan was the first man to shatter the spell. As soon as Behrens lurched forward with helpful hand outstretched he leapt into the open. He was shouting even as Chikwanda's head swivelled, startled. An animal surprised.

'NO, Sammy . . .'

But Sammy didn't hesitate. A pal was a pal if he was for real; while if 'e wasn't. . . . Them hairy monsters or green elephants or even shiny black fantasy-savidges — they wus all quite harmless too, once you'd learned to cope wi' 'em.

''S'all right, Mister Sullivan,' he beamed, reaching matily for the axe. 'Chicky don't mind. Chicky's glad to let me help 'im with 'is fire drill.'

'Noooooo, Sammy!'

The end of Greaser Behrens was mercifully swift. Triggered by that roar of warning Chikwanda's brain exploded again, his terror burst in a primitive shriek, there was a flash ... and Sammy Behrens was dead before any man could place a foot on the now unguarded ladder. But it didn't take them long, not galvanised by their fury and their own primeval anxiety to survive.

Sammy's blank stare still bore a trace of disillusionment. A lot've happy times with shipmates; a lot've drinks; a lot've faith in long-familiar spectres, yet now ... Even Slimy Simmieson had let him down in the end. Disappearin' like he'd done.

Or maybe Slimy hadn't. Maybe Slimy was already up there. Waiting for Sammy ...

The Bridge was careering towards them ever faster; beginning to drift gigantically above their heads. Not more than two minutes left.

Chief Officer Temple fought blindly through the melee as Chikwanda finally went down, cornered and pitiful under the blood-lust of ordinary men now driven far beyond the accepted bounds of reason. But Temple didn't have time for compassion.

Chief Steward Sullivan was still behind him though, with the tears streaming unashamedly down his ashen face and only the last shadows of his former determination keeping him going. 'Oh God,' he kept repeating as they scrambled frantically for the ladders to the upper decks; but everyone has a breaking point, even the brave.

'Oh God oh God oh dear *God*!'

Maybe ninety seconds left ...

It was a living nightmare now, only Chief Officer Temple knew beyond any doubt that he was wide awake. He knew that, because you can't feel pain through a dream; not real pain — yet he did. The chill of his body was fading but it wasn't simply the sweat of muscles pushed to the limit of endurance; there was a growing sensation of retained heat; a burning within.

Up the next ladder to the boat deck and past the galley, the crew mess, the provisions store where it must all have begun. Then he saw something ahead; something flaccid and awful, barely able to drag itself over the coaming leading from the crew heads — Holmquist. Chief Cook Holmquist waved pitifully up at their approach with an expression of quivering revulsion; the haunted look of a man who discovers he has embraced the contamination of the Plague and is already lost.

'Help me, Chief Stewart. Help meeeee . . .'

Time . . . No time!

Up again towards the officers' deck; Sullivan labouring, falling gradually astern while Temple's legs screamed for mercy and his lungs blared a stertorous agony . . . an' someone else! Virtually unrecognisable this time, crucified on the deck, a bloodied starfish of self-mutilation gazing dead-eyed to the sky — Garvie. Third Officer Garvie who, bereft of supervision, must have slashed himself a hundred times before he died, and who still clutched the razor-edged proof of his immolation in one outflung hand.

Upwards again; but now a sobbing wail of despair which detonated into a harrowing shriek as the accommodation door burst open and yet another of the Obsessed squirmed out and collapsed at his feet. Radio Operator MacNally. Pivoting on one shoulder, a Catherine wheel of maddened pain twisting and crying, 'The Fire . . . Oh God but the Fire's *insiiiiide* me!'

Leap over and across the poor bastard! Run, Temple, run! Only one minute left now if you're lucky, an' the Forth Railway Bridge filling your whole horizon; sweeping over you like a massive shroud . . . dwarfing *Auriga* herself; crushing her already by its sheer immensity.

Up again — the last ladder of all. Temple never even felt his fingernails splinter as he flung himself forward, scrabbling for the strength to mount that interminable obstacle to survival. Yet miraculously help might be at hand . . . there were two figures waiting for him at the top. Two figures seemingly clinging to each other like shimmering lovers. Temple reached imploringly towards them. 'Port the wheel,' he cried. 'Hard aport the wheel.'

'It's very nice up here,' one of the figures said, and it sounded just like the invariably doleful voice of Bosun Peak. Which meant it couldn't be, because it was happy now. Contented. As if everything had worked out nicely despite all that had happened, despite the death of his old friend.

Then Chief Officer Temple's black-shadowed stare focused on the second man who waited there. He was sagging slightly, held erect only by the naked arm hooked stiffly around Bosun Peak's scraggy neck.

'I brought 'im up here, Mister Temple,' the Bosun explained in a reasonable way. 'It's sunny up 'ere on the bridge. An' the sun's good for you when you're not feelin' too well.'

But they would never find out if the change really *was* doing the second sunbather any good. Because David Temple suddenly realised he'd been gazing blankly into the milk-glazed stare of the one and only friend the Bosun had ever had; into the rigor-grinning death mask of Donkeyman Trott.

That was when Temple, too, first heard The Madness! A satanic peal of laughter drowning the shrill fright of the seabirds scattering from within the great girders, and the rolling crash of displacing water now pushing ahead of *Auriga* to break against the green-slimed stone piers of the north cantilever almost hidden by the bows.

A terrible rage burst within him. He lunged in abhorrence, fighting to cling to precious sanity; separating Bosun Peak from his limpet shipmate. 'Keep away from me, you ghoulish bastaaaaard.'

Then he heard the chanting. Whirling, he faced inboard.

'*Aye, Lord, we are coming. Open Thy gates to Heaven for we are about to breach the stronghold of The Devil . . .*'

A tableau of waxen images within the wheelhouse. Second Officer Yancy kneeling in muttering devotion; Quartermaster Mulholland erect at the helm with his eyes gazing up at the Bridge and a look of Beatification smoothing away his fear . . . and finally, the Captain. Charles Mowat, Master of *Auriga* before God. And indeed he was, with the battered red Bible clasped between his hands in prayer, and his strong head held unflinchingly to meet the fury of Mammon with the steadfast courage that had already carried him and his crew through storm and tempest, and the tumultuous violence of a North Sea winter.

A brave man. A most gallant, resolute and kindly man. A mad man.

'*Have mercy on us, Dear Jesus, as we enter The Valley Of The Shadow Of Death.*'

Thirty seconds . . .

Quartermaster Mulholland shrieked as Temple hit him with his shoulder, smashing him away, tumbling him and Bill Yancy into a sprawl of dazed incomprehension. The Captain didn't even stir; only his appeal rose louder, more impassioned.

'*Lucifer is upon us, Lord. The Demon has risen from Pandemonium. Send us down Your Divine BLESSING.*'

Chief Officer Temple spun the wheel frantically. The rudder indicator slammed hard to port and his eyes switched to the great Bridge ahead. He stopped breathing; stopped shaking; stopped sobbing; stopped every bloody thing in his own silent prayer for the ship.

Twenty seconds to impact. *Fifteen*. Ten.

Auriga began to turn the other way at last; swinging slowly to port as if very, very tired. Gradually the breaking waters of the Firth of Forth could again be detected slipping outside her beautifull flared bow . . . and the lattice gargantua was broadsiding too. Gathering speed; sliding steadily across the wheelhouse windows but to starboard this time as the ship fought to save herself even against the will of Captain Mowat's God.

Five seconds only — and the world ahead now totally blanked by the Bridge.

Someone was crying as Temple flung himself down — Mulholland? — while Bill Yancy's eyes gazed blankly into his at deck level. He understood, even in that most fearful moment, that Second Officer Yancy was dead, his body corroded beyond endurance by the assault of The Madness he had withstood so bravely until then.

An explosive, shearing detonation from forr'ad — the foremast? Didn't that mean that *Auriga*'s bows had already passed under the lowest part of the Bridge? Temple dragged himself back to his feet with wheelhouse spinning and the vomit sticky against his cheek, and stared ahead and upwards. Another crash from forward as the starboard *Liebherr* crane struck a forge of sparks against the soaring underside of the mighty cantilever supports. SMASH! The after crane impacting into twisted yellow metal and tottering ruin, keeling terrifyingly as it spun on its mounting . . .

He began to laugh hysterically — they were going through, f'r God's sake . . . f'r Satan's sake? Through and clear and what matter if the ship was wounded in its juggernaut career towards survival?

A sickening lurch as her stern, still pivoting on full rudder, slammed hugely into the piers . . . but five thousand long-dead Scottish craftsmen had done their work assiduously, and the great Forth Railway Bridge held firm.

Hold the wheel . . . keep it hard to port, laddie.

Someone else tumbling into the wheelhouse; crouching like a hunched dwarf with eyes averted to encompass the cathedral roof passing over their heads; but the newcomer, too, was grinning and yowling unrestrainedly with the exhilarating promise of being able to live a little longer. Sullivan! Chief Steward Arthur Sullivan, once his most dedicated adversary, now slapping him on the back and frenzied in the joy of salvation . . .

Another bang and a rending screech — but above and behind them this time as the rim of the funnel, the whole of the mainmast and most of the rest of *Auriga*'s tophamper swept aft to bounce clear of the poop deck and be swallowed by the Firth of Forth. Her Red Ensign would be gone too, now. Temple was sorry she'd lost her Ensign.

One final cacophony of frustrated malice. Glass tinkling down from the steaming light; aerial wires dragging crazily across the deck above, uprooting ventilators and cowlings an' . . .

. . . and then the sun coming out again. Dazzling! Wonderful! Racing towards them and driving the shadow of the Bridge before it until it finally burst upon them, exploding into *Auriga*'s wheelhouse in a triumphant flare of brilliance . . .

They were safe!

Chapter Nineteen

As *Auriga* burst clear of the Goliath which had so nearly crushed her she was still turning, still broadsiding crazily to port. Her starboard side was a buckled mutilation and her decks a tangle of wreckage; but she was still whole, still a ship.

And still under the control of her Chief Officer.

And it was still a lovely day. With the sun a great big smile over the blue waters of the Firth of Forth.

She only had to stop now. And anchor.

That was all.

Temple was still grinning idiotically in his gratitude; clinging to the wheel, edging *Auriga* back into mid-channel.

His mind was a riot of urgency. Someone would have to get down to the engineroom before they could stop her. They would have to cope with the unknown horror which had destroyed Fourth Engineer Bench's reason and which surely had been the end of poor Chief Webster. And it would have to be done quickly. They were still careering at seventeen knots; there was little sea room left.

He half-turned, opened his mouth to shout to Sullivan but hesitated as he observed the Captain, and the look in the Captain's eyes. Lost. Suddenly old and lost and staring dully into some black void which no proud man should ever be called upon to view; while the Chief Steward stood with him in awed compassion, uselessly comforting him in his trembling arms as he had already done for so many of their shipmates.

That was the moment when a terrible lassitude overcame Chief Officer Temple. In the very moment of his victory he felt exhausted; helpless as a child as every trace of the resolution which had carried him so far drained abruptly into a gutter of apathy.

Right then. Even while *Auriga* was still swinging hard to port; cutting well into the main channel already and sheering faster and faster towards the opposite bank, now less than a mile away.

He was tumbling into a time and distance nightmare again. One mile. Seventeen plus knots. Three minutes at most left to control the on-going legacy of The Madness. Time ... bloody *time* pressing down on his shoulders yet again. Only his shoulders were bowed, now. Unable to carry any more weight.

He tried to centre the wheel, but couldn't. Slack-jawed, he struggled to focus on the hazards ahead: a crowded police launch roaring towards them from Rosyth; the low grey line of a Royal Navy frigate drawing from the Dockyard outer jetty in belated

215

response to some frantic alert, a fishery-protection vessel pushing a white bow wave as she hastily worked up revolutions to clear the Naval base approaches; two tugs steaming doggedly down-river, black stumpy silhouettes against the sweep of the distant Scottish mountains.

And he was still swinging hard to port; broadsiding across the Forth, an' there wasn't a bloody thing he could do to prevent it because he was too *tired*. He began to appreciate how funny it was; all those frantic vessels taking action now. At this stage of the game . . . he heard himself laughing.

'Go away! Hell, but we've saved your Bridge, you slow-witted bastards. We've saved your bloody great Railway Bridge an' it's all over. The panic's over, don't you see? I'll bring her up in a minute. Steer into the channel in a minute when I've had a rest an' . . .'

Sullivan appeared to be shouting too, now. But why was Arthur Sullivan shouting like a . . . like a bloody maniac?

Temple leaned on the hard-over wheel and reflected on this curious matter. He ignored the steady click of the steering compass as the ship continued her monstrous circle, merely leering drunkenly at the waving Chief Steward — just like Greaser Sammy Behrens had leered blearily at Able Seaman Chikwanda.

Before Able Seaman Chikwanda chopped him in half.

'What're you pointing at, Sully? There's no need to point like that an' get all scared again. It's all over, Sully. Anyway, pointing's a rude thing to do . . .'

It didn't seem to help, because Chief Steward Sullivan still grasped Temple's slouched shoulders, and shook him like a rag doll, and roared through blanched lips, 'The Bridge, Dave. The bloody Bridge!'

David Temple giggled deprecatingly as The Madness stood beside him. 'S'alright. We missed the bridge, Sully, ol' man. We saved their precious Bridge f'r 'em . . .'

Until the shock hit him; slammed him back against the wheel as Sullivan's ravings finally penetrated his drowning brain.

'There's still the *other* Bridge. You're steering us straight for the south pillars of the ROAD Bridge!'

Whereupon Chief Officer Temple of the Motor Vessel *Auriga* spun round with the imminence of death again clutching his spine.

216

And gazed up and up. And saw the second great Bridge spanning the River Forth already looming above him.

The Forth Road Bridge is an awesome giant too; a monument of a much more recent era, which lies only a short distance up-river from the venerable cantilevers of legend.

It is a suspension Bridge under which carefully navigated ships can pass with ample clearance and, while its twenty-one thousand tons of steelwork and the sixteen miles of socketed wire rope hangers which retain it in the sky are, perhaps, a little less overwhelming than its elder sister of the railways it is, nevertheless, still a massive threat to hold over any seaman's head.

Even its twin-towered supports represent five thousand six hundred tons of immovable majesty. Immovable, that is, unless something huge in itself and travelling at a good seventeen knots collides with one of them . . . something like, say, the Motor Vessel *Auriga*.

As David Temple whirled in belated horror he found that the south towers of the Bridge now rose sheer on the bow; still a little to port admittedly but *Auriga* was still turning to port; describing precisely the same arc as had already steered her clear of the northern buttress of the earlier Bridge . . .

Sullivan was so scared he was just looking. Not moving; just looking. And shouting.

'Starboard, then,' he bawled frantically. 'Starboard your WHEEL, man!'

Temple blinked dazedly, his clutch white on the helm. Why can't Sullivan *help* me? Dear God I need help even to move this wheel one spoke . . . two spokes . . . three . . .

Then he saw the cat.

It was an ordinary cat; black mostly, with brown ears and a bit of white round the paws and the tip of its long furry tail. Yet as soon as he saw it David Temple knew it must be the cat which had frightened Donkeyman Trott to death all that time ago, only he couldn't see why. It was such a . . . well, such an ordinary cat.

The ship continued to turn. To port.

Definitely an ordinary cat, David reflected vaguely. Though it did look a bit mangy, and its fur was all wet or something; sticking out in spikes in a rather unpleasant way ... and if you looked closely enough, wasn't there a trace of foam flecking the corners of its cruel little mouth? And a touch of madness about its almond eyes ... those luminous, penetrating almond eyes which kept staring at him?

Auriga still continued to shudder and thresh her monstrous passage across, instead of up, the River Forth — while her bows swung closer and closer to a heading for the slender southern towers of the suspension Bridge which now reared almost vertically above her.

By now Arthur Sullivan had stopped shouting and making a nuisance of himself, and was also gazing at the cat in the wheelhouse doorway ... and that was when perhaps the oddest thing of all the odd things that had happened under the spell of The Madness began to take place.

As had happened to the Captain and Yancy over the Forth Bridge Lucifer, Temple and Chief Steward Sullivan both began to witness a vision. But in their case it was one which had already been seen aboard *Auriga* a long time before; and which had driven one man on to, and another man clean over, the brink of death. Temple and Sullivan suddenly discovered what had caused Donkeyman Trott's old heart to stop, and Seaman Grainger's mind finally to disintegrate.

The little cat started to grow as they watched. Larger and larger. As it bloated to a monstrous form so it began to spit, and its maw gaped wide with sabre teeth razor-sharp and slavering with malevolence. And then its rippling fur became infested with millions of squirming insects too small to be detected by the naked eye but inflating in their awful detail while their parent loathsomeness continued to swell and swell and swell.

... until the little cat was as big as a leopard and growing ever larger and until, for Chief Officer Temple and Chief Steward Sullivan, there existed no threat from anything so awful as from that tumescent spectre before them. And there was no prospect of salvation from any other man on that bridge: because Yancy was already dead; and Quartermaster Mulholland — who wouldn't have acted on his own without an order anyway — was curled in a foetal, tearful ball; and Bosun Peak was still out on the splintered

218

starboard wing enjoying the warm sun and carrying on a somewhat one-way conversation with his good friend and shipmate Donkeyman Trott; and Trotty, for his part, wasn't concerned either with the cat or the coming death because *he'd* already met them both.

Which left Captain Charles Mowat to share the responsibility; only the Captain would never sail his ship again for he had lost his Faith, and had become a human vegetable.

So when the cat crouched in wiry hatred, and then finally sprang screeching and scratching and berserk towards them, neither Temple nor Sullivan had any way of knowing that the monster was experiencing *its* death agony, too. For The Madness affects all varieties of living things. Birds, animals, human beings ... even fish that swim in blissful ignorance; as the crew of *Auriga* had done during their passage across the North Sea.

Chief Officer David Temple didn't die as mercifully as Trotty had when the cat impacted against his raised arms.

He had a few more seconds to live.

At that moment the base of the Forth Road Bridge towers were still a good fifty feet ahead of his ship ...

Epilogue

Auriga was still steaming at over seventeen knots when she hit.

She collided precisely at right angles; with the length of the Bridge suspended directly above her. Her forward momentum caused her to smash through and partly mount the stone piers at water level. As the two separate vertical Bridge supports were just in excess of two road widths apart, and that dimension somewhat less than the beam — the overall breadth — of *Auriga*'s hull with its ideally wedge-shaped forward end, she then continued to drive irresistibly onward between the 155 metre high interconnected twin towers, thus forcing them apart; detonating their welded togetherness into collapsing giants.

The Road Bridge over the Forth is a triumph of flexibility. Under the pressures of the Scottish gales sweeping down the valley it can give way some twenty feet at its centre; but it was never designed to withstand assault from the water itself.

The three thousand three hundred foot long middle span of the aerial highway fell out of the sky with a lingering rumble of thunder. A large part of it — fabricated steel, miles of snaking wire, hundreds of tons of fragmenting carriageway — fell squarely upon what had once been the Motor Vessel *Auriga*, flattening her vertically into the gouting waters of the Forth. And it continued to fall for what seemed a very long time in a ribbon of roaring violence until there was no Bridge, no ship . . . no Madness.

There were no survivors either; not from a cataclysm like that. But no one else outwith the now compacted hulk of *Auriga* was lost, which was a blessing. The authorities had closed the Bridge to traffic as soon as the pilot cutter had screamed a warning over her V.H.F. radio.

So only her crew and a pilot and a doctor died in the end, when a ship went mad. All the newspapers revelled in it for the next few days. Of course it was to be a long time before the divers could burrow below the waters of the Forth to recover such grisly samples as were required by the waiting pathologists. And even longer before those pathologists were able to publish their findings, and at last identify the true cause of The *Auriga* Madness.

But the public cannot wait for the facts; speculation can provide a more satisfying basis for wonderment. And nearly every newspaper felt it profitable to feed that mass impatience. Some of them even got close to the truth.

One particular journalist, with a medical background and a talent for research, burned the midnight oil in pre-empting official conjecture. His office desk was strewn with toxicological references; all suggesting bizarre reasons why healthy and balanced men such as those who sailed *Auriga* should suddenly have gone insane.

Two publications attracted his closest attention. The first was that highly authoritative work by John Glaister; *Medical Jurisprudence and Toxicology*. Thoughtfully he had underlined passages of particular note:

> . . . *her arms began to ache, her skin to itch, and her fingers to swell. Her left index finger became cold and showed cyanosis at the tip. The remaining fingers of this hand and also those of the other hand became similarly affected, and later several of them became gangrenous as far as the distal joints . . .*

And also:

> . . . *the disease may occur in epidemic form, as at Manchester some years ago when upwards of two hundred persons were affected. In 1951 in France, some two hundred persons suffered from . . .*

That diligent researcher had also traced a copy of the British medical journal *The Lancet*, dated the 8th of September 1951. In one article it contained quite a lot of information which captured his interest and caused his typewriter to rattle.

> . . . *It is interesting that France should again be the scene of an*

outbreak of a disease which, in epidemic form, has been almost unknown for centuries.

Since Aug, 17 more than 200 people at Pont St Espirit, near Avignon, have been taken ill: 4 of them have died and 15 are said to be temporarily insane. The cause of their illness has been traced to bread sold by a local baker, and numbers of animals — chickens, ducks, dogs, cats, goats and even fish — which had eaten this bread have sickened and often died . . .

Followed, most particularly, by the sentence:

Most of the victims have suffered from pains in the throat and stomach, vomiting, and pains and sensations of cold in the limbs; while some have had delirium, mania, and bizarre hallucinations and delusions . . .

It wasn't conclusive; but nothing could be until the pathologists had completed their macabre assessment; analysed what really *did* spawn The Madness which drove *Auriga* to destruction.

The journalist lit yet another cigarette, then began a long article on what might have happened aboard the Motor Vessel *Auriga* in the hours before she impacted against the twin towers of the Road Bridge spanning the River Forth.

He suggested, very astutely, that it might have been the result of a specialised type of vegetable poisoning — as written in the bible of Dr Glaister — due to *Claviceps Purpurea*, a fungus parasitic on the rye plant. Its modern medical name is that of ERGOTISM, or ERGOT POISONING.

He also, however, remarked that The Madness had possessed many other descriptions, dating as far back in time to six hundred years before the birth of Christ, in which an Assyrian tablet referred to *a noxious pustule found on ears of grain*. And that for centuries, during its depredations through Europe, it had been given a name which had its grim origin in the form of agony it inflicted upon its victims.

In those medieval days they called The Madness *St Anthony's Fire*.

And that, had he not already passed beyond the power of satisfaction, would have been a source of pleasure to a certain Third

Engineer Wimpy Jennings; lately a crew member of a ship called *Auriga* ...

That excellent and hard-working journalist's article on the monstrous consequences of ergot poisoning and its possible existence aboard *Auriga* was syndicated world wide. Among the many national newspapers which published it was one based in Helsinki, Finland.

So it *was* rather a pity that Olga the nubile Finn never actually bothered to read about St Anthony's Fire, and the *Auriga*'s Madness.

There aren't all *that* many girls who have helped to kill thirty eight men and a cat ...

Fontana Paperbacks

Fontana is a leading paperback publisher of fiction and non-fiction, with authors ranging from Alistair MacLean, Agatha Christie and Desmond Bagley to Solzhenitsyn and Pasternak, from Gerald Durrell and Joy Adamson to the famous Modern Masters series.

In addition to a wide-ranging collection of internationally popular writers of fiction, Fontana also has an outstanding reputation for history, natural history, military history, psychology, psychiatry, politics, economics, religion and the social sciences.

All Fontana books are available at your bookshop or newsagent; or can be ordered direct. Just fill in the form and list the titles you want.

FONTANA BOOKS, Cash Sales Department, G.P.O. Box 29, Douglas, Isle of Man, British Isles. Please send purchase price, plus 8p per book. Customers outside the U.K. send purchase price, plus 10p per book. Cheque, postal or money order. No currency.

NAME (Block letters) _____

ADDRESS _____

_____

_____